ANOTHER MAN'S
Treasure

Bardolf & Company

Another Man's Treasure

ISBN 978-1-938842-15-3
Copyright © 2013 by Charles R. Hall

Published by Bardolf & Company
    5430 Colewood Pl.
    Sarasota, FL 34232
    941-232-0113
    www.bardolfandcompany.com

Cover design by Charles R. Hall
Layout by Cathleen Shaw

To My Father

a man of meager beginnings
and successful endings,
who taught me the
power of dreams,
the necessity of hard work,
and the value of perseverance.

ANOTHER MAN'S
Treasure

Charles R. Hall

Bardolf & Company
Sarasota, Florida

A good man out of the good treasure of his heart brings forth good things, and an evil man out of the evil treasure brings forth evil things.

—Matthew 12:35

Chapter 1

The slow paced red beeping light stood out in stark contrast to the bland green wall behind the bed. His pale skin made the redness in his eyes seem deeper and their blue color more haunting. It had been several years since *the* accident, but the multitude of operations had finally gotten the better of him. The beeps on the machine were slowing. The end was near. He had one more thing to say but had neither the strength nor the words. Last words are not always uttered. Sometimes they are written.

He did his best to motion toward a jewelry box on the bedside table, and after many exhausting gyrations was finally able to make his desire clear. Several puzzled looks were exchanged, but the nurse in blue eventually understood his request. Deliberately, she grabbed the box, then inspected it indifferently and gently put it on his chest. His thin, stiff hands clawed through the wrinkled papers in the box with equally wrinkled and scarred fingers.

The flap inside the clear plastic cylinder of oxygen picked up its pace as he expended what little life he had left. His jaw jutted in frustration while his fingers continued their dry scraping through the small wooden box. His free hand pulled at the pesky tube in his nose that allowed him to breathe. When he found the proper paper, he rubbed it slowly with a once finely manicured thumb, now tarnished yellow from the concoction of chemicals pumped into his veins. His red-rimmed eyes sagged with moisture as he stared at the blurred blue ink. With one last motion, he pushed the worn paper into his son's hand and stiffened.

A steady, piercing flat line signaled the end.

Though the father's heart had stopped beating, his son's was pumping at three times its normal pace. The young man became light-headed from the unusual amount of blood flowing through his brain. All he could think was: What was appropriate to do?

He moved close and pressed his lips on his father's forehead. To give the doctors room to do the tedious tasks of organizing his father's body, he stepped back and allowed for the propriety that follows death.

Working his way toward the swinging double doors of the waiting room, he found a chair in the midst of strangers. He sat down slowly and stared at similar expressions—faces filled with the pain of having lost or preparing to lose a loved one.

A man, the father he barely knew, had summoned him to be at his side for his last moments. Yet the reason why was still unclear. So many unanswered questions. He rubbed the sweating palm of his right hand on his corduroy pants leg. The other hand was still balled in a fist that held his father's dying words.

He glanced around the room and saw nothing but indifference from those surrounding him. A long release of air expelled from his lungs as he slowly opened his hand. He straightened out the wrinkled paper. "Nearvana. Two hands, two fingers up stage right off the main spot" were the only words written on it.

The son folded the worn, wrinkled paper neatly and settled it into his plaid shirt pocket. He reached to his back pants pocket and produced a pair of airline tickets. On top was a used boarding pass that read, "Toronto (YYZ) nonstop to Youngstown (YNG)."

Another sigh of air expelled from his lungs as he moved the boarding pass to the bottom to reveal an unused ticket that read, "Youngstown (YNG) nonstop to Tampa (TPA)."

A single tear from one of his incredibly blue eyes streamed down his cheek.

The first leg of the journey was done.

Now on to the second leg, just as his father had requested.

The drone of the dial tone held a portion of his concentration while he fiddled with the rotary phone. He knew this would be a conversation that would raise his already high blood pressure, so he kept himself from calling in too much of a hurry. His eyes studied the row of pictures, some black-and-white, some in color, and the plaques that decorated the walls of his plush real estate office.

A slow drip of wax rolled down the side of a silver candle, leaving a heavy cream smell to fade into the air. The rhythmic ticking of an unbalanced ceiling fan was the only accompaniment to the sound of his dialing in the dark office. The blades pulled a thick gray mix of Ybor City cigar and candle smoke toward a heavily stained ceiling. After he dialed the last number, he rubbed the edge of his thumb over the shiny gold nameplate that read Lawrence R. Kronis, GRE. After three annoying rings, the friendly voice of a man who seemed to be expecting a call piped up.

"Congratulations, Mr. Kronis!" boomed into the earpiece. "I'm sure you're very proud, sir. Awards like these are certainly wonderful achievements. Definitely hard to come by, sir."

The man's protruding lips tightened around a mouthful of unusually white teeth, and his tension pressed his chin closer against the phone. "He's dead, Sam."

"Sir?" came the uncertain reply.

"He's dead," Kronis shot back.

A long silence…and then a click.

The intersecting circles rippled the water as they bumped into one another. With each encounter, the circles would change in some way. Some were big and some were small. Some were round and some were not. It was the differences in them that made them the same.

"Plop, plop," Rudy yelled, hurling another crab back into the water of the bay.

"Fizz, fizz," Lucy answered with a half-grin as she studied the bubbles of the salty water seeking the humid air.

On cue, they looked at each other like two singers performing a well-practiced act. "Oh, what a relief it is!" they chimed in together and looked skyward in harmony.

This well-choreographed ritual was repeated every time a catch was returned to the water as a mock offering to the gods of the sea. The gods may have been pleased, but still one more crab was left with one less claw.

While Rudy finished picking a clump of stickers off his tube sock from an earlier sandspur fight, Lucy decided it was time to drop one more line and watch the sun go down. A jagged, concrete seawall snaked along the bay, providing a platform for Lucy and Rudy to do their fishing and crabbing.

Crabs were generally easier to catch than the blind hope of hooking a fish. Stone crabs, the easiest of all. The prehistoric looking creatures clung to the side of the seawall and could be pulled up quickly with a net. With ease came limitations. Florida law only allowed a single claw to be removed from any captured crab.

"You think it hurts real bad?"

"What?" asked Lucy.

"Getting your claw ripped off?" mumbled Rudy while sucking his thumb, bloodied from the sandspur removal. He jumped to his feet and assumed a crab-like stance and said, "I mean, imagine if we got swooped up, and someone ripped off our arm?" His face got angry and twisted as he acted out his own mutilation.

"Probably like a tooth," Lucy mused after some thought. "Kinda hurts at first. One quick rip, and then it's all over. Yeah, like a tooth. Ya know? That *good* hurt." Her face seemed more complacent regarding the surgical nuances of declawing. "Besides, they grow back. It's not like an arm, where we wouldn't have it anymore."

Rudy stared into the water, his gaze skipping over the waves as he digested the information from his fishing buddy. He watched three pelicans flying over Sunset Beach and admired their beauty. The sky was a smear of pastel orange, purple and blue. A slight breeze of warm air pushed the bay water into the seawall, and it made a lapping noise against the barnacles and rocks.

The end of just another perfect day in paradise. Though, this day was different than any other up to that point. This was the day before Lucy's twelfth birthday.

"Nixon Fires Top Aides Hall-de-man and Earl-lick-man," Lucy said, stiffly reciting the newspaper headline.

A blank look grew over Rudy's face.

"So whatta ya think about the Dolphins' chances this season?" he asked with a swipe at the sweat gathering on his forehead.

"Shoes'll do it. Pretty hard to match the perfection from last season, though," answered Lucy in a voice well versed in sports jargon. "But I'm not sure I'm really ready for football this season."

She stared at the setting sun for a moment and then looked back down at the newspaper with a pair of eager eyes.

"Ko...Ho...Tek Comet should be visible this summer," she mumbled as she read another headline. "Comet of the century, some astronomers believe."

"Not ready for football! Are you sick, Loose? I mean, we're talking the Fins here, right?"

Lucy returned her gaze toward the setting sun with longing.

"No, Rude."

"Why are you reading the front...page?"

"I think I'm getting to the age where I should start learning about the world," she answered, placing a hand flat on her chest. "When you get as old as me, you might find it necessary to stay up on current events, too."

Rudy expelled a long breath through his nostrils as he pushed his chin onto his chest, wincing.

"I'll be your age in a few months, and I'm still gonna read the sports section, Loose."

As the last of the sun melted into the dancing shine of the Gulf, the two gathered up their fishing gear and headed up to Sunset Tavern where their dads were sipping their usual flat draft beers. This time of day often made Rudy most anxious. Just after it got dark was the time when most of the tavern regulars were working up their daily drunken tune. It was the same old tune for Rudy.

"I tell ya, Gene, I think we should openna joint," Bill slurred. "Na jes' any place, the bigges'n the bes' joint on the beach. Women. Put women'n short shorts. Asses put asses in the seats. Gene...?" He cupped his hands into mock breasts over his chest.

Lucy's father nodded politely as he listened to Bill's plans. Plans he had heard for years. Plans that would not be as farfetched if they did not fade into the obscurity of the next morning's hangover.

"Can't be in the junk business forever," Bill slurred.

"Yeah, that would be something, wouldn't it?" answered Gene. "I'd like to see that happen, Bill. I'd really like to see that happen."

A rusty metal sign hanging on the side of Sunset Tavern hinted at the age of the beaten-down joint. Despite its decrepit appearance, the place had somehow weathered more than one storm. Hurricane Agnes had paid a visit the previous summer. A six-foot-high watermark by the pool table, the tavern's lone trophy from the storm surge, was coated in polyurethane to preserve it as a conversation piece.

With some good storms and destruction comes insurance money, and the tavern's salty owner, Wally, had used every penny of it to refurbish the inside of his popular dive.

"Another, Gene?" barked Wally, whose favorite claim to fame was being stationed in the same unit as Joe DiMaggio in the Second World War—a novelty that seemed to find its way into almost every conversation.

"I'm good," answered Gene, covering a nearly empty glass of beer with his hand.

"You're good," Wally stated stiffly.

"I'll have 'nother, Wall," muttered Bill.

"'Course you will."

Rudy's face sank. His dad was slurring already and the sun had just gone down. He decided not to bother his dad with "When we gonna leave?" It would keep him in a better mood.

Lucy sat on a pickle bucket and continued to educate herself about the world affairs of the day.

"Any luck, hon?" Gene asked his daughter.

"No, Dad. Just a coupla bites," she replied, not looking up from the newspaper. "Crabs were kinda small, too."

"Din't catch nuthin' yet, Rudy?" mumbled Bill.

"No, Dad. Maybe I'll have more luck with the blue crabs."

He smiled sadly toward Lucy.

Bill's head bobbed as he continued to look at his son. With a slow, lazy wink he hunched further over his beer. "Whas amatta—losin' yer touch, Son?"

"Time to go, honey?" Gene said, motioning to his daughter.

"Yeah, Dad," Lucy said. "See ya, Rude."

Rudy only nodded, knowing it would be a long solo night from here. Any word uttered might have come close to a sob.

Gene and Lucy hopped into their Sedan DeVille and drove off, stirring up dust in the sandy parking lot.

Rudy looked after them, then glanced up at the snowy, black-and-white television over the bar.

"Local real estate mogul was honored today for his charitable work in the community. Lawrence Kronis received the Humanitarian of the Year award from the St. Petersburg Beach Rotary Club," announced a news reporter.

A man with jet-black hair and a huge white smile walked across a stage to a podium and accepted a large wood-and-gold plaque. He nodded politely to the crowd that was on its feet, clapping. Periodically, he turned to give the audience a chance to bathe his body in white flashes of light—pictures that would become further testimony to his greatness.

"This is getting to be a yearly piece of hardware for this fine gentleman," the news anchorwoman commented with a laugh.

"That's right, Karen. When's my turn?" joked the male anchor as he segued into another story.

"Phhh," Bill mumbled into his drink after a lengthy cross-eyed stare at the television. "That sonofabitch. Humanitarian? Gotta be a goddamned human first."

Wally looked blankly at Bill. A Joe Dimaggio anecdote was on the tip of his tongue, but he saw that it would be wasted. The alcohol was already enveloping Bill's mind. He rubbed the bar with a wet towel instead and asked, "'Nother?"

Bill struggled to push his head up. He slid his glass toward Wally and shook his head back and forth, but said, "Yeah, 'nother."

Chapter 2

Whenever it happened, Rudy would study the bathroom mirror and try to distinguish the sweat beads from the tears. The pain sometimes would be so unbearable that his head would go numb from holding his breath and then grow into a slow pounding throb.

"Gawwwwd," he exhaled. His long, brown, curly hair, matted against his forehead, resembled the form-fitted slope of a bicycle helmet.

"You almost done in there?" prodded a monotone whisper from the other side.

"Uhh…," Rudy responded. "Uh, yeah. Yes, Mom. I'll be out in a sec." He coughed softly to cover a whimper.

A bland housedress with two skinny arms protruding hung loosely on Lillian's body. The paleness of her long neck gave her the appearance of a delicate porcelain doll. Her simple face, with traces of hidden beauty, was now masked with years of concern and worry. A tight bun sitting neatly on the top of her head allowed a few stray hairs to spill down behind each ear.

Occasionally stealing a glance at the dirty clock on the wall, she paced nervously between the living room and the hallway, her slippers shuffling along the beaten down carpet while barely staying on her feet. A sink full of dirty dishes, a pile of empty beer cans on the counter, and a trail of stained socks and worn-soled shoes reminded her that she was way behind schedule. Bill would be up soon, and nothing was done yet.

"Are you sure everything's okay in there?" she asked again in a heightened pitch.

"I'm okay," Rudy answered in a shaky voice as he emerged from the bathroom. "Is there anything for breakfast?"

"Eggs," she rasped, scurrying back to the kitchen to tend to a smoking pan on the stove. "Only a couple, though. I was holding those for your father. Please stay quiet. He's still sleeping. How 'bout a glass of milk?"

"No, thank you," Rudy replied, disappointed, yet with the proper respect owed to his mother. "I'll just get something while I'm out. Maybe Wally's got leftover waffles."

He grabbed a worn Dolphins hat and slid it on his still wet head. Lillian watched her son roll up his *Mad Magazine* and put it in his backpack with deliberate care. A rare smile was about to blossom on her face when the untimely clang of an alarm clock bell interrupted.

"Goddamnit, Lil!" bellowed a tobacco tar-coated voice from the bedroom. "Where the hell are my slippers? I can't find anything in this house."

"Just a minute, Bill. I'll be right there!"

Lillian turned away from the noise in the back of the duplex and looked sympathetically at her son. "You try to have fun today," she said, giving him a tired smile.

Walking Rudy to the front door, she admired how innocently he went about his life. She longed to be back at that place herself.

Returning to the kitchen, she wiped her running nose with a tissue. Then she grabbed a glass of water and swallowed the pill that had been moistening in her palm for the last fifteen minutes.

"Lillian…Lillian…!"

"In a minute, Bill…just a minute." Her voice ascended in agitation with each impatient prompt.

There is something special about the morning you wake up on your birthday when you are a kid. The air seems to smell fresher. The sheets feel softer. The sun finds its way to your pillow and hits your face, making your eyes squint with pain and happiness at the same time.

Normally, Lucy had a hard time waking up. Her dad, a notoriously early riser, would have to nudge her three or four times before she would even think about stirring. But this was her twelfth birthday, and she was up before her dad even had a chance to roust her once!

Lucy hopped to her feet to go to the full-length mirror on her bedroom door. The air conditioning made the terrazzo painfully cold, and she tip-toed gingerly across the floor. She wanted to see if she somehow looked any different. She had always heard how a young lady starts to change at the age of twelve, and she wondered if any developments had taken place during the night. Getting a side view, she ran her hands down her chest and over her stomach and back up her chest again.

"They're never gonna get here," she said unhappily.

Many of the girls in her class had already grown partial signs of womanhood, and some of them had even started their period the year before. Lucy felt that she was somehow missing out on all the fun. Perhaps this twelfth birthday was not going to be the special one she had anticipated.

Digging through a pile of clothes, she reluctantly slipped on a loose pair of faded Wranglers. Pulling a worn T-shirt over her head, she found her face in the mirror and frowned at her poor sense of style. "Is this how a lady should dress?" she mumbled to herself. A pair of red, white and blue tennis shoes completed the clumsy ensemble.

A singular ray of sun drew a bright line across the countertop of the neatly kept kitchen. A folded dish towel hung on a hook over two freshly washed pans. A pot bubbled on the stove, emitting the smell of recently brewed coffee.

From the doorway, Lucy took in the glass of foamy orange juice towering over a pile of pancakes, sausage and toast, which were laid smartly on a blue plate, waiting for her. The silver fork, knife and spoon next to them glinted on the flat white napkin.

She watched as her dad licked his thumb when he finished with the front page and slowly opened the newspaper. The tavern in the evenings and his morning breakfast were his two respites from the mundane activities of running a twenty-unit motel. If Gene had to choose, it was the mornings he found more relaxing. He could achieve a sense of tranquility preparing an elaborate breakfast and enjoying the warm feeling of two or three cups of coffee.

Lucy sat down and leaned over to give her dad a kiss on the cheek. Prodding the pillar of pancakes with the fork and slicing into it with the knife caused a steady flow of buttery syrup to pour down into the gash she'd made.

"Anything good going on today?" Gene asked playfully.

"Not much. Probably gonna go down to Sunset Tavern and see how the fish are running. Crab a bit. See what Rudy's up to."

"Ahh, just another day." Gene sat back to admire his daughter as he took a long sip of coffee.

"Yep," Lucy said tersely, not looking up from her pile of food.

Gene put down his mug and pushed his chair back. He reached down to his feet and pulled a brightly wrapped, rectangular box with a big red bow from under the table.

"Happy Birthday!"

Lucy put down her fork and did her best to suppress a smile. "What is it?"

"Why is it everyone asks 'What is it?'" Gene said, laughing. "Just open it up and find out."

Lucy tugged at the red bow, which gave way without much effort. "Did you wrap this?"

Gene answered with a shrug.

Carefully pulling away the pretty wrapping paper, Lucy found a white box underneath. Slowly she lifted the lid and peeled back the tissue paper.

"Wow!" she gasped. "It's beautiful."

Gene's face lit up as she held up a lacy white dress admiringly. He grinned when she giggled over the pair of high heels she eventually found tucked under a second layer of tissue paper. He beamed when she hugged and kissed him and called the gifts "perfect."

A rattle from the bells on the office door broke their embrace.

"Gotta get to work, I guess, honey. I hope you have a happy birthday today."

"Thank you, Dad. Thanks for the dress, too. I think I'll save it for a special occasion," Lucy said, running her hand over the soft, white lace.

Gene downed the last gulp of coffee in his cup, wiped his mouth with a napkin and patted Lucy's shoulder.

"Looks like someone needs a room. We'll get together later on this afternoon."

Lucy gave her dad a knowing look and offered him her cheek to kiss. Watching him walk out of the door, she could not help but think how lucky she was to have such a good father. Especially with her mother gone. He was everything to her. She did her best to reciprocate the love he showed, but not nearly as often as she should.

When Lucy was done with her breakfast, she gently placed her blue plate into the sink and picked up her new dress and shoes on the way to the office. It was always a game to inspect the new people who were checking in to the motel. Mainly, she was interested to see if they had any kids.

The motel camaraderie Lucy developed with the children of guests was unique. She was able to make friends from all over the country, the world even, but it would usually only last for about two weeks. The first couple of days would be awkward, but then the next ten would be great fun. She would bring her new friend to the tavern and meet up with Rudy. There would be fishing, swimming and pinball. The last two days would get awkward again. A sense of aloofness or a series of minor arguments would ensue. The tension often helped to ease the pain of ending the relationship as guests were concluding their stay at the motel.

Lucy yanked at the door of the office confidently and shimmied past the narrow opening. She stopped in surprise to see a clean-cut young man in his early twenties bending over the desk. His pale face, corduroy pants and flannel shirt suggested that he was from up North.

Lucy watched as the man signed his name on the rental agreement. His long fingers and nails were finely manicured and moved with a grace she had not seen before. They seemed to be the hands of a man who had not done a day of manual labor in his life.

When he was finished filling out the paperwork for the rental, he looked up at Lucy with a pair of the most radiant blue eyes she had ever seen.

"Hello," he said.

Startled by the fact that he had noticed her, she could only muster a barely audible, "Haigh."

A long silence followed, punctuated by some fidgeting and eyes darting back and forth. The seconds felt like minutes to Lucy as she stood transfixed by the attractive guest. Embarrassed by her behavior, she spun away from the office and dashed into her room.

"Omigod! What was that?" she said under her breath.

This was a new feeling that Lucy had never felt before. Her stomach burned warmly. While it hurt, it felt good. It was a good pain.

She placed her new white dress softly on the bed, picked up her smiling Skipper doll and shook her head at it. "What was that?" she asked again.

"Okay, Mr. uh, Hughes," Gene said, looking over a pair of reading glasses at the man. "You're in room 17, next to the swimming pool."

The man looked over his shoulder to see where the proprietor was pointing his finger.

"Adjacent to the shuffleboard court," Gene added with an enthusiastic voice.

He was always proud to show off this prized guest recreation area, since it was his first and only construction effort to improve the motel and served as a landmark for navigating his guests around the property.

"Please, call me Orel," said the man.

"Well, sure thing, Orel. Nice to meet you," Gene replied as he reached out his hand. "Gene. Gene Lewis."

"The pleasure's mine, Gene."

"Canadian…I detect there, Orel?"

"Uh, yes, sir. Toronto." Orel pointed to his driver's license before pocketing it.

"Great. We have many Canadians staying with us throughout the year, and they seem to love it." Gene's voice took on a south-of-the-border twang. "Hope you enjoy your stay at the Gulfside Oasis."

"Thank you, sir. I intend to," Orel answered, smiling, as he picked up his red plaid bag.

About to walk out of the office, he reached in his chest pocket and pulled out a crumbled piece of paper. He looked down for a few seconds, then spun back toward Gene.

"Can you point me in the direction of"—he stopped to look at his note again—"the Near-van-ah…," he stuttered phonetically.

"Nearvana. Sure, it's north on Gulf Boulevard for two miles, then a left on Coquina, and you'll see it on the right hand side just up Sunset Way," Gene recited like a tour guide pulling from his repertoire.

With an appreciative nod Orel exited the jalousie-windowed office door into the courtyard of the motel in search of room 17.

The finely kept grounds of the Oasis were a big reason guests stayed with Gene. Sloping coconut trees hugged the motel rooms' entrances. Brick walkways adorned with beautiful yellow and pink flowers wound around small fountains and fish pools. A wooden deck with a gazebo overlooked the large swimming pool, which was surrounded by lush bamboo bushes. During the busy season, it was the center of activity.

On weekends, Gene would book bands to play for the entertainment of his guests. The parties, which often lasted late into the night, were the highlight of the week for many of the visiting tourists and another reason Gene had such strong return clientele.

Lucy stuck her head back in the office. "All right, Dad, I'm heading down to the seawall after I do my chores."

"Okay, sweetie. Stay dry down there," advised Gene without looking up from scribbling in his ledger. "And don't forget to have a good birthday today, honey."

Lucy walked to the counter, leaned over and kissed her dad. Then she skipped out the door. "I will. Thanks."

She headed for the courtyard where cups, napkins, soda cans and cigarette butts littered the beautiful landscape. Although it was a dirty job, somebody had to make it paradise again, and that was Lucy's responsibility—even on her birthday.

She methodically deposited the trash into a large, plastic garbage bag that hung on the back of a chaise lounge. She saved the ashtrays and cigarette butts scattered on the tables for last. One by one, Lucy segregated the cigarette butts from the ashes and gum wrappers and put them into a small sandwich-sized plastic bag.

"Marlboro. Nice. Kool." Lucy smiled as she itemized the barely smoked cigarettes. "Those are keepers."

When the grounds were once again pristine, she headed to the bathroom to wash her hands and get ready for a day full of fun.

With the regulars either at work or sleeping off a cocktail flu, the Sunset Tavern was a much calmer and quieter place. In the unforgiving daylight, it looked like a funhouse with the lights turned off. Unlit neon beer signs were but shadows of the gleaming beauties they became at night. The walls were dotted with different colored paint, each shade covering a mark left by a drunken stumble or a clumsy pool stick. Most noticeably, the inside had a daytime smell of dirty mop and hot bleach water.

Although it lacked the nighttime romance, Lucy and Rudy loved being at the tavern during the day. It was the only time that unsupervised children had unfettered access to the adult establishment normally cluttered with burned-out hippies and tired old men, and they relished their chance to play pool and listen to their own music.

"Six up high, Rude," Lucy said, eyeing her next shot on the table.

"Anything you wanna hear on your birthday, Loose?" Rudy asked, inspecting the wealth of choices on the jukebox.

Although he had memorized all the selections, he always searched for a new card, which would not have yellow nicotine stains yet. He would play the selection over and over and enjoyed watching Wally's blood pressure rise, as the owner grumbled about "the goddamned music the kids listen to these days."

"How 'bout 'Brother Louie,' Rude?" Lucy requested as she circled the table, sizing up her next shot.

"Right on, Loose," he answered, knowing that it was her favorite song because she could change the words to fit her name.

"You're up, Rude," Lucy said after she muffed her try at the six.

"High balls?"

"Yup."

Rudy was an average pool player at best. His height made longer shots difficult. Many times when he was actually doing well, he'd buckle under the pressure and lose his composure. He would forget to chalk his stick and end up mishitting an important shot or making a bad decision on which ball to play.

"Eleven in the corner," he said pointing to the red-striped ball snug up against the jutting green edge. Leaning over the table as far as he could, he reached toward the ball with one foot completely off the floor. A puff of blue and white chalk stained the felt table as he banked the eleven off the side and into the center.

"Dang it!"

"Still can't hit the rail shot, huh, Rude?" chided Lucy in between crooning verses of "Loosie Loosie Loosie Looseeee."

Rudy dejectedly hung up his pool cue and said, "Let's go."

The air outside the tavern already hinted at the muggy May afternoon to come. The late starting mullet boats gave off a familiar smell of gas and saltwater as they made their way through the channel. A few fishermen had already gathered along the seawall in expectation of the high tide.

On the far side of the wall, a grassy area covered in sea oats formed a natural barrier between the Sunset Tavern regulars and those just fishing. Usually this was where the black folks would wade into the water up to their hips, angling for saltwater cats with their bamboo poles. Rudy and Lucy enjoyed going past the high grass because it gave them some privacy from the people they knew.

"What'd ya get, Loose?" Rudy asked when they finally settled behind one of the larger sea oats.

"Lemme see. Two Marlboros, a Camel, a Benson and Hedges, and three Kools," tallied Lucy, peeking into the small plastic bag.

"Kools! I get the Kools," Rudy yelped excitedly.

"You always get the Kools. I like 'em too, ya know."

It was the menthol the kids coveted. The minty tasting cigarettes were easier to smoke and made their breath seem so fresh that they thought no one could tell what they'd been doing.

After agreeing to split the Kools and save one for later, they lit the half-smoked butts and leaned back on the sand to enjoy the view in between violent coughs.

"So, how's it feel to be twelve?" Rudy asked, squinting through his own murky exhalation.

"Pretty much the same as it felt to be eleven, I guess."

This was the third year they played this question and answer game, and the third year Rudy would have to wait six months to find out how it felt to be her age. His November birthday remained the problem. Normally, it didn't matter, but on Lucy's birthday in May, he always felt so much younger than her. Though the day before they were the same age, for six months she would be twelve and he would still be eleven. At that age, it often proved a significant difference.

"Hey, Rude," Lucy started, drawing a line in the sand with her toe. "You ever see me as a female?"

Rudy's face looked as if he were suddenly wrestling with lungs full of smoke. It was a question for which he had no immediate answer. His eyes became slits and the hole that opened in his lips pushed out a long stream of white smoke, followed by a suppressed cough.

"A female?" he asked, feigning disinterest.

"Yeah," she persisted. "Like someone other than just a buddy to hang around with. A girl."

Rudy looked sideways at Lucy and exhaled another puff of smoke in her direction. The odd question left him uncharacteristically speechless. He leaned back on the sand dune, putting his head on his hand as he pulled the cigarette to his lips, the way he had seen it done on television.

A long silence ensued, though not an uncomfortable one. Normally, it was easy to be around Lucy. She never complained about putting worms on hooks or cutting up a pinfish for bait or ripping the claw off a crab for Rudy. She knew the name of the water boy for the Miami Dolphins and Jim Palmer's win-loss record and ERA for the past three years, and even his underwear size. She also knew the precise way to gig a stingray without breaking her pole. But now, she wanted to know if Rudy had ever seen her as a girl.

"Well, Loose," he started with a giggle. "I guess—"

Before he could finish speaking, the sound of a beeping horn in the distance peppered the air. Rudy stood up and pushed aside the sea oats. At first, all he could make out was a billowing cloud of sandy dust. Then he realized it was his dad's old red Ford pick-up truck that was making all the commotion as it approached the seawall.

"Loose, it's my dad!" he exclaimed.

"Your dad!" Lucy gasped as she quickly gathered up the remainder of the cigarette butts they had not yet smoked. "What's he doing, coming here at this hour?"

"I dunno…he should be making his rounds right now," said Rudy. "He can't be done with work already, can he?"

Bill pulled his truck into the tavern parking lot and swerved toward the kids with his arm hanging out of the driver's side window. Lucy noticed that there was someone in the passenger seat next to him.

"Who's with him, Rude?"

"Is it your dad, Loose?"

The two exchanged puzzled looks, realizing that Gene was sitting in the truck with Bill. Their puzzlement turned to disbelief when Gene climbed out of the rolling truck and waved excitedly to the children.

"Happy birthday, Lucy!" he shouted in a giddy manner not often heard. "Hop in! We're goin' to have a party!"

"A party," said Rudy, giggling as he ran to the bed of the truck. "Hey, Loose, there's hay in the back! It's a hayride!"

"Hayride?"

"Sure, sweetie. Hay ain't just for horses, ya know," Gene yelled, slapping his knee and laughing extra loud to drive home the joke.

Lucy grinned and hopped in the back of the truck with Rudy. It was strange to see the old Ford hauling something besides garbage—a stark contrast to its traditional payload of broken box springs, smashed televisions or dirty toilet bowls.

"Ahhright, Bill, let's go!" Gene shouted with a wink to his buddy.

"Where we gonna go?" asked Bill.

"Well…take a ride down past the Oasis. Let Lucy show off in front of the guests," Gene instructed, motioning with his arm in different directions. "We'll spin around the beach for a bit. Then…Three Swings. Yeah, Three Swings for pizza!"

"Wanna go to the Three Swings, kids?" yelled Bill, leaning out of the window.

"All right! Three Swings!" Rudy yelped.

Lucy's face lit up with excitement, as she hastily pushed the sandwich bag of cigarettes deep inside her bleached pair of Wranglers to hide their habit.

"Yeah, Three Swings!" she joined in.

Bill turned the truck down Palm Way on his way past the Oasis. "Pool's looking kinda slow. You pretty empty, Gene?" he asked.

"Yeah. It flattened out a bit the past few days, but I welcome that from time to time. Gives me a chance to get some jobs done and spend more time with Lucy."

As the truck motored loudly past the motel, Lucy saw the new guest getting out of the pool and drying off. His pale body was so white, it almost seemed to reflect the sun. His dark brown hair got darker when it was wet. Though his frame was slender, his sinewy shoulders, legs and brief swimsuit indicated that he may have been a swimmer at some point in his life.

"Hey, Loose, check out the speedo boy at your motel," Rudy said. "Geez, what's with wanting to wear one of those things?"

Lucy smiled as she looked at the man's bathing suit.

"Weenie Bender!" Rudy exclaimed, laughing. "Guy's wearing a Weenie Bender!"

Reluctantly she joined in. "Looks more like a marble sack," she said, giggling.

Yet, somehow she could not stop looking in the direction of the man as they drove past the Oasis.

The red truck struggled down the boulevard to the entrance of Three Swings, which sported a sign with the name of the place and a list of all it had to offer.

There was something for everyone. Rudy and Lucy's eyes widened when they saw "Miniature Golf, Game Room, Batting Cages." Gene was looking forward to "Pizza." And Bill's mouth was already watering at the promise of "Coldest Beer in Town!"

Lucy caught the reflection of her dad's face in the passenger side rear view mirror. His smile was big and his eyes gleamed with excitement. She thought of how much he had done for her over the years. This surprise hayride and party was just another example. Finally Gene noticed Lucy watching him in the mirror. He smiled and he gave her a loving wink. It was then that Lucy realized this would be her most special birthday.

The Red Room in the back of the restaurant was dark with the exception of two intricate chandeliers and some sconce lights pointing toward the ceiling. Sepia photos of deceased family members of the restaurant and city dignitaries hung on the red velvet walls. A rustic tile bar was on one side of the room. Behind it, liquor bottles were lined up neatly on shelves bordered by stucco arches.

Waiters in black trousers, red vests and white long sleeve shirts placed a napkin onto the lap of each guest as he took his seat. Then they removed the presentation china and poured Sangria into every glass on the table.

The invitation to the quarterly meeting was only extended to the well-connected, a periodic opportunity for the Tampa Bay area elite to network. The food was always the main attraction at these gatherings. Arroz con Pollo, large slabs of Mahi Mahi, plates of Ropa Vieja and chorizo sausage in sauteed onions, bowls of Cuban black bean soup and wine bottles of various vintages crowded every table.

"I never get tired of coming to these things, Mr. Kronis."

The heavyset man nodded slightly in agreement. But his concentration was more focused on the man at the head table rather than worry about his dining partner.

"See that guy over there?" Kronis said pointing with his forehead while using both hands to wipe his mouth with the cloth napkin. "Runs this entire state."

Sam looked toward the old, balding man with coke bottle glasses at the head table. He returned to his meal with a half a nod, acknowledging that he recognized him.

"He runs the whole goddamned state from the south side of the beach," Kronis elaborated, continuing to fix his eyes on the unassuming figure laughing with his table mates. "The same beach we live on. He can buy and sell both of us three or four times and not even feel a dent in his wallet."

Sam's chewing slowed as he sensed a rise in his boss's intensity.

"He does all this…" Kronis paused, knowing his words would run away with him if he did not compose himself. He took a deep breath and started anew, "Listen, Jonny's dead."

Sam put down his fork knowing the conversation had turned to business and would require his full attention.

"Yes, sir," he said. "Took a little longer than we expected, but that was the desired outcome, was it not?"

Kronis worked a fork and knife through the middle of the chorizo as he pondered Sam's question. The long silence dangled in the air till the surgery was complete and Kronis was able to slide the piece of meat into his mouth.

Sam's face tightened, hoping he had not upset the man with poorly chosen words. A nervous twitch danced on his mouth as he waited for Kronis to formulate a reply.

"Desired outcome," Kronis mumbled, laughing, through a half-chewed sausage. "Desired outcome? Well, Mr. Eisenrad, the desired outcome would have been for me to have retrieved what was mine."

Sam tugged at his shirtsleeve in obvious discomfort. Kronis was not only using his last name, but also what he'd just said. Never a good sign. Sam had seen other guys on the wrong end of this conversation before.

"The desired result…," Kronis started again, his eyelids squinting, "would have been to retain some dignity. The desired result would have been able to retain some control." Kronis' dark face reddened as his voice rose. "The desired result would have been to not get swindled by…a goddamned piano player!"

Sam froze as he saw a few men from another table look in their direction. He knew it was best at events like these to be seen, but not heard, to be viewed as a cool customer. An icy glance at the nosy rubberneckers returned them to the business of eating their meals.

"So, where do we go from here?" Sam asked in a hushed tone, hoping to diffuse Kronis' anger.

Without looking up from his plate, where he was dismembering a second sausage, Kronis said, "The places."

Sam's eyebrows contracted as he attempted to define Kronis' meaning.

"We start by gutting the places. Sand Dollar, Gulf Breeze… Nearvana. Tear them apart and start over." Kronis speared the remains of the mangled sausage with his fork and put them into his mouth. "Sink a little bit of dough into them and get new meat in there. This will accomplish two goals. New tenants in the old burned out joints, which means cash flow to rebuild the lost capital."

His words were somewhat garbled from chewing and mixing his food with a sip of red wine. Sam concentrated hard to follow along.

"The second goal would be to get some answers."

"Okay, sir. When shall we start?"

"First thing Monday morning we'll–"

Kronis was interrupted by a tap on his shoulder.

"Lawrence! How the hell are you?" came a confident booming voice from behind him.

Kronis turned and looked up at a tall, gray-haired man in his early sixties in a finely creased suit and a tightly knotted tie.

"Senator!" he said enthusiastically and stood up to shake the man's hand and pat his shoulder "How long has it been?"

"Too long," the Senator responded with a dazzling smile, clasping Kronis' hand between two of his own. "I saw you on the news the other day and just had to stop by and say congratulations."

Kronis nodded in appreciation. "Thank you, sir. That's very kind."

"Let me introduce you to a friend of mine," the Senator said as the two walked over to the bar near the head table to grab a drink.

As he worked his way toward the exit of the restaurant, Sam looked back over his shoulder to see the Senator leading Kronis to a seat next to the balding man with the coke bottle glasses.

Chapter 3

The late spring air was hotter than he expected. This journey had seemed like a good idea when he started. Of course, it was only 10:30 in the morning then, and by now the noon sun was causing the humidity to rise. Dress shoes, corduroy slacks and a long sleeve shirt were also a poor choice of attire for the trip.

It was lucky he had brought one of the motel towels with him on the walk. By now, the shirt, opened to the fourth button and its sleeves rolled up above his elbows, was soaked with sweat. After some consideration, he found that draping the towel around his neck helped to keep him cooler.

In the distance, several blocks down the road, he could make out the shape of the old building. As he got closer, he noticed that the parking lot was empty and covered with overgrown bushes and weeds. The wooden exterior of the place showed dry rot everywhere, and most of the windows were boarded up.

A once-fancy sign swayed sideways from a pair of rusty hinges, giving the impression that one stiff breeze might make it fall at any moment. Turning his head sideways he read, "Nearvana Fine Dining" in scripted lettering framed by an oval of clear light bulbs.

Orel stopped momentarily and reached into his pocket to pull out the soft paper. He unfolded it carefully, afraid it might rip. He wiped at the sweat beads on his brow and upper lip. "Two hands…," he whispered, his voice fading to mouthing the words. "Two fingers…"

A melancholic feeling in the pit of his stomach accompanied the rush of vague memories associated with the decrepit building. The longer he stared at it, the clearer they echoed through his mind.

"Daddy, who's that man?"
"That's Mr. Kronis, Orie."
"He looks kinda scary, Daddy. Is he a bad guy?"
"Nah…he just tries to look that way…. That's the Boss's job."

Orel found one window that had a board loose enough to pry off, so he could look inside. Years of accumulated filth covered the window, making it nearly impossible to see through. He glanced around briefly, then felt for the towel around his neck. With a circular swipe he made a round clear spot, which allowed him to get a veiled view of the inside. A mere glimpse of the place that was…a mere glimpse of his past.

Water spewed so high it hit the ceiling and dripped down onto Gene's head. Only when his hair was really wet was it noticeable that it had been thinning. His velour shirt and khaki trousers were drenched and discolored from the leaking water, which gushed out of the PVC pipe ascending from the top of the pool pump. The room, a combination pool house and laundromat for the maid, was soon covered with linty, chlorine puddles.

"How we gonna get this taken care of, Mista Lewis?" asked Joyce rolling her eyes and biting her lip. Her twenty years of service with the Oasis were longer than the nine and a half that Gene had owned it. She was a fixture that had come with the purchase of the motel. Her tenure allowed Joyce more confidence in times of stress. She was at her best when Gene was at his worst and over his head in a certain project.

"Better call Phil da pool man, Mista Lewis."

"Ya know, Phil is just gonna say it needs a new coupling, Joyce. It's notta problem…I got it," Gene replied as he raked his head pensively. His fingers kept pulling at some of the wet strands, hoping to make them appear more voluminous.

Gene tended to glom onto a specific word when he was trying to solve a problem. Suddenly "coupling" became the recurring word of choice. After the fifth "coupling" issued from his mouth, he was interrupted by a familiar voice.

"Hello, hello," came a greeting from the door.

"Yeah, we're here, hon. Watcha need?" Joyce yelled through the din of the pump and leaking water.

Orel walked gingerly through the puddles to get closer to Joyce and Gene. His face was beaded with sweat and his soaked undershirt hung transparently on his pale skin. Not paying much attention to the commotion erupting from the pool pump, he turned his blue eyes to Joyce.

"Uh, hello. I was wondering if I could get another towel for my room. I've soiled this one," he said, looking at her apologetically.

"Dang it!" yelled Gene in the background.

"Oh, I'm sorry. It should come clean," responded a startled Orel, pointing to the light dirt on the towel. "And if not, I will gladly reimburse you for its replacement."

"Wha…?" Gene looked puzzled in Orel's direction. "Oh…not the towel! This doggone leak seems to be getting worse. I think it's gonna need a coupling." He turned back to survey the gushing mess.

"Ahh, that's quite a geyser there, eh?" remarked Orel, grinning as he moved in to get a closer look. Suddenly, his face came in direct contact with the spray. "This water's just what you need after a good walk," he said appreciatively.

Gene scowled his disapproval at his new guest's levity regarding what he considered a serious situation. "With all due respect, sir, there's a whole pool of it outside the door, if you want the full effect."

"I think you need a new seat on this valve and your problems should be over," said Orel assessing the damage through a steady stream of water.

"Seat?" said Gene, mystified, his face covered in water beads.

"Yeah, the heavy chlorine in the pool water wears them out over time and they need replacing periodically," offered Orel "Same thing used to happen to our rigs in Canada. It'd drive my uncle crazy."

Joyce kept pace folding towels and doing her best to keep them out of the water. Every now and then, she glanced up to hear what Orel had to say, just in case Gene was missing any of it.

"They only cost about a little over an American dollar in the tool store. But they save a peck of headaches," continued Orel.

"Seats? Seats, Joyce. Sounds like we need some new seats in our valves," said Gene, not realizing she was paying attention to the conversation. "I'm gonna head down to Ace and pick up some seats. Yes! Seats, that's what I thought."

"Better turn off the pump for a bit to stop the leaking for now, sir," advised the Canadian.

"Yeah, I was gonna do that," replied Gene. "I just had it on to see where the leak was coming from."

"Well, I think that should do the trick," said Orel, flipping the switch on the pump to off. Then he turned toward Joyce. "Could I please have that towel now, ma'am?"

"Yassir! One towel coming up. And try not ta soil dis one," said Joyce, breaking into a toothy smile.

As Orel walked away from the laundry room, he noticed that Gene was already heading out of the office door with his car keys in hand.

"Off to the hardware store to buy some seats," yelled Gene to Lucy, who was lying next to the pool. "Be right back, honey."

"Seats," mouthed Lucy to herself, trying to understand why her dad was going to the hardware store to buy chairs when there was a closet full in the hall. She waved unenthusiastically as Gene drove off and returned to her *Tiger Beat* magazine, but her concentration was interrupted by a warm voice.

"Lovely day to sit around the pool, eh?"

Lucy held her hand up to shield her face from the sun and closed one eye to make out a silhouette.

"Yeah…yes, it is," she winced, realizing it was the new guest standing over her.

In his corduroy pants, soaked T-shirt and flannel shirt wrapped around his waist he reminded her of a scarecrow.

"I was thinking about coming out too, but I needed to get a new towel and put on my swim trunks first," he said, motioning to the unseasonable clothing he was wearing.

Lucy nodded and started to turn her attention back to her magazine, though she found it odd that he called a Speedo "trunks."

"Orel. Orel Hughes," he said, extending a hand.

"Hi. I'm Lucy," she answered bashfully, yet offered him her hand politely. "Nicetameetcha."

"Pleasure's mine, Lucyball," Orel said, grinning. "I'll be right back. Lemme go change."

As Orel turned to go back to his room, Lucy followed him with her eyes. She noticed the fine lines of his broad shoulders and otherwise thin frame and admired his short haircut, which was met at the base of his neck with freshly pinked skin from his morning walk in the Florida sun.

"Wanna cold drink, Lucyball?" he yelled, spinning around quickly.

"Uh uhhh—no thanks," she answered nervously, turning her eyes away from him.

"I'll get one for myself then. Too hot out here," Orel said and then walked the remainder of the way back to his room.

Butterflies flitted in her stomach as she thought of how oddly he said her name. They had met only minutes earlier and already he had given her a nickname.

On his way back, Orel continued to make himself familiar with the grounds of the Oasis. His light step and somewhat curious demeanor made him an interesting character to watch. As he passed the fishpond, he stopped to drop something into the water, then laughed. When he finally made his way back to where Lucy was sitting, he held out a bag of Pepperidge Farm Goldfish.

"Wanna Goldfish, Lucyball?" asked Orel. "The guppies in the gully over there seem to like them."

Her polite smile at the joke turned into a broad grin when she saw that he was wearing his Weenie Bender swim trunks.

"No thank you, sir," she said, quickly hiding her face in the magazine.

"Sir? My father is 'sir.' I'm just plain Orel, Lucyball," he mocked. His eyes wandered around the finely maintained courtyard of the motel as he continued to pop one Goldfish after another into his mouth. "So what's fun to do around here? Seems kinda quiet."

Maintaining her feigned focus on the magazine, Lucy asked, "You like fishing, Orel?"

"Fishing? Sure. Ice fishing's probably my favorite."

"Ice fishing? What's that?"

"We do it in Canada. Usually go into a shack that's on a frozen lake. Cut a hole in the ice and drop a line down. Wait for a bit, and if you're lucky, you pull up a keeper," said Orel as he popped another Goldfish in his mouth.

"Oh. That sounds neat. Cold, though. I don't think I'd like that. I enjoy fishing in the summer, 'cause even if you don't catch any fish, at least you can get some sun."

"So where you go fishing around here, Lucyball?"

"We have a seawall near a place called the Sunset Tavern where we do most of our fishing. There are also stone crabs and blue crabs down there. It's a great place!"

"Oh, yeah? I'll have to check that out later on. Sure you don't want a Goldfish, Lucyball?"

"Sure, why not? I'd love one." As she extended the palm of her hand, she said, "'Cause Pepperidge Fa'am remembas…that's why."

"I beg your pardon?"

"Oh nothing. Just something we say from TV." Lucy giggled, grinning. Then she stuck her nose back in her *Tiger Beat*.

Silence hung heavy in the air of the duplex at night in anticipation of when Bill would finally get home from his route. His frustration with career and life only intensified when he stumbled through the door, reeking of other people's garbage and found his wife on the couch staring straight ahead—in the same position he had left her that morning.

A sharp pain would grow in Rudy's stomach then. Sometimes it reached all the way from his belly to his back.

A twisted lip, huff and head shake at Lillian accompanied Bill tossing his keys onto the kitchen counter next to a disarray of bills and collection notices. The sudden slam of metal on Formica jolted Lillian from her trance.

"Oh hon, how was your day?" she said in a monotone whisper, barely glancing in his direction.

"'Nother day of pickin up other people's garbage. How do you think it was?" Bill responded, followed by a series of mumbled and indefinable words.

With each remark, Rudy could feel the vice tighten. Glassy shards stabbed at his back, radiated up his spine and thrust to the top of his skull.

Dinner routinely commenced with little conversation other than more small talk about work. A few downed Rob Roys would either sedate or fuel Bill's anger and frustration—a nightly crap shoot of which emotion would triumph. The finale came when Bill took off his smelly work boots and plopped into the worn Lazy Boy, which over time had retained so much of his odor that it was marked as his territory only.

"I'm gonna get a few winks," he mumbled, drifting off.

"Mm hmm," Lil acknowledged, clearing the dinner table quietly so as not to disturb him.

"Need help, Mom?" offered Rudy in a whisper.

"No, honey. You just do what you're doing."

The duplex was a simple dwelling which was sparsely, yet tastefully decorated. It was essentially one main space with a dining room attached and a small kitchen off to the side. Bill and Lillian slept in the "master" bedroom while Rudy had grown accustomed, of necessity, to a wiry-mattress pull-out bed over-looking the television.

After almost 30 minutes had passed, Rudy could see his father stir in the Lazy Boy. One side of his face was lined white-and-red from the chair's fabric pressed against his cheek, and his hair swirled in circles around a salt and pepper cowlick. Opening his puffy eyes, he looked around until he found the eyes of his well-behaved son sitting on a folding chair in the corner of the nearly vacant room.

"Rudy, you goin ta tha tavern with me?" he growled with a mucous laden throat.

"Yeah, Dad," replied Rudy, his attention still on the television which was broadcasting the Watergate hearings.

"Well, let's get outta here then. See ya later, Lil," Bill said.

He took one more mouthful of Rob Roy-stained ice and walked out the door with Rudy one step behind.

It was only 6:30, but the Sunset Tavern was already abuzz. Cars were pulling in and people were finding places to sit and enjoy the sunset. Rudy quickly scanned the seawall for Lucy and ran over to join her. Bill found Gene, who ordered up a round for those drinking at the exterior bar of the tavern.

The regulars were as reliable as the setting sun they had come to see. On the inside of the bar sat Dorothy. A former runner-up in the 1927 Miss Florida pageant, she was doing her best—along with periodic plastic surgeries—to fight the fading of her once brilliant good looks. Her dyed-black hair had the texture of cotton candy, while her makeup seemed to be a glazed mix of skin tones and blues. Forty years of smoking had made her skin drawn and her lips wrinkled. She sat stirring her Dewar's while she surveyed the three long-haired construction workers who were playing pool.

"One in the middle's kinda cute," she whispered through Scotch coated lips to the man seated beside her.

Winston did not answer but only nodded nervously. He was a quiet man who kept to himself. It was unclear whether he was skittish by nature or due to the hazards of being an electrician.

Oftentimes, the men on the outside of the tavern would involve Winston in their conversations just to make him feel like he was part of the crowd. Other times, they'd simply yell, "Isn't that right, Winston?" Invariably, Winston would nod, quietly giggle and fumble for the pack of Marlboros in his shirt pocket. Then he'd slouch over the bar and cautiously put a cigarette in his mouth while his eyes darted around the room to see if anyone else was laughing with or at him.

The outside of the tavern was washed in the jovial conversation of the regulars swapping stories of the day, with Gene leading the way.

"So I'm thinking, I've got to change a coupling or two. Water spewing everywhere. Then the Canadian down in 17 tells me it's a seat. I gotta change a danged seat. So I change the seat and the pump's as good as new," said Gene as he wrapped up his story.

"I coulda gotten you some seats, Gene," offered Bill. "I run across 'em all the time out there on the route."

"That's okay. The seat only cost me a coupla bucks and the pump works like a charm."

The busy tavern chatter was momentarily interrupted by the sounds of a dilapidated car making its way through the maze of vehicles. An eggshell 1960 Ford Fairlane rumbled closer to the tavern and then came to a slow stall in a space in front of the bar.

"Einstein," mumbled Gene, with a subtle eye roll toward Bill.

A gentle whirlpool of sandy dust spun around the driver's side door opening with a loud creak and whining moan. As the dust cleared, the white rear end of a man eased its way backwards out of the vehicle. With a long push, he stood upright, all six feet five inches of him. His body was pointed at the elbows, shoulders and knees. A white T-shirt exposed a farmer's tan and his white pants were dotted with the colors of nearly every house he had ever painted and the stains of every drink that had missed his mouth.

Slowly he reached for a stick in the backseat, which caused a chain reaction of turmoil among a pile of paint cans and brushes. Deliberately, the man worked the stick out of the car until he was able to free it completely. Varying degrees of dark marks hashed the surface of the stick.

With long hairy fingers, the man pried open the dented gas tank cover and carefully inserted the stick. His eyes turned skyward as he felt for the bottom. When he was satisfied he had hit the mark, he pulled the piece of wood back out slowly and felt it with his hand. Then he put his equally hairy nostrils to the stick and smiled, satisfied.

"'Nuff to get home," he whispered to himself.

James Rose was a Sunset Tavern fixture, but it had been years since anyone called him anything but Einstein. It was unclear why he had acquired the nickname. Some attributed it to the creative ideas he had in fixing commonplace problems. Others blamed it on his appearance.

Since the headliner in his car was a sagging piece of nylon, it created a slight static electricity arc with his thin gray hair. After prolonged drives, friction made it stand straight up on his head.

His appearance certainly earned him the moniker of the famous genius, whether his brains deserved it or not.

After returning the gas stick to his jalopy, he wobbled his way toward the outside bar of the tavern.

"What's the word, Einstein?" Gene asked without prompting.

"Thunderbird!" Einstein shouted, laughing, as he brushed some dried paint from his overgrown gray mustache.

"What'll ya have, Einstein?" asked Wally as he looked over the bar to where the crowd was congregating.

"Let's start it off on a Cutty and see where the sails take us," came the reply with a wrinkled smile.

As soon as it appeared before him, Einstein swiped the cold, thin glass off the counter. He lifted it toward his buddies, downed it in one gulp and slid it back toward Wally.

"This glass is no good, Wall. It's empty," he joked, working the crowd like a stand up comedian.

As he brought the second glass to his lips, his attention was directed to a young blonde-haired girl staring up in his direction. "Lucy…how long you been staring up my gut?"

"Long enough to watch you burn some paint off your nose hairs, I think, Mr. Rose," jabbed Lucy, who was less than enthusiastic in her dealings with the painter.

"Lovely little girl you have here, Gene. She always makes me laugh," Einstein commented as he patted Lucy on the head.

"Dad, we have a guest here," Lucy said, ignoring him while motioning to her father with the top of her head and signaling with her eyes toward a new arrival to the group.

Looking over his shoulder, Gene noticed the familiar face of the stranger who had helped him out of a jam a few hours earlier.

"Orel, what brings you here?" he shouted in an excited voice.

"Your daughter, Lucy said this is a great place. So I figured I'd see how great it really was for myself," said Orel, taking in the sights of the tavern.

"Yes, it is a fine place to come and watch the sun go down and enjoy a beer with some fine friends," bragged Gene, nodding to some people across the bar. "And by the way, thanks for helping me out this morning. Fellas, this is the guy I was telling you about that helped me with the seats on the pool pump."

Einstein raised his second drink in greeting to Orel.

"You look familiar to me, Orel. Din't I see your face on a poster in the post office?" he quipped. He was so tickled by his humorous remark that he rounded it off with a self-satisfied laugh.

A polite, smiling nod brought Orel closer to the group and further away from the man in the painted white trousers.

"To tell you the truth, I thought you were bee-essing me about the seats in the pump, Orel," Gene said. "But sure enough, that was the problem."

"It's like my Uncle Roy always said: 'It's easier to know how to do something the right way today, than to BS about the wrong way tomorrow,'" replied Orel.

Bill straightened from his hunched position over his beer to reach out a hand to Orel. "What brings you to this part of Florida, partner?"

"I came down to get away from the cold weather and find out what direction I should take my life, I suppose," answered the Canadian. "I believe I'm at a bit of a fork in the road."

"Find yourself? Isn't that what the kids are calling it these days?" Wally piped up from his side of the bar. "In my day, no one had to goddamned find themselves, 'cause we never got lost. For cries sake, Joe Dimaggio. Stationed in my unit. Got drafted in the goddamned Army. WWII. He didn't get lost. Nowadays it's all this 'find yourself' shit and 'feel good' crap."

"And that's Wally. Owner of this fine establishment," Gene whispered apologetically. "He has a way with words, wouldn't you say?"

"Fellas like that bring color to the world, Gene," the Canadian replied with a half smile.

"'Scuse me, Orel," interrupted Lucy. "There's someone I'd like you to meet."

Orel nodded politely in the direction of his newfound friends and extended an arm toward Lucy. "Show me the way, Lucyball."

In the distance, he could make out a figure of a boy on the seawall working with something in his hands. When they got closer, it became clear that he was wrestling in frustration with a ball of tangled fishing line that had gotten knotted within his reel.

"Doesn't appear that the gods of fishing are smiling on you right now," Orel observed as he came closer.

"Nahh," answered Rudy shortly without looking up.

"I've had many of those in my fishing career and found that the best remedy is a good pair of scissors and a nearby tackle shop," Orel advised.

"Uhh, Rude, this is Orel. He's staying at the motel with us for a while," Lucy said.

Her face pleaded for him to be nice to the guest. She knew how mean he could be when things were not going his way. And at this point he was obviously losing the battle with his fishing reel.

Rudy looked up long enough to remark with a sarcastic grin, "Yeah, the guy in the Weenie Bender, right?"

Orel, confused, looked to Lucy for assistance.

"Yes, Rude. This is the man who we saw by the pool yesterday on the way to 'Swings,'" said Lucy in an effort to clue Orel in regarding the smart aleck comment. "He will be staying with us for a few weeks."

"Weenie Bender...? Aaahh-haa-ha," Orel started with a crisp laugh. "Yeah, I get that in the States a lot. Especially in Florida, for some reason." His eyes watered from the chuckles and coughs brought on by the comment. "Seems we Canucks prefer our swim trousers a bit briefer than you surfer types down here," he continued in a self-deprecating manner, which Lucy found very attractive.

The sun was now making a silhouette of the trio as it sank further into the Gulf. Only about an inch of burnt orange sky kept the ball from touching the water. This meant that there was only about 15 minutes of daylight left for Rudy to toil and save his reel. He picked up the pace dramatically.

"Would you like me to take that back to my room and work on it for you tonight, Rudy?" inquired Orel politely, hands in his pockets. "Not much to do in the room after dark. It might be a very therapeutic way for me to spend the evening."

Rudy cautiously glanced at Lucy for approval, knowing that his dad would never let him bring his rod and reel into the house.

"You think you could fix this?" he asked shyly.

"I think I may be able to work my way through that tangled web you've got there," Orel said and nodded with a crooked grin. "I've been in tougher pickles than that, my friend."

"Pickles?" Rudy exclaimed, giggling. "You really have a funny way of talking."

"Let 'im give it a try, Rude. You know how your dad gets when he sees your reel tangled like that," Lucy said.

"Yeah," answered Rudy with a serious stare into the blackening water. He then confidently handed his fishing gear to Orel. "I'd appreciate if you could get me out of this pickle," he said, chuckling.

As the last sliver of sun melted into the gulf, Orel took one final glance around the tavern. "You're right, Lucyball—this place is great," he said. He grabbed Rudy's reel and headed off into the darkening night.

Chapter 4

The harsh ringing of the phone just minutes prior to the equally annoying blare of the alarm clock's wail pierced Rudy's sleep. Since it was the beginning of summer, he was not concerned with getting up at any specific hour. However, it seemed somebody on the other end of the phone expected his household to already be awake.

Since no one else seemed concerned with answering the ring, Rudy struggled out of the cool sheets and stumbled into the kitchen.

"Hello?" he asked into the receiver.

"Yeah, Bill?"

"Um, no—just a minute, please," answered Rudy. "Lemme go get him."

Rudy wiped the sleep from his eyes, scratched his nappy hair and made his way through the living area. He tapped lightly on his parents' partially open bedroom door.

"Dad, there's a phone call for you," he said softly. "Dad!"

"Hmmnay…whaa…?" Bills choked groggily.

"There's a man on the phone who needs to talk to you, Dad,"

"Ahhight. Tell 'em I'll be there inna minute, Son," Bill rasped.

Muscling his way out of the bed, he glanced toward the bedroom mirror and saw the familiar red, puffy eyes and mussed hair that usually accompanied his hangovers in the morning. He looked at the clock mumbling, "Who's calling at this hour? They've got some nerve!"

On the way to the phone, he cleared his raspy voice to give the impression that he had been up for hours.

"Heeelooo, this is Bill," he warbled in a mock professional voice that even fooled Rudy on occasion. "What can I do ya for?"

"Bill...Sam Eisenrad." The voice at the other end of the line was loud enough for Rudy to follow the conversation.

"Sam," bellowed Bill. "How are you and that fine humanitarian doing this morning?"

"I'm fine, thank you. And Mr. Kronis is doing fine also, I'm sure. Good to see your smartass attitude wakes up as early as the rest of you."

"What do you need, Sam?"

"Well, Bill, it's one of those good news-bad news scenarios. Which do you want first?"

After a long pause, Bill forced an answer, with the palm of his hand pressing hard against one eye. "I'm feeling kinda foggy this morning," he growled. "Bad news."

Sam started reluctantly. "It's your mortgage—I need the two months' delinquent payments by the end of the week or the bank is talking serious foreclosure on you, buddy."

"You are an unsympathetic bastard, aren't you?" chided Bill. "You know this is my slow season."

"Slow season?" Sam started. "Didn't realize junk had a slow season, Bill. People not throwing out as much trash this time of year?"

"Well, it does when I lose a couple of accounts," answered Bill, his voice starting to rise.

"Perhaps if your customer relations department was better trained, you wouldn't be losing clients," Sam replied, matching his pitch.

"Look, ya sonofabitch, you called me!"

Rudy snuck into the bathroom when he heard his father's voice get louder.

"Look, I'm not the bad guy on this one, Bill. I have people that are busting my chops, too, over this mortgage thing," pleaded Sam on the other end. "The banks enter into loans with the expectation that they will be repaid."

Bill exhaled into the phone, which Sam took as a sign of submission.

A long silence ensued.

"Are we through?" Bill finally asked, impatiently.

"Well, here's the good news," Sam said, laughing. "Harry Covington finally is giving up his grip on the Nearvana. The title struggle and power of attorney nonsense may be coming to an end. Well, that's not good news for him, but it could be for you. There may be some steals in his place that you could walk away with. Mr. Kronis is interested in getting it cleaned out as soon as possible."

"Why you telling me this shit? You know I don't have that kind of capital to buy out a completely outfitted restaurant."

"I'm offering you a deal if you are interested."

Bill dug around in the junk drawer searching for a silver capped lighter which was wedged between a deck of cards and a bottle of aspirin. A sulfur flame ignited a glow on the end of the white cigarette and bought him a few seconds to clear his head with some nicotine.

"Deal? What kinda deal?" he said flatly through a veil of smoke.

"Maybe I can help you with your situation, Bill," Sam offered.

"What would you say if I gave you a loan that wouldn't have to be repaid until after you got back on your feet? I'll cover you on the two months of your mortgage. Pay me back when you can. I just need the place cleaned out as soon as possible."

Bill's lip twisted at the thought of taking any charity from Sam. "A loan to pay a loan?" he asked anxiously. "What's your angle, Sam?"

"The appliances and fixtures are dated. You clean it out and we go fifty-fifty on whatever you sell. My angle is: We get the joints cleared out for renovation as quickly as we can."

Bill began to pace with the phone in hand, taking it to the limits of its cord as he worked out the details of the offer between drags on the cigarette.

"Sand Dollar, Gulf Breeze, along with the Nearvana—all need to be gutted," Sam continued.

"Sam, let me think about this for a little bit and get back to you on it."

"What's there to think about? It's a no-brainer," returned Sam. "But you think it over, Bill. Don't wait too long, 'cause I've got these bankers breathing down my throat."

"Yeah, Sam, I hear ya. Give me a few hours."

Bill hung up and stared at the wall for several seconds, mentally rehashing the conversation.

Rudy stuck his head out of the bathroom. Cautiously he worked his way past his father into the television area and sat on his unmade bed.

"Why you so sweaty, Rudy?" asked Bill pointedly.

"I…I just washed my face with a hot towel and sometimes that makes me look sweaty," Rudy replied, focusing his attention on a television show to avoid any more discussion about his appearance.

Bill nodded but did not listen to Rudy's answer. "Why'n you get dressed and go out and play? I've got some thinking to do."

Rudy nodded and pulled his pajama top over his head.

A shave and a haircut knock at the door interrupted their conversation.

"Geez, who can that be now? So much for a quiet start to my day," complained Bill as he strode to the door, aggravated. "Better not be a damned salesman or I'll drop his ass right on the front step!"

He jerked the door open and saw the angular figure of Gene's guest standing on his front porch, holding a fishing rod.

"Pardon my dropping by so early," Orel said, smiling, "but Lucy Lewis from the inn I'm staying at gave me directions on how to get to your place. Just thought I'd drop off your son's reel, in case he wanted to get an early start on his fishing this morning."

Bill squinted at the figure chattering on his doorstep, responsible for so much light invading his dark duplex.

"Uhhhh…yeaahhh. Orel, right?" Bill stammered as he turned toward Rudy. "It's for you Son."

"Hey Rudy!" Orel called inside. "I took some liberties with your rod and reel. Hope you don't mind. I found this nicely colored filament down at the bait shop and thought it might brighten your rig up a bit."

Rudy made his way past his father and took hold of the shining fishing pole with the bright, fluorescent green line on its reel. He studied it carefully to make sure it was the one he had given Orel. The inside of the spool was shinier than he remembered and the handle spun with greater ease. The knobs were all greasy and slipped when Rudy touched them. He did finally make a positive identification that it was his reel when he spotted the broken eye in the third position, which he had snagged on the seawall trying to gig a horseshoe crab earlier that spring.

"I would have fixed that bent line hole on your pole if I could only locate the proper one for ya. Man at the bait shop said he could order it. Would take a few days," Orel said, smiling. His deep blue eyes gleamed as he looked at Rudy for approval. "So, what'd ya think?"

"Wow…is what I think!" Rudy exclaimed. "Thank you, sir. I thought all you were gonna do was get the knot out. I had no idea you'd do all this."

"Well, it's like my Aunt Mabel used to say: 'What's the sense in doing a job half arsed when it takes a complete arse to do it,'" said Orel with a quick wink and a bite of his tongue. "Maybe you should take it out for a spin and see if that funny colored string helps you catch more fish."

He patted Rudy on the head, gave a wave to Bill and turned to walk down the duplex pathway.

"Maybe I'll see you at the Sunset Tavern tonight at sundown, fellas," he called back.

"Yes, you will," answered Bill, bewildered. He put an arm around Rudy and closed the door behind him. "Is this a new pole?"

"No, Daddy, it's the one you picked up for me on your route," replied Rudy. "Orel just took a knot out of it for me and, I guess, cleaned it up a little bit, too."

"Damned Orel's got a hunk of junkman in him, I suppose," said Bill.

The cowbells rang out loudly as she let the door swing shut behind her. A heavy mixture of smells overwhelmed Lucy while she shuffled slowly along the dingy wooden floor. It took a few seconds for her eyes to make the adjustment from the bright sunshine to the dark purple strobe inside The Outta Sight Shop.

She noticed a long-haired person behind the counter but was unsure whether it was a man or a woman. When the person made eye contact, Lucy quickly spun in the opposite direction and walked down an aisle. Her clammy hands reached on the shelf to feign confidence in her being there. She found a candle and pulled it toward her nose to enjoy the smell. Oblivious at first to what she was touching, she pulled her head back in horror when she realized the candle's shape was that of a male penis.

A feeling of regret flushed her body and made her face tingle with apprehension. The Outta Sight Shop was the biggest head shop on the beach. She and Rudy always laughed about the place whenever they rode past it on their bikes. Now she was alone in its inner sanctum.

A curtain of beads slightly concealed two people sitting on beanbags in a small room in the back illuminated by black light. One seemed to be a man whose limp body had become affected by something other than oxygen. The other, a woman, rocked back and forth gently to the rhythm of the music which piped softly out of a foamy speaker above her head. Occasionally, a grin would spread over her face and the rocking would slow to a mere tremor. A strobe light, which changed its staccato rhythm from time to time, made her movements and shadows on the black wall even creepier. From another beaded room a slow giggle grew into laughter, punctuated by calls of "No way!" and "Far out!"

Lucy rubbed her eyes. A pungent blend of cherry candles and vanilla incense had somehow found its way to the palm of her hand. Perhaps it was some musk from the manly thing she had touched. Slowly she pulled her hand away from her face. Her olfactory concern was forgotten as she was startled to see a green frog, which was giving her the finger. She stared at the poster for a long moment and wondered why the frog was angry. But the longer she looked, the more she realized that it was not angry at all. For some reason, she got the joke.

Maybe it was the sights, sounds and smells of The Outta Sight Shop having its affect on her.

This was the place where the hippies would come to get anything they needed to make their experimental experiences that much better. Whether it was bongs, rolling papers, mirrors or roach clips, The Outta Sight Shop had it all. An eclectic collection of counter culture paraphernalia, it stood out on the beach like the middle finger on the green frog. Over the years, the city council tried repeatedly to have it closed, but for some reason a last-minute hitch in the proceedings always blocked it from happening.

A spinning display offered various shapes, colors and styles of sunglasses. Lucy tried them on one by one and looked around the shop at the sights.

On a gray and green textured wall was a poster of Richard Nixon sitting on a toilet with his pants down and two peace signs over his head. There were anti-Vietnam slogans, "Abortion is Legal" documents, "KISSinger MY ASS" bumper stickers, cartoons of Vice President Spiro Agnew smoking marijuana, and rolls of toilet paper in the design of dollar bills.

And flags. American flags were everywhere. Old Glory was visible on hats, on shorts and even on rolling papers. The Outta Sight Shop was where people would go to bask in their own expression of Free Speech.

Lucy decided that since she was now twelve years old, she was mature enough to handle this place on her own. Slowly she walked through the aisles touching the velvet, braiding the fringe, smelling the candles. One fragrance in particular brought her back in time.

"Mommy, what's that smell?"
"Vanilla, my dear."
"Like ice cream, Mommy?"
"Yes, it's like the ice cream.
Just makes you feel a little
warmer than ice cream, sweetie."
"I like that smell, Mommy."
"I do too, honey."

Lucy's belly burned a little when she recalled the smell. A nervousness made her pulse quicken and she felt the urge to run to the bathroom. The feelings subsided when her reverie was interrupted by a mellow female voice.

At the counter she noticed some daisy barrettes and sticks of incense. She grabbed two barrettes and placed them next to the round pair of blue sunglasses that she pulled off her face.

"Will there be anything else, sunshine?" asked the thin woman behind the counter as she placed the sunglasses and daisy barrettes into a paper bag.

"No, thank you, ma'am. That'll be all for today," answered Lucy, hoping to sound like a repeat customer older than her years.

"Then thirty-five cents is your change, sunshine."

Lucy reached for the change and nearly fumbled it on the wooden counter when a noise rang out that startled everyone. The cowbells were crashing against the glass of the front door so loudly that it made the hippies in the back room nearly fall out of their beanbags.

When Lucy finally swung her head around she saw an over-weight man, dressed in a camouflage jacket and ripped jeans, lying on the beaten wooden floor of the store. He had apparently lost his balance on the way in and fallen through the entrance. The woman behind the counter ran over to him.

"Are you okay, love?" she asked.

The hairy-faced man rolled over and sat up to look first at Lucy and then the lady with a look of terror in his eyes. "IN THE HOLE! FIRE IN THE HOLE!" he screamed and uttered a long cry that turned into a shriek of laughter. He wiped his long, sweaty hair from his face and gave a deep sigh. His dark eyes stared at the cowbells until they finished wobbling alongside the glass door.

The woman from the counter pulled back as the man flailed his arms in her direction, in the door's direction and then back toward her again.

"Doorbells," he exhaled as his body relaxed back onto the floor. He lay there for a few moments working his way through it, his chest heaving rapidly.

Lucy could see that his left leg was not there, though the man grabbed at the nothingness as if it were. Her belly burned again and she wanted to run, but the crippled man blocked the en-trance. The room spun around her and she stood frozen in fear.

"Stinkin' doorbells," he said, breaking into a slow laugh.

"Acid'n one leg ain't a good mix," said the counter woman with a half smirk and a sense of relief.

A crowd quickly encircled the helpless man on the floor. As more people came closer, Lucy could feel the room getting smaller. In every direction, she saw strange and ugly faces looking at him.

She quickly picked up her bag and the change she had dropped on the floor and walked briskly toward the door. When she got close to the man, she briefly stared at his hands clutching the air just below his knee. He seemed to be scared, amused and lost at the same time. Lucy crashed through the door and reawakened the cowbells. She kept walking without looking back, jumped on her bike and pedaled…out of sight.

As he cast the bright, florescent green filament, water droplets flew in all directions. The sun hit the shine on Rudy's pole and made it look like it was studded with diamonds. His hands worked in unison with the well-oiled spool as he cast out line after line. Rudy almost did not care if he got a bite. He just wanted to feel and see the beauty of his newly fashioned rig.

"Rude, what's up?" came a call from far off.

Rudy looked over his shoulder to see Lucy struggling to pedal her bike through the heavy sand.

"Loose!" he yelled back, eager to show her the changes to his old rod and reel. "You gotta check this out!"

She finally gave up her struggle and walked her bike the rest of the way.

"That guy. Ya know. Weenie Bender," Rudy said.

Lucy stared blankly at him, annoyed.

"He redid my pole. Check it out! It's all clean and smooth now," he said, almost unable to catch his breath. "And look at this line. It's green. Green! Can you believe that? Whoever heard of green line?"

"Orel," said Lucy flatly.

"Huh?"

"His name is Orel," she repeated dryly, "not Weenie Bender."

"Whatever his name is, can you believe what he did to my pole?" Rudy continued. "Only thing he didn't do was fix the eye, but the man at the bait shop woulda had to order it, and it would take a few days and…Orel," he said, measuring his tone and properly pronouncing the pole fixer's name, "decided to wait and…look at this line, would ya?"

"So, do these glasses make me look mature?" Lucy asked as she donned her new purchase and flipped her hair to one side.

Rudy tilted his head at Lucy as she continued modeling. "Mature? Whatta you wanna look mature for?" he asked.

"I'm twelve now, and I think it's about time I start acting like a twelve year old," Lucy continued, as she pulled a yellow daisy barrette from the paper bag.

Rudy gave Lucy a sideways glance and then returned to his fishing pole. He watched as the green line danced over the waves left in the wake of the mullet boats.

"Rude, you shoulda seen this guy at the Outta Sight Shop. He fell through the door and started screaming about a fire or something. I think he was in Vietnam, 'cause he was in those green pants and only had one leg. He looked pretty scared. Scared me, too."

"You went to the Outta Sight Shop, Loose?" Rudy asked, astonished. "Your dad would not be happy if he knew you went in there. And especially by yourself."

"Well, it's time I start doing some things on my own," Lucy answered, pulling back her hair and snapping the daisy onto her head much like she had seen her mom do many times. "Besides, Dad and I have an understanding about such matters."

"Yeah. You better do what he says. Understand?"

"No, Rude, that's your dad," Lucy said, catching his eye and giving him a wink.

Trays full of ashes and a collection of condensation rings cluttered the bar where Winston had obviously been spending some of his time. His red-rimmed eyes and glazed skin told the tale of a full day of liquor consumption. Dorothy was in her customary spot to Winston's left, and the two shared minimal conversation. Most of the noise was coming from behind the bar, from Wally, with his usual complaints about the "goddamned president and the lazy asses who don't give a damn about doing a day's work."

It was slower than a usual Sunday night at the tavern, which meant the only competition for Wally's rants was the occasional clack of the cue ball being struck.

Einstein was early and sat alone on a barstool at the outside portion of the tavern. He was much more reserved when his buddies were not there to work up his comic bravado. His time this evening seemed more inclined toward study. The object of his attention most notably seemed to be Winston. The painter watched the electrician with an interest known only to him.

A warm breeze blew through the outside bar and made the hanging lights spin in small circles. The water by the seawall seemed calmer than earlier, as Lucy and Rudy were taking turns throwing crabs and stones into the air. With each toss, the two would sing out the Alka Seltzer song. It was apparent that Lucy had taken a break from acting "mature" and was happily twelve again for the time being.

Across the parking lot, a cloud of dust rose as Bill's red pickup truck approached Lucy and Rudy. When Bill pulled up next to them and gave a grunt from the window, Rudy jumped up and ran over to him.

"Don't get wet, Son. You know how your mother hates to do laundry," Bill quipped, squinting and smiling.

"I won't, Daddy. We're just playing with the crabs."

"And how are you, young lady?" Bill asked Lucy.

"Fine, Mr. Connor. Just doing a little crabbing this evening, sir," Lucy answered, amazed that Bill even cared how she was doing.

"Well, that's great, dear," Bill replied and made a half smirking expression toward his son. "I'll be over here talking to the fellas for awhile, if you need me."

It looked like Rob Roy had been kind to Bill this evening.

"Okay, Daddy, I'll be out here if you need me, too," Rudy answered with exaggerated enthusiasm.

Lucy followed with a wave and a feigned smile.

As Bill pulled his car away from the kids and into a spot in front of the tavern, Rudy and Lucy exchanged looks of disbelief. They then returned to what they were doing before they were interrupted.

Einstein swung his gray head around and noticed that Bill was making his way toward the outside bar. The two exchanged nods.

"Business good?"

"Ahhh, just out there painting the world, Bill. Painting the world."

"Yeah, I hear ya, my friend. I can't complain either. Nobody'd listen," Bill said, as he gave a nod through the window to Winston and a four-fingered wave to Dorothy. "How's my favorite beauty queen this fine evening?"

"Nothing that a little Scotch and Rose Milk can't cure, sweetie," Dorothy rasped, wiping Scotch from her smile as smoke streamed out of her nose.

Bill returned an uncharacteristic smile and continued his banter with Einstein.

Gene's Cadillac next entered the parking lot. First, it stopped by the two children playing at the seawall, and the passenger door opened to allow a slender figure to disembark. Then, it pulled into a spot outside the bar. The driver's door opened and Gene emerged, straightening his shirt and pants along the way.

"Who's with the kids?" Bill asked Gene.

"My guest, Orel. Got a lot of energy. Seems to really enjoy being around the children."

Lucy's face flushed when she watched Orel take a turn at casting Rudy's green-strung pole. The tackle flew in circles against the setting sun and plopped into the water with a bubbly splash.

"My dad got a new job today," Rudy said, looking over Orel's shoulder to follow another long cast into the rapid current. "Guy called on the phone. A Mr. Eisenrad, I think he said. Cleaning up a few of the places down the beach."

Lucy looked toward Rudy with minimal interest.

"My dad was talking loud on the phone and I could hear the other guy, too," Rudy continued. "Sand Dollar and the Gulf Breeze were the places."

Cool gusts off the bay accompanied the names of the once-vintage establishments.

"And Nearvana," he added chewing the inside of his cheek.

Orel's roll on the reel slowed at the sound of the name. Without moving his eyes from his hands, he tilted his head toward the conversation. His motion remained steady but his mind raced his beating heart. The mere mention of the Nearvana always brought out a myriad of emotions in the young Canadian.

"Sounds like he's gotta clean up the places," Rudy continued, "but I'm not even sure what that means."

Orel's ruddy cheeks became more flushed as he listened to the young boy describe the conversation he had overheard. His hands trembled as he slowly finished reeling in his last cast. He gave the pole back to Rudy and excused himself.

"I'm going to walk up to the tavern for a bit," he said. "Can I get you anything?"

The children both shook their heads and then watched the lanky Canadian walk through the deep sand.

"Orel," came a bellow from the outside bar. Bill was leading the way in the greeting committee this evening. "Enjoying your trip so far?"

"Well, sir, it has been wonderful up to this point. But I get a little nervous if I don't keep myself busy," Orel answered politely as he walked up and tried to flag down the bartender. "Not used to all this free time. I really would love a chance to work up a good sweat doing something other than just walking down the street in this humidity, eh?"

"Is that right? I appreciate a man who's not afraid of a day's work," said Bill.

Orel's raised index finger finally got Wally's attention and a club soda soon appeared before him. Orel pulled out a barstool and worked his way into a comfortable position next to the three men.

"You're in salvage, eh?"

Bill looked puzzled initially, then realized Orel was talking about junk. "Yes, sir. Been in the junk game since I can remember," he said. "There's one thing I know, and that's the value of garbage." His voice trailed as the reality of his job seemed to become all too clear.

"Always found the salvage business to be very intriguing," reflected Orel as he lifted his glass of clear bubbly water to the group in a toast. "After all, it's like my Uncle Lou always said: 'One man's junk is…another man's treasure.' I always found that to be true, too. Wouldn't mind trying my hand at it one day as well, eh?"

Bill nodded at Orel, not sure whether it was homage to the junk business or the patronizing of a someone who was practically a stranger. He confidently turned his attention to Gene who had just gotten himself a beer.

"So, Gene, if you have a minute, I gotta talk to you about a proposition," he whispered.

Since Bill was speaking with a slight slur, Gene assumed it was that time of night where the conversation would turn to "asses putting asses in the seats." But he played along. "A proposition. Whatta you have in mind, Bill?"

"'Scuse me, fellas," Bill said as he pulled at Gene's shoulder and took him aside to explain the conversation he had with Eisenrad.

Allowing the men to go their way, Orel slid his stool next to the remaining soul at his end of the bar. "So, Mr. Einstein, how are you doing tonight?"

"Na too bad, Mr. Findingyourself. Any luck on your search?"

Orel grinned, realizing that he had inadvertently gotten himself in a verbal toe-to-toe with a master sparring partner, but before the painter could land another blow, the round was interrupted.

"Orel, would you like to take me on?" yelled a sweet voice from the picnic tables by the seawall.

Lucy's bright smile and blonde hair shone in the sun as she beckoned.

"Pardon me, Mr. Einstein," Orel said as he got up from his barstool. He walked over to Lucy. "Take you on? Not sure what you mean."

"In pool. I'll play you in pool."

"Ohhh, billiards! I fancy billiards."

"You what? Fancy?"

"I—ahh-ha-haa—enjoy playing what you Americans call pool," Orel explained. "Sure, I'd love to play a game of pool, Lucyball."

Heading over to the pool table, they passed Bill and Gene who were still huddled in their private conversation and paid no attention to them.

"Sounds like a great plan to me, but you gotta be careful of that Sam. He can be a snake in the grass if you don't watch his every move," Gene warned as the two men walked back to join Einstein for another drink. "Kronis. He's another story altogether. I've heard way too many things about him over the years. He's got some interesting friends over in Tampa, from what they say."

"Yeah. I thought the same. Kronis doesn't part with a dime unless he's gonna make a quarter out of it. Or unless there's an award to win."

"You're gonna need help if you do this, Bill. You won't be able to handle all that stuff by yourself," Gene advised, rubbing his cheek and chin.

Lucy was inside the tavern lining up her next shot. As she walked around the table, Orel watched how she deftly cued her stick without taking her eyes from the playing surface. Her look shifted from the cue ball to the object ball as she got ready to hit. It was obvious to Orel that Lucy had played this game many times before.

"Five in the side," she confidently announced as she softly pushed the white ball into the red one. Without looking up, she continued, "Three in the corner."

"Lucyball, I do believe you've taken me for a pigeon," Orel complained.

Dorothy repositioned herself on the stool so she could watch the youngster taking the Canadian "to school."

After she dropped the three, Lucy rose up from her crouch and reached again for the blue chalk. "Eight down low off the rail," she said with eyes half open and a sideways grin.

Dorothy was amused by Lucy's behavior, since all she had ever witnessed was a tomboy running through the tavern with Rudy stuck to her hip.

"WOW, Lucyball! I am truly impressed! Where'd you learn how to play billiard…I mean pool, like that?" Orel exclaimed.

"I suppose I get a lot of practice from being here," Lucy answered as she finished knocking his balls off the table.

"I mean, you don't just play a good game, you talk one, too," he continued.

The men outside were deep into planning mode on what approach to take with the Eisenrad proposition. Overhearing the need for physical labor, Einstein joined the conversation.

"If you need help, Bill, why don't you get Mr. Findinghimself in there, who's flirting with Gene's daughter, to give you some ass and elbows?" he quipped. "I'm sure that back of his has got a few fridge lifts in it."

Offended by Einstein's slight of his daughter, Gene dropped his lower lip and squinted. "Rose, you sack of sh…" he started, but was interrupted.

"You know, Einstein, notta bad idea," Bill interjected. "Kid seems to wanna work."

Orel was racking up balls for another game of pool with Lucy when Bill's gruff voice broke his attention.

"OREL! Hey, Orel!"

The Canadian looked up from the rack, "Yes sir, Mr. Connor?"

"You wanna give me a hand on the route starting tomorrow?" Bill asked in a voice loud enough for the entire tavern to hear.

"Gotta little more work than I can handle myself. Need to clean out a few restaurants down the road."

Lucy's face lit up at the prospect of Orel working for Bill. This job might increase the length of his stay.

Spinning the pool rack on his pinkie in apparent contemplation, Orel finally responded, "Well, I don't see a problem with that. It may give me chance to really get to know some of the folks around here."

"Well, it's a deal then," answered Bill. "I'll pick you up at the Oasis at 7 a.m. Plan on getting dirty."

Lucy's enthusiasm with the turn of events was evident by the smile that spread across her face. She did her best to look down at the floor so that no one could see that she cared one way or the other if Orel took a job with Bill.

"Are we gonna play or what, Orel?" she chided, bringing herself back to earth.

"Uh, sure, Lucyball. Just gotta rack 'em, sweetie."

Dorothy turned back to the bar with a long drag on her cigarette and took a slow sip of Scotch. "Looks like our little Lucy's got herself an Orel fixation," she drawled. "Wouldn't you say, Winston?"

Winston nodded with a nervous smile and reached in his pocket for a Marlboro.

Chapter 5

Waves lapped the beach, leaving a foamy line on the sand with each trip to the shore. Sandpipers performed a repetitive dance with the highs and lows of the approaching surge to keep from getting their feet wet. Every now and then, the small birds were able to find a morsel to eat in the frothy water. Pelicans dropped from the sky like rocks into the deeper, wavy sea in search of breakfast. The dawn fog was giving way to the glow of the emerging orange ball. Palm trees were wrapped with its warm glow as the shadows shrunk and the light grew.

Orel tugged at his shirt pocket and pulled out the crumbled piece of paper. He pushed at it and noticed how the paper was beginning to feel more like cloth. Slowly he ran his fingers over the scrawled words inked on its surface.

"Two hands two fingers stage right off the main spot, two hands two fingers up," he whispered reading the note.

The handwriting seemed hastily scrawled. It had a sense of purpose. It had a sense of urgency. He recalled how crisp the paper felt when it was first placed in his hand. How cold it was to the touch.

Orel kicked the sand from his feet as he concluded his early morning walk.

A few feet from him was a black-and-white seagull hard at work, doing its best to pry a french fry from a discarded McDonald's bag.

Bill greeted this morning with more enthusiasm than he had in quite some time. He woke before the alarm and had already had his first cup of coffee by the time he would normally be hitting the snooze button for the third time. Perhaps it was the excitement of the Eisenrad offer or just the fact that he hadn't drunk as much as usual at the tavern the night before.

"You gonna be long in there, Son?" he asked at the bathroom door.

"Uh no, Dad. Be out in a minute."

Rudy had been in the bathroom since before Bill had woken. Though this seemed odd to Bill, he sensed that this was just something that young boys go through.

"Sorry, Dad," Rudy said as he finally emerged. He tried to slink past his father in the tight hallway, but Bill grabbed him by the arm.

"Sweaty again, Rudy?" he asked. "What the hell you doin' in there that's making you so sweaty, Son?"

A ray of light from one of the two windows in the duplex caught Rudy just below the forehead, causing him to shut one eye as he looked up at Bill. "Nothing, Dad. Just going to the bathroom, I guess."

"Ya? Well, I've gotta get going, Son. See ya when I get home."

"Is Orel helping you today, Daddy?"

"The, uh…yeah, the uh…Canadian is gonna ride the route with me today," Bill said, grabbing his wallet and keys off the counter.

"I'd like to ride the route with you sometime, Daddy," Rudy mumbled, still struggling to see past the annoying ray of light.

Bill turned his head slightly and gave his son a surprised look. "You would? Lotta work out there, Son. You think you've got what it takes to be a junkman?"

Rudy's face lit up at the thought of riding the route next to his dad. "Yeeeah! Maybe a junk boy," he said with a laugh.

Bill looked at Rudy with a rare smile and made his way toward the door. "See ya when I get home."

The old Ford started after a few tries and pulled out of the gravel driveway, leaving a warming oil smell as it moved. Bill lit a cigarette with his left hand, found second gear with his right, pushed the clutch with his left foot, pressed the gas with his right and somehow found a knee available to do the steering. It was a well-orchestrated dance of coordination.

Years of neglect and cigarette smoke inside the truck had left a filmy, gray residue on the windshield that made seeing down the road somewhat difficult. Though Bill had grown accustomed to his limited vision, the rising sun on this particular morning made looking ahead even more difficult than usual.

As he drove down Palm Way, he saw the slender figure of Orel leaning against a planter with his arms crossed. Bill pulled his truck up close and reached across the seat to open the passenger door. Opening it from the outside was no longer possible.

"Nice to see that somebody cares about being on time," said Bill, smirking.

"Yes, sir, like my grandpa Rufus used to say: 'Being late is just the same as saying I don't give a damn.'"

"Can't argue with that one there, Orel," Bill said as he gave a wave to Gene, who was also up early cleaning the pool with Lucy.

Gene returned the wave and watched the red pickup drive off.

"Dad, whatta you think of Orel helping Mr. Connor?" Lucy asked, taking a break from cleaning the tile to watch the truck disappear in a sea of sunlight and mist.

"That Orel's a good guy. He'll do well to help Bill out, I'm sure, sweetie."

"Yeah, he is a good guy, huh?" Lucy kept staring in the direction of where the truck had vanished.

Bill looked up from the pool broom and glanced in Lucy's direction. "Good looking, too, huh?"

Lucy quickly turned her attention to the job of scrubbing the suntan lotion off the tiles with a toilet brush. Gene could see a nervous smile making a crease on her cheek. Noticing her discomfort, he quickly changed the subject to something that would put her more at ease.

"So, the Dolphins gonna win 'em all again, ya think?"

"Yeah, I guess...

She scrubbed the tiles with less enthusiasm than before Orel left and paused for a moment. "Dad, why did Mom leave?"

Gene eased up on the piece of gum he'd been chewing vigorously and searched for the appropriate answer. He had known this question was going to come. He had even practiced an answer in anticipation for over eight years. But for some reason, perhaps the shock of the moment, he found himself speechless.

"I mean why'd she just leave? Why didn't she stay my mom like Rudy's mom does?" Lucy pressed on.

"I don't know, honey. Sometimes people get scared of things, I guess. I don't know..."

"Scared? Of what?"

"I'm not really sure, honey. Your mom was...is...a very special person. I think she just needed to go out and prove to the world how special she really is. And staying here with us—she was scared that she would never get that opportunity, I guess," Gene said as his eyes developed a faraway look.

Black smoke poured out of the tailpipe and gray smoke billowed out of the driver's window as the old pickup struggled down the boulevard on its way to Harry Covington's place.

"So, Orel, we never really did get a good chance to get to know each other. What's your family's line of work, son?" Bill asked, squinting through his exhaled cigarette fumes.

"Drilling. Wells. For hydro…ya know, water," Orel said, as he searched for a crank to roll down his window. "Uncle's business, really."

"Handle broke on that thing awhile back. Crack your vent window there, son. These jobs tend to pile up on me."

"Yes, sir. Entropy is one thing that doesn't sleep," responded Orel, twisting his lip and wiping his eyes.

"No, I suppose it doesn't," agreed Bill, not exactly sure what he was agreeing to.

The tires on the pickup made a comforting noise as they rubbed the gravel driveway of the closed restaurant. Though the building had few windows, the ones that were noticeable out front were speckled with cracked or completely broken panes. A sign hanging sideways from the eaves announced NEARVANA.

Orel tilted his head to look at the name.

The place had not always looked this way. In the late '60s, it had been an exclusive hangout for the spring baseball ballplayers and the occasional Brat Packer who found his way to the beach. Now, it was just another sign with a clever pun that stood there as a reminder of heydays long gone.

Though Harry Covington, the original owner, had been an apparently hard-working WASP, there were the occasional whispers of his involvement in shady dealings and rumors of connections to the Mob.

"Veal," Bill said.

"Hmm?"

"Best veal I ever put in my mouth," Bill continued. "Cov knew his way around a kitchen. Least his cooks did."

"Baby cows," Orel said, still fiddling with the broken handle in the truck. "Never could see the desire to eat a baby cow. Kill the poor thing before it gets a chance to live a full life of standing in one spot eating a grass patch till it's bare."

Bill's eyes darted in Orel's direction, searching for a response. When none came, he returned to his nostalgic stare.

"Nice to see punctuality is still a quality you give a damn about, Connor," came a raspy voice out of the bright heat of the morning. "People just don't seem to give a shit about being on time anymore."

"Always on time, if there's a buck to be made, Eisenrad," Bill responded.

"Or a beer to be drank," chided Sam, his lips enfolding the end of an already sloppy cigar.

Bill clambered out of the truck and mosied over to where Sam stood, eyeing him. "Eisenrad, nice to see you're not missing any meals," he said

"A belly's a sign of success, Connor."

"Well, from the looks of things, you're pretty damned successful," Bill quipped as he offered a handshake.

"Who's the help?" Sam asked, looking in Orel's direction. "Has the enterprise gotten so big you need employees?"

"This is Orel," announced Bill.

"Hughes, Orel Hughes!" proudly piped the Canadian.

"He's gonna give me some help cleaning out this rathole," Bill continued.

"Pleasure's mine, Hughes," Sam said, not used to using first names where matters of business were concerned. "Lemme show you what needs to be done in a relatively short period of time."

As Sam got near the door of the old restaurant, he reached into his polyester pants pocket and pulled out a wad of keys of various shapes, colors and sizes.

"If a belly was a sign of success," Orel thought, "the number of keys a man owns is an indication he can open a lot of doors."

When Sam finally found the right combination of key and lock, he pushed open the heavy red door and exposed a dank-smelling, dark foyer with a large, tiled floor and deep-brown wood walls. From the ceiling hung a yellow lamp attached to a black swag chain.

"Aaafftta yoo," Sam offered. He pulled the soggy cigar from his lips, and picked the pieces of tobacco off his tongue. He watched the two men walk cautiously into the building. "Haven't been in this joint in a few months. Hate to think the neglect has made it worse than it was the last time I was in here."

"Smells worse than your goddamned breath, Eisenrad," Bill said.

Orel followed closely behind Bill as the two carefully stepped into the darkness. Bill put a flat hand on the wall searching for a way to brighten things up. His palm bumped against a switch, but when he flipped it, nothing came on.

"Power's been off for sometime. Here…," Sam said, extending a flashlight to Orel.

The Canadian grabbed it with one hand while he wiped his face to remove a spider web with the other. He pointed the light over Bill's shoulder into the main part of the restaurant. Through a beam dancing with specks of dust, Bill could make out the bar where he had spent many an evening and even more dollars.

"Best part of this joint was the wait. Sometimes you had to wait hours for a table," Bill reminisced. "Not that I like the idea of waiting for a seat, but this bar was the best place to do it."

Orel shifted the flashlight to take in Bill's profile and saw a man with faraway eyes.

"Manhattans. Tony had a way of making those damned things better'n anybody I seen," Bill said.

"Tony? That sonofabitch beat me outta five hundred and skipped town," Sam complained, his voice getting louder as he went on about the old bartender. "Last I heard, that bastard dropped the dime to the cops to get himself out of a jam. Never liked an informer. Look, Connor, I hate to be the red light on your trip down memory lane, but we have some things to work out here."

Bill snapped out of his trance and glanced over his shoulder at Sam.

Orel followed the beam of his flashlight to a seat next to the "best Manhattan bar on the beach" and sat down. He looked around the place to take it all in. It was smaller than he had been told. Stories always make things sound bigger. He did his best to picture what it was like when it was in full swing during its heyday, filled with music and laughter. A smile grew over his face when he saw a stage over by the shadowy dance floor. He stared closely at its elevated wooden floor, which was a simple pattern of tongue and groove slats. With a glance toward the ceiling, he took in lights of various sizes with a particularly large one toward the middle. Again, his eyes wandered back to the stage and its construction.

Bill and Sam gingerly stepped over a broken glass and garbage as they made their way across the dining area. As the two men joined Orel at the bar, Sam popped the cigar back into his mouth.

"Dis plathe needs ta be gutted by dee enda da monthhh," he lisped. "Tho we don't have much time." After removing the cigar from his mouth once again, he stated more clearly. "So here's my offer to you, Connor. I don't have the time, nor desire, to deal in matters of junk. Since you seem to have dedicated your life to garbage, I am offering you the opportunity to clear the whole kit and kaboodle, so they can renovate this old dump in a few weeks."

Bill's eyes widened as he heard Sam's barely discernible words.

"Now," continued Sam, "while I have no desire to pay your ass, everything you take out of here will be yours. In addition to the money you repay me for the two months mortgage, I get half of everything you make off the fixtures. That's the deal."

"The whole thing?" Bill asked eagerly. "The fridges, the stoves, the toilets?" He pointed in every direction of the restaurant. "The whole kit–"

"–and kaboothle," interrupted Sam, his shrinking cigar back in his mouth and his face half illuminated by the flashlight that Orel had laid on the bar.

"So, Eisenrad. You're telling me that every fixture in this place is mine as long as I do the job of getting it out of here by the end of the month?"

"Half, Connor. I get half. Can I make myself any clearer?"

"Perhaps by removing the cigar when you speak," Orel sniped quietly in an innocent tone.

Sam's head swung slowly toward him and then back to Bill.

"And it won't cost me a dime?" Bill asked.

"Notta penny. Just get it cleaned out so the bulldozers can level it by the first of July. Capeeth?" Sam punctuated his remarks by piercing his lips with the thumb-length cigar.

"Capeesh," answered Bill and offered a hurried handshake. "When do we start?"

"Have at it. Place is yours," Sam said and reached in his pocket. "Here's your key."

Bill caught the light gold key with a flat hand as Sam's pitch bounced it off his round, taut belly. His other hand remained locked with Sam's to seal the deal.

Chapter 6

The medical examiner described it as a fat metal wire with spirals, which acted as a conductor. The detectives were more specific, calling it the lowest octave C bass piano string from a Baldwin baby grand. While both used deliberately antiseptic terms to explain the weapon of choice in the self-inflicted death, neither could give a logical reason why it happened.

Dorothy's eyes were welled bags of wrinkles. Her bottom lip quivered as she scissor-fingered a cigarette to her mouth. Her hand cupped a lipstick stained glass of Scotch to numb the pain. Her hope was that the drink would give her answers.

"Maybe he was a homo," Wally whispered as he wiped a collection of beer circles from the bar. "Joe D. and I had a homo in our outfit. Not even sure how the hell he got in. They didn't let fags defend our country in dem days."

Einstein eyed Wally with furry eyebrows as he sat outside the tavern and watched Dorothy through the smoke from her stale cigarette.

"Did he have any family, Dot?" he asked, trying to sound sympathetic. "Will there be a memorial?"

Dorothy answered with a blank stare and a sniffle into a tissue. Her eyes became more watery as she thought of Winston and how she'd first met him. He had walked into the tavern in his neatly pressed Larry's 'Lectric uniform. She thought of how the same uniform had been burned slightly around the collar from the electrical charge that went up the piano wire and into his neck. She thought of how he never would drink when he drove a vehicle for fear that he may harm someone. She thought of how quiet and drunk he got the night after his mother died. All through the pale gray cigarette smoke and amber Dewar's, she thought.

"Ohh, whatta relief it is!" Rudy screamed into Lucy's ear.

"Say it, don't spray it, Rude," complained Lucy, somewhat irritated by his proximity.

Rudy walked down the seawall looking for more crabs while he wiped the residue of the previous catch from his dirty hands. A warm breeze made the palm trees sway against the orange and blue sky. Lucy sat on a car bumper and seemed to be thinking of something other than crabbing.

"So did Orel go with your dad today, Rude?" she asked.

"The what?" responded Rudy who had gotten on his belly to see if any crabs were under a piece of old, broken seawall.

"I said, 'You smell pretty bad today, Rude.'"

"Loose, you should see the size of this stoner down here," Rudy yelled. "Claw on this one would be a whole meal."

"Rude, why don't we let it live another day? I've had enough crabbing for now."

"You sure, Loose? It's humongous."

"I'm sure. Let's go back to the motel and swim."

The motor on the truck could be heard for blocks before its smoke could be seen. Rudy knew the sound. Sometimes it made his stomach hurt. This time it did not.

"My dad's heading back, Loose!" he shouted excitedly.

Lucy's face lit up, since she knew Orel would be in the truck. "Race ya, Rude!"

"Last one there has to kiss Danny Partridge!"

"Eeeeeyyuuuu," yelled Lucy at Rudy's waving hair.

As they rounded the corner, they could see a murky mix of sandy dust and oily smoke enveloping Bill's red pickup. The passenger door was opening and a figure emerged.

When the dust settled, the children could make out the tall thin body of Orel. His white T-shirt was smeared with grease and dirt. His jeans were speckled with white dots, big and small, and his face was covered with a wet mix of sweat, oil and saw dust. His smile was the only clean part of him when he greeted Rudy and Lucy running toward the truck.

"Well, look what the cat dragged in," Orel remarked, somewhat ironically.

"Hello, Orel. How are you?" Lucy said self-importantly, trying to sound adult.

"To tell you the truth, Lucyball, I've been a lot cleaner," he quipped, holding up his right hand and exposing another area of grease and dirt.

"Orel, thanks for the hand. Same time tomorrow," said Bill. "I'm off to the tavern to celebrate. Maybe I'll see you later."

After a few grinding noises and some vigorous pushing on the clutch, Bill had the red pickup on its way.

"Let's go swimming, Loose," Rudy said.

Lucy had her eyes fixed on the vein that ran up Orel's bicep and did not hear Rudy until the Canadian responded for her.

"Swimming? I wonder if your father would appreciate me getting his pool all dirty, Lucyball? Sounds like a great plan, Rudy.

I'll be out in a jiff. Just let me go to my room and get the first layer of gunk off my body."

Lucy's gaze wandered from the vein and sleeve to Orel's eyes. She smiled uncomfortably when he looked back at her.

"Wouldn't want to mess up any of your father's seats again now would we, Lucyball?" he said

"Seeee? Aaah…no…no, we wouldn't," answered Lucy with a giggle as she figured out what Orel meant.

"Meetcha in the deep end in about fifteen minutes," Orel said.

"Okay," Rudy yelled. "Last one in kisses Edith Bunker on the lips!"

Orel and Lucy watched as Rudy ran toward the pool dropping sneakers and socks along the path. Orel glanced down at Lucy and gave her a wink.

"Be out in a bit, darling," he said. Lucy followed him with her eyes as he walked in his peculiar prance down the sidewalk, stopping to smell a hibiscus flower on his way.

"You comin' in, Loose?" Rudy yelled from the top of the pool slide.

"Yeah, Rude, as soon as I put on a bathing suit."

"What's the matter with what you're wearing?" he asked.

Lucy looked down at her tight, lime green shorts and orange blouse, which had been stained with a mixture of crab slime and dirt. Then she examined her nails and found more remnants of crab slime. Looking back up to Rudy, she decided not to say something she would either regret or have to explain.

"I'll be out in a sec, Rude," she said and then walked briskly, yet ladylike to her room.

Rudy watched Lucy leave and shrugged it off as "a girl thing." It really did not matter much to him, though. Usually Rudy enjoyed moments alone like this because it gave him the chance to go off in his imagination without being interrupted. Sometimes, he would be a jet pilot giving air support to the ground forces in Vietnam. At other times, he would be the army guy on the ground calling in air support.

This time, however, he was in the water, the toughest guy he had seen on the news reports. He was a Navy Seal. He had heard stories of how the Seals would become human logs and float in the water until the enemy stumbled upon them. And then "POW da da daa daaa daaa daa. DIE, YOU COMMIE PIG!!!"

The dark water and murky seaweed hung on the Seal as he took down all the Vietnam guys. "Air support! WE'VE GOT CHAR-LIE ALL OVER US. INCOMING! AHHRRRGGRRRHHH! KablAAAAAMMM."

Stillness, nothingness.

"RUDY! GEEZUS, RUDY!" Orel yelled, pulling at Rudy's motionless body in the pool.

"Phhlaaa…" puffed Rudy as he expelled imaginary seaweed and Viet Cong body parts from his lungs, only to be pulled out of the war by a guy wearing a…Weenie Bender?

"Are you okay? You bumped your head and fell off the slide. I saw you floating. Thought you were dead! " Orel continued to rant until Rudy interrupted.

"Oh, sorry, Orel. I was…I was just playing Army."

"Army? Christ! Army?" Orel complained. "One of these days I'll understand the American affinity for war."

Rudy looked up with his brown eyes, not sure what Orel was telling him.

"You…you people just don't seem to be happy unless you're arguing. Or blowing something up…or killing something!"

Orel continued until he realized he was preaching to an eleven-year-old boy who was doing nothing more than wishing to be a young man. He let out a laugh. When Rudy saw things were okay, he joined in. Before long, the two were laughing harder and harder, neither remembering why they were laughing in the first place.

Just as they were getting over the shock and horror of pretend war, they heard the motel office door swing open with a jingle, followed by a slam. Both turned their heads and saw the slender figure of Lucy walking in their direction.

Rudy pursed his lips and cocked an eyebrow to make out what she was wearing. "A bikini?" he whispered under his breath.

As Lucy got closer, he noticed that her hair was bouncing from side to side, rather than clinging to her head as usual. And she was wearing round blue sunglasses.

"Sunglasses?" he whispered again. "Oh, geez. Outta Sight."

Even the way Lucy walked was different. It appeared that she made an effort to make one foot go over the top of her other shin and foot. Orel took notice of Lucy's appearance and bit back a grin.

"Gentlemen," Lucy purred when she got to where the two were sitting.

"Gentle...? Loose, what's with the glasses and the hair?" Rudy asked. "And the walk? You freaking out on me?"

"No, Rudeee, I'm not freakin' out!" Lucy barked, slipping out of character for a moment before catching herself. "Maybe you're freakin' out!"

Rudy's silence was deafening.

Orel did not look up from the blueness of the pool. The awkwardness of the moment would not let him. "You should have seen me just make a fool out of myself, Lucyball," Orel started in an effort to change the subject. "I came out here to find you guys and instead found young Rudy floating in the pool half dead."

"What?" gasped Lucy pulling her sunglasses down.

"Yeah, it seems Rudy was in a battle with some bad guys, and I pulled him out right before they killed him," Orel continued in a serious tone.

Rudy, sensing the joke, nodded from behind like a wrestler's sidekick.

Lucy's eyes darted back and forth between Orel telling the story and Rudy looking silly. Then she asked, "Anybody up for Marco Polo?"

"Now we're talking, Loose," yelped Rudy.

Orel looked at Rudy and gave him a wink. It was apparent that the war story had been enough to jolt Lucy back to reality. At least for the moment.

The driver's side door of the red pickup made a squeak as Bill swung it open. A puff of dust flew off his shoe when it hit the sand of the tavern parking lot. As Bill made his way up to the outside bar, he could see Einstein sitting next to Dorothy inside.

"What's the good word, Einstein?" he yelled as he threw his worn wallet on the bar.

Einstein swung his chin toward the sky slowly in acknowledgement of Bill's greeting.

"What's the matter with you, ya fuck? Who died?" chastised Bill.

Einstein's erect chin slowly dipped toward his chest while his eyes pointed to his left. Taking a last drag on his cigarette, he rose from the bar, patted Dorothy on the back and made his way to the outside bar where Bill was sitting.

"Connor, for cries sake," he whispered when he got close enough for Bill to hear without Dorothy seeing that they were talking.

"What? What's your problem?" Bill snarled.

Reaching into his shirt pocket, Einstein pulled out a tattered pack of Camels and dug a thick hairy finger around inside it until he found a cigarette. Placing it between his lips, he began to speak slowly. "You know Winston?" he asked.

"Yeah," Bill said with a shrug and a turned down mouth. "Skinny guy who usually sits next to Dorothy. Electrician."

"Sonofabitch killed himself last night."

Bill's eyebrows contracted. Stealing a look over at Dorothy, he now noticed that she looked visibly shaken.

"How'd he–?"

"Goddamned piano wire," interrupted Einstein.

Bill looked on in astonishment.

"A hunk of rope tied to a ceiling beam would have done the trick," Einstein continued. He looked left and right, sizing up his audience to see who else was listening.

"Oh, he used a rope. Marine rope like they use on, ya know, boats. Ties it to an eye hook in the ceiling and throws a loop of it around his neck. But that wasn't all for this guy. He strings a piano wire under a light bulb in the socket and wraps the other end around his neck. Puts the chain from the wire under the noose, and voila."

Einstein seemed to revel in the gory details.

"A piano wire," repeated Bill, staring straight ahead, trying to picture the scene.

"Yep," acknowledged Einstein. "And when he jumped off the chair and the noose tightened, the chain turned on the power to the light." Einstein's whispers grew raspier as he puffed on the bent cigarette. "His foot landed in a bucket of water underneath him and he was toast after that."

"Jesus!" mumbled Bill. "If he didn't die from choking, he was sure gonna die from the electrocution."

"Poor bastard wanted outta here, that's for sure," Einstein said as smoke poured from his nose. "Funny, an electrician dying from electricity, huh?" His face lit up as he contemplated the irony of it all.

"Hmmm…oh well," piped Bill. "I guess some folks just don't know how to cope anymore."

"How's the new clean-out going?" Einstein asked, changing topics as if the previous story had never been never part of their conversation.

"Good. Couple of joints and Covington's place," Bill offered, though his mind was still working through the details of Winston's death.

"Covington, huh?" interrupted Wally who was wiping up their side of the bar as much as eavesdropping. "Harry knew his shit. Knew how to get people in the door. And he knew veal."

"Best veal you ever put in your mouth," Bill said, nodding.

"I was sorry to see Cov close up shop. Sure, he was competition. But he was a helluva nice guy," Wally reminisced.

Einstein and Bill exchanged smirks. This was the first time they had heard Wally say nice words about anyone.

"Yeah, so I gut the joint and then the 'dozers knock it down," Bill said.

"Sorry to see it happen. The Nearvana was a landmark. They just don't leave anything alone anymore," Wally rambled on, pushing his towel down the bar till he happened upon another customer in need of a drink.

"Yeah, I'm sorry to see it going away, too," came a voice from behind the two men.

"Gene!" yelled Bill when he turned and saw who was speaking.

"Bill, Einstein. How are you fine gentlemen doing this evening?"

"Better'n Winston," joked Einstein.

"Uhh, yeah. I heard about that earlier today," Gene said. "Sad situation. Did they rule out foul play?"

Bill looked up, surprised at Gene's question.

Einstein remained hunched over his drink. "It was a suicide," he flatly responded. "Guy just killed himself, that's all."

Gene took a long look in the painter's direction, studying his certainty. A pull off his drink brought him back to a more sociable conversation.

"So, Orel tells me you closed the deal with Eisenrad this morning."

"Yeah, we're gonna be working on cleaning out Covington's whole place and a few others on the beach," explained Bill. "Gut the whole joint. Eisenrad's giving me all the fixtures. Lotta work, but it's a good trade out, since I can turn those appliances into cash in a hurry."

"Hmmm. Shame you don't have capital," joked Gene.

"Money? I don't need it. He's giving me all the shit in the place for my labor," Bill said. "Splitting what I sell."

"No, I mean to buy the joint. You know you're always talking about opening a place of your own one day. 'Women in short shorts. Asses put asses in the seats.' You know—the whole dream thing. The Nearvana would be a great location for something like that. Tailor made."

Bill bit his lip as he laughed off the notion of owning his own bar. "Yeah, that'd be something, huh?" he snorted as he popped a cigarette in his mouth and returned to his beer. "Asses *would* put asses in the seats, ya know."

Einstein gave Bill a sympathetic wink.

"Where is Orel, anyway?" asked Bill. "I need to work out a payment arrangement with him."

"He was swimming with the kids and said he was gonna stop by a little later," Gene said.

Lucy was looking into the clear blue of the water for answers when she decided to ask Orel the question.

"What do you think happens when you die, Orel?"

Orel thought for a moment. He didn't want to make light of the question or produce an answer with too much gravity.

"Well, Lucyball, I don't know for sure. But I'd like to think we go somewhere nice," he said, hoping to appease her curiosity.

"Nice?" she prodded.

"Yeah, nice. Heaven. Well, what's the best thing you can think of in the world?"

"Rocky Road ice cream!" Rudy yelled, hanging from the handrail of the steps with the top of his head in the pool water.

Orel smiled and raised two thumbs skyward toward Rudy.

"Rocky Road ice cream it is. Imagine you get to do nothing but eat Rocky Road ice cream from the minute you wake up till the minute you go to bed."

"Sounds like it might get a little boring after awhile," Lucy said. "I mean, wouldn't you get sick of doing nothing but eating ice cream all day long?"

"Not me," Rudy said, eyes upside down and hair floating in the water. "I could eat ice cream seven days a week, twenty-four hours a day."

"Sure, maybe it could get boring," Orel said, chewing his cheek. "Perhaps that's why life is so exciting. It's full of different things that constantly excite us." His lips became redder and fuller as he spoke. "So many things to do and experience and feel. There are mountains to climb. People to meet. Things to invent."

Lucy looked at Orel with appreciative and adoring eyes. There was something about the way he spoke with such a zest for life that made her want to go out and do something special herself right at that moment.

"Why are you so worried about what's happening after we die?" Orel asked.

Lucy looked down at the skimmer drain gasping for water as if it were oxygen.

"There was this man at the tavern," Lucy started. "Well, he used to be at the tavern. I was in the bathroom there today, and I heard two ladies talking about how he killed himself last night."

"Oh my..." Orel winced and laid a comforting hand on Lucy's back.

"Wonder if Winston's eating Rocky Road right now?" Rudy joked, his hair still floating in the pool.

"Winston?" asked Orel.

"Yeah that is...was his name," said Lucy, shaking her head at Rudy for his comment. "He never said much. Just kinda sat there and leaned on the bar every time I saw him. Come to think of it, I don't think I ever heard him say a word. Not even sure what his voice sounded like. He always kinda freaked me out."

"Well, I'm sure Winston is doing okay right now," Orel assured her. "Some people just don't get a chance to ripple the pond as much as others in this life. But I think they get another chance down the road to get it right."

Rudy pushed off the ladder and kicked like an otter till he got to where Lucy and Orel were sitting on the side of the pool.

"Ripple the pond?" Lucy asked.

Rudy held his mouth under water and let air bubbles seep out one by one as he stared at the two of them.

"Yeah—ripple the pond, Lucyball," Orel repeated, as he noticed his audience had grown by one, with Rudy pulling himself out of the water to sit on the side of the pool.

Orel stood and walked over to a planter holding a small palm tree that bent across the sidewalk. He reached down and picked up a handful of stones. He walked back to where the two children were sitting, winked at Rudy and sat back down. Opening his palm, Lucy and Rudy could see that Orel had many stones of different sizes and colors.

"Imagine that each of these stones is a different person," he started. Slowly he passed his flat hand full of pebbles before each child so each could see his point. "And the pool," he said, while pointing with his free hand, "is life."

With a small grunt he swung his left arm in the air and released the stones. Some flew high, others barely made it off the ground, but all eventually landed in the pool with varying size splashes. Some made loud noises while others caused a more muffled "plop" as they entered the water.

"Now this is what I'm talking about," Orel said as he stood at the pool's edge pointing at the water. "See the circles. Each stone made a circle. A ripple."

Rudy got on his belly by the side of the pool to get a closer look. He giggled as he listened to Orel continue his monologue.

"See how the circles bump into each other? If you watch long enough, every circle will bump into every other circle in the water."

Lucy squinted her eyes and shaded her face to cut the glare of the sunlight dancing on top of each of the circles. Every now and then she'd grin when two of the circles had their ripples touch.

"That's the way I see it," said Orel. "Don't worry about the dying part, Lucyball. As long as you go out there and ripple the pond, everything will be fine, sweetie. I think you get a bigger bowl of Rocky Road the more you ripple the pond."

Lucy looked up at Orel who seemed to be in another place as he finished sharing his thoughts.

"You think Winston rippled the pond, Orel?" asked Lucy.

"Winston?" thought Orel. "Unfortunately, I think some people wait till they die to ripple the pond. And somehow, I think Winston may have been one of those people."

Lucy looked at Orel with a nod of understanding.

"Well, enough of that. We better get these stones out of the pool before your dad blames us for breaking his pool pump," warned Orel as he dove into the water and headed straight for the bottom.

Rudy grinned at Lucy. "Time to ripple Orel's pond. CANNONBALL!" he yelled, leapt and landed with a splash on top of Orel.

Orel pushed off the bottom and grabbed Rudy by the ankle and pulled him under.

"Looooose! Help meeeee," gurgled a laughing Rudy as he bobbed up and down.

"There's no help for you, Rude," said Lucy.

She grinned at her friend and continued to think about Orel's words.

Chapter 7

The upside down Santa in the first week of June sat as a stale reminder that Bill loved his parties. He hated to see them end. What made it worse was the thought that this Santa might have been a leftover from two or three Christmases prior.

Orel kept polishing the ashy red paint till it gave off a reflection not seen since the truck was almost new. When he got to the door he lightly wiped over the newly applied cursive letters on the side of the pickup.

The white towel pulled away to reveal the words: Another Man's Treasure.

"Geezus, what time is it?" came Bill's sandpaper voice as he emerged from the pre-dawn darkness. He was doing his best to wipe the previous evening's carousing from his eyes. His wrinkled shirt was covered with the remainders of the chilly dog he'd had for dinner at the tavern.

"Six forty-five," answered Orel with a glance at his watch.

"Why didn't you wake me sooner? We need to get to the site."

"We're in good shape. I got doughnuts and coffee and washed and waxed the rig," Orel said proudly. "Only thing we gotta do is start it up and hit the road."

"Yeah, if it starts," said Bill. Scratching his tangled, wavy hair, he walked to the side of the truck.

Orel buffed the final remnants of wax from the driver's side and snapped the towel at the new logo with pride. "She's purring like a kitten. I changed the plugs and air filter right before I washed and waxed her."

"A kitten," Bill chortled, then looked at the sign. "What the hell is this? Another man's traysure. What in cries sake is that?"

"That is the new name of your company," Orel gushed. "It's like my Uncle Lou used to say about stuff at the tag sales: 'One man's junk…is another man's treasure.'" He circled the shiny red truck like a used car salesman. "I think in our line of work it fits like a glove."

"Our line of work?! You spend one day helping me clean out an old restaurant and suddenly you're a goddamned junkman. What the hell do you know about the garbage business?"

"Well, sir, with all due respect, it all seems pretty simple," Orel said. "You take something that once had value but was neglected. Give it some attention, and then it has a new value. Kinda like this truck. Some minor maintenance and she's almost good as new. Just a little piled up neglect is all."

He scratched some caked up wax off the rearview mirror with his thumbnail.

"Yeahhh?" Bill drawled, unsure what to make of his new business name or his new business partner. "We'd better get to the site before Eisenrad's busting my balls about being late."

Orel resumed wiping the truck.

Bill walked past him and playfully pointed out a spot the Canadian had overlooked. When he got to the screen door of the duplex, he noticed that Rudy was awake already and limping around the living room.

"You're up? What's the matter with you now, Son?"

"Not sure. I think I got into some sand fleas or ants last night," Rudy said, rubbing his swollen ankles. "Must be allergic or something."

"You better have your mother put some calamine on that."

"I'll be okay."

Rudy looked his dad in the eyes, not something he did often. "You said I might be able to go with you and Orel one of these days to help out on the route."

"Yeah. Why don't you...," Bill started, focusing on Rudy's eyebrows—direct eye contact made him uneasy—"...have your mother look at those ankles."

A long silence hung between them.

"I need to get a little more comfortable with this Orel before we add another character to the show," he said and walked outside.

Rudy got up and followed him to the screen door. He watched his father slide in the truck alongside Orel. They almost looked like a father and son, even acted like a regular father and son.

He pictured with envy what they would eat for lunch. He wondered what they might joke about. He wondered what his dad would teach Orel. What Orel would teach his dad.

Rudy was startled when he noticed Orel looking in his direction and waving. Orel was trying to yell something out of the passenger side door, but Rudy couldn't understand what he was saying. He pushed the screen door open and hobbled toward the truck. Orel tried again, but the motor drowned out his voice. Rudy made a silly face, waved back and watched the shiny, red pickup pull out of the driveway.

The truck stopped short of the street. Orel was now gesturing and speaking vigorously to Bill. From Bill's expression, it was obvious he did not agree with what Orel was telling him. Eventually, he bowed his head on the steering wheel, flung his hand in the air in acquiescence and turned off the engine.

"Rudy!" Orel yelled from the truck window. "Your dad said he wants you to come and give us a hand today."

"Ohhhh kayy!" Rudy yelled back and ran back to his room to change out of his pajamas.

In a matter of minutes, Rudy bolted from the duplex with no sign of his ankles bothering him. He jumped into the back of the pickup and settled in, suppressing a grin.

Bill squinted at Orel and started the engine.

"Purring like a kitten," the Canadian said.

Bill backed the truck into the street. "Never did like cats," he muttered.

The darkness absorbed the light as the crease of the open door widened. Gradually, cobwebs and mold could be seen draped where Babe Ruth or Sinatra once sipped whiskey or Scotch. As more light poured in, it became obvious to the three figures entering that this was not going to be an easy task. Although Orel and Bill had gotten some work done the previous day, they had barely scratched the surface.

Rudy tiptoed around scattered tables and chairs in the restaurant until he found his way to the video and pinball games. He was very young the last time he had been to the Nearvana with his parents. His memory was uncanny when it came to arcade game rooms, though. Sure enough, there was foosball, air hockey and Ball Four—the last, the ultimate challenge of man against machine.

While Orel made his way past the dining room onto the dance floor, Bill pried open the breaker box in order to get some electrical power into the restaurant. After several snaps that produced no result, the entire place suddenly lit up. Light gained equaled lost allure.

The black-and-white checkered floor showed age and dirt. The walls and corners of the ceiling sported watermarks from a leaky pipe and roof. The dance floor was scuffed and bowed.

The game room came to light in front of Rudy's eyes. It sparkled and pinged with red lights, blue lights, yellow lights, bells and pops. The air hockey game gave off a whir of crowd noise with an occasional "Booo!" As Rudy took it all in, he heard the three familiar words, "PLAY BALL FOUR!"

"Okay, Orel. Today we'll start by getting these tables and chairs out," Bill said. "That'll clear a path to work our way to da kitchen. Need ta git those pieces out pronto."

Orel nodded at his boss from the dance floor.

"Rudy, I need you sweeping behind Orel," Bill ordered. "That way we don't track this crap floor all over and end up doin' twice da work."

Reluctantly, Rudy turned away from the games and got to work. He knew it was important to please his father if he wanted to come along again.

After several hours of work, the dining room area had been cleared, except for a few stray chairs. The air was heavy with dust from all the sweeping Rudy had done.

Bill had tackled the electrical outlets. Bare sockets filled with exposed wires dotted the walls. The switch plates which had covered them were lined up in a cardboard box. Next to that box was a smaller box filled with a variety of colored screw caps. An even smaller box contained different sized screws. Everything was organized according to size. The floor resembled a used hardware store. Nothing was out of place. It was evident that Bill was a good junkman. He knew the value of his garbage.

As he finished unscrewing the final switch plate, he turned to his crew and shouted, "LUNCH! Why don't you guys relax, and I'll run out and get us a pizza."

"Okay, Dad. We'll be here," Rudy called out. He looked at Orel and smiled. "Got any quarters?"

"As a matter a fact, I do."

"Take you on in some air hockey."

"American against a Canuck in hockey? You're kidding, right?"

"Bring it on! And make sure those coins are American or they'll break the machine."

Orel pursed his lips, walked over to the air hockey machine and inserted a quarter. "You know, you Americans can put a man on the moon, but you still can't figure out a way to get machines to take our money," he griped.

Rudy grabbed his round hockey mallet and looked around the room, making sure his father had left the building. "What'd you say to my dad to make him change his mind about letting me come today?" he asked.

Orel continued to make selections for the hockey game. When he was happy with his choices, he looked up. "Well, I told him that you wouldn't be a kid forever. And that these are the most precious years of your life with him. And it would be a good experience for you to work with him every now and then. And that there's nothing more important than the relationship between a father and a son."

"And that's when he said it was okay to come?"

"Well, that and…and when I finally told him that I'd work for half a day's wages today if you could come is when he seemed open to the idea."

Orel dropped the puck on the table and laughed. "You're going down, Yankeedoodledandy."

By the time Bill returned forty-five minutes later, the effects of mental body checks and verbal sparring were obvious in Orel's demeanor and physical appearance. The Yankee was doing a dandy job of mopping the air hockey floor with his Canadian counterpart.

Bill put down a huge square pizza box and a six-pack of Cokes he was balancing.

"Yay, pizza!" Rudy yelled and ran over to help. Carefully, he grabbed the Cokes and gave his dad a gentle pat on the back. Bill glanced at his son, unaccustomed to signs of affection.

"Napkins in my back pocket" was all he could muster.

Though a long line of booths remained, the three decided in unison that it made more sense to eat on the floor.

"I haven't had pizza in quite a long time," Orel volunteered.

"You haven't?" Rudy squealed. "We have it every Friday night."

Orel smiled at Rudy.

"I love Friday nights when we have pizza," Rudy mumbled, struggling through a mouthful of crust and cheese.

"So, Bill, I was thinking during my hockey match with your boy," Orel started. "Seems we have a huge task here. I am not one to tell someone how to do their business, but it would make sense to me to do this systematically. I think we would be able to get more accomplished if the two of us split up. You and Rudy could work out here in the restaurant area and I could attack, say, the back room and office."

Bill swished his tongue around his mouth looking as if in search of a wayward piece of pepperoni or the proper answer for Orel.

Orel discovered a packet of Parmesan cheese and worked to get it open while Bill digested the proposition.

"I think that will work," he said after considerable thought and added, as if it were his own idea, "We'll do the main restaurant area while you work on the back room and office."

Orel nodded at his boss in approval.

Rudy looked deeply into his piece of pizza.

By the time the day grew old, the three were making some headway in cleaning and clearing the restaurant. Bill and Rudy worked on removing dining area fixtures and had not seen Orel since lunch. Still, they knew he was busy from all the hammering and prying noise coming from the back room. Bill had instructed him to remove the wallboard from the entire office. From the racket Bill could only assume he was making progress.

"How's it goin' in there, Son?" asked Bill, a soggy cigarette hanging from one corner of his mouth.

After several seconds of no response, he got up and headed toward the office. "Yeeeohh, Orrrrelll?"

"Uhhhh, yeeeahh, almost done, sir," answered the preoccupied Canadian. "I'll be out in two shakes."

"Two shakes?" giggled Rudy. "Now I'm getting hungry again."

"Yeah, those Mapleleafs sure talk funny," agreed Bill, poking his head in the door. "We gotta get a move on here, Son."

"If you'd like to go ahead and leave, I'll just finish up at my leisure," Orel said, wiping a fine mix of white powder and sweat from his forehead. "I'll catch up with you at the tavern for a beer when I'm done."

"You don't needa ride?" asked Bill, inspecting the work of his helper.

Three of the walls in the office were a skeleton of two by fours. The fourth, which was still partially covered in wallboard, was where the safe was anchored. This seemed to be the object of Orel's attention.

"Nahh, the walk would do me good. Get some of this dust out of my lungs, to be exact," he joked.

Bill cast another glance toward the safe and said, "Suit yourself, Son. Never stand in the way of a man willing to do more work than me. Just lock up when you're done. We'll see you after awhile." He stalked past Rudy who took a long stare at Orel from the doorway, nodded and turned to join his father on his way out.

Orel called after him, "Work on that rail shot, Rudy. I'll be looking for some revenge for the hockey beating you gave me this afternoon."

"Okay," Rudy said as he negotiated his way through the maze of boxes of fixtures on the floor and headed outside.

Orel went to one of the windows and watched until the truck drove off. Then he ducked back to the spot in front of the wall with the safe. He squatted down and thrust the claw of the hammer between a two by four and the remaining piece of sheetrock. It did not come off as easily as the other sheets had, but with some coaxing, it finally gave way.

The wall was now bare and the safe was free with the exception of some fasteners against a heavy piece of wire lath. Some wire cutters and a crowbar would take care of that.

Orel stood up slowly and worked some of the stiffness out of his knees. Wiping the sweat from his forehead and dust off his cheek, he looked around for the proper tools. Cautiously, he walked through the clutter of the office to the toolbox in the main area of the restaurant.

The toolbox gave off the pungent smell of dirty hands as he shuffled though the mess of pliers, screwdrivers, wrenches and hammers. When Orel finally found tools to his liking, he took them to the window for one more look outside. The white-hot Florida late afternoon revealed nothing in the parking lot but burning sand and a pair of tire tracks.

A nervous heat filled Orel's belly. He took a deep breath and reached into his pocket for the worn out piece of paper. Two greasy fingers tweezered the paper and added one more stain to its tarnished surface. He placed the tools down and read the note slowly aloud to himself. "Two hands two fingers…"

He looked around the room. "Two hands two fingers stage right off the main spot."

Orel folded the paper in his left hand and scanned the dining area. He slowly plodded across the checkerboard floor to the foot of the stage. The darkness made it difficult to discern the breaker box and light panel he had seen earlier in the day.

After several frustrating minutes of groping for switches, he finally found one that seemed to be big enough to light the stage. With a slow and deliberate push, he threw the switch. A loud click and a single light made a circular spot in the middle of the stage floor.

Orel walked carefully to the light and stopped a few feet in front of it. Again he unfolded the paper, which had become moist from the sweat in his palm.

"Two hands, two fingers…stage right off the main spot," he whispered. Since he was looking toward the stage as an audience member would, he realized his point of view was backwards. A pivot on one heel turned him back to the unlit chairs from where guests would have watched the show. Now, his right was also stage right.

He closed his eyes as he felt the warm burn again in his belly. Carefully kneeling on the stage floor, he laid the paper next to the lighted area and dropped the tools behind him with an echoing thud. He placed his greasy left hand palm down with the little finger at the center of the round light spot. Then he put his right hand next to the left, eyeballed two additional fingers' worth, and marked the spot with a grease smudge.

He picked up the piece of paper again. "Two hands, two fingers up," he whispered.

Orel looked around and decided which way was upstage. He searched the floor for the grease smudge. Carefully he took his right hand and spread it wide from the mark. Repeating the earlier process, he placed his left hand next to the right. With a leap-frog motion, he placed two fingers from his right hand next to his left. One more smudge marked the spot, which was centered on a peculiarly short piece of tongue-and-groove flooring.

Though the room was empty, Orel unconsciously glanced over his shoulder to make sure no one was watching. He reached for the crowbar and hammer. He lined the claw of the crowbar against the side of the short piece of wooden floor board. One sharp hit, but nothing gave way. Another. Then, a third. Still nothing happened.

Finally, after a dozen hits, the board popped out of its space, spun into the air and landed on the wooden stage with a splintery noise. The adjacent pieces slid out more easily. Before long, the narrow space became a hole.

When it was big enough to reach inside, Orel pulled his head back from the hole. A small beam of light from the main spot spilled into the opening, revealing a small green man. Orel squinted. It was a green man with a pipe, smiling.

Swiping away some of the dust, Orel could see that the green man with the pipe was part of a large bag and had something on his finger—a small, brown ball. "Celtics," he mumbled. "Boston…Celtics…basketball."

The green man on the gym bag kept smiling as Orel worked to free it from the stage floor. When he finally managed to dislodge it, the green and white leather pouch fell to the stage with a solid bang.

His breath quickened and he went to each window and checked that nobody had pulled into the parking lot while he was doing all the banging. Beads of sweat fell into his eyes causing a salty burn, blinding him momentarily.

He quickly ran back to the stage to the weathered gym bag and the green, smiling man. He knelt down and, lifting one side of the bag slightly off the stage, pulled at the rusty zipper. To his surprise, it moved easily, making a warm popping noise as it opened.

A silky cloth immediately below the zipper protected the contents. Orel could feel something bumpy underneath. His pulse quickened and beads of sweat formed on his upper lip as he pulled the cloth away. He could see rectangles. Stacks of rectangles wrapped with rubber bands. Green stacks. Too many to count.

Grabbing one of the stacks, he thumbed its corner and fanned through the contents. The number 100 danced like a green animation until he got to the end of the stack. He picked up a second stack. Same result. A third and a fourth try told Orel that there was a lot of money in the gym bag.

He dug into the pile of wrapped bills and found a manila envelope. With trembling hands he pulled at the red string wound around a tab on the backside. Inside were some black-and-white photos and papers. The photos showed men in suits standing on the street, in restaurants and at various gatherings. At first glance, Orel did not recognize any of them. The papers appeared to be deeds and legal documents. There was also a single, sealed, white business envelope that simply read "Lawrence Kronis."

Once more, Orel dipped into the bag. Pushing the stacks of money aside, he could make out a book at the bottom. A gentle pull loosened it from its hiding place. On the cover of the worn, brown leather binding was the title, *The Journal of Jonny Hughes*.

"A message—from my father," Orel mouthed to himself. As he opened the book, a heave of emotion racked his body. He rubbed the words on the first page as if that would somehow help him. Tears started to run down his cheeks, and his breath spluttered from his lungs.

The small scribbles on the next few pages were barely legible. On the fourth was the first dated entry.

> *6/23/49*
>
> *Not sure what I'm doing. Guys in the band said to write things down. Great way to blow off steam. Maybe help to loosen a few song lyrics.*

Orel read on for a few more pages.

> *5/29/51*
>
> *Got a nice gig a few weeks back. Fellow named Lawrence hooked me up with another nice guy, Harry. Steady piano playing at his restaurant.*

He leaned back and released a quivering breath that wobbled. The journal of the man who had sent him away all those years ago should have been a page-turner. But Orel felt mostly betrayed and also dirty for intruding on his father's personal account.

He glanced at the green man on the gym bag, whose frozen smile and wink seemed to mock him. He put down the journal and reached for the contents of the manila envelope.

His first discovery was a legal document that read, "Jonathon Marcus Hughes hereby grants power of attorney to Orel Benjamin Hughes, should grantor become incapacitated." A second document was a deed of ownership to a property. The place was simply listed as Parcel 57.

Orel found nothing of interest among the rest of the papers and moved on to the black-and-white photos. A small, faded one appeared to be his father at a piano. In the background, several men stood in dark suits and plain black ties. One man in particular seemed very happy. He smiled broadly and had his arm around the piano player.

Another, larger photo was a portrait of a tall, well-built man who was proudly holding a shotgun off his hip, pointed straight into the air. His face seemed familiar, but youth shrouded its identity. Photo by photo, Orel searched for a meaning, but neither the snapshots nor the bag of money and memories revealed any.

Under the last photo lay a piece of paper ripped from a notebook. The scrawled handwriting read:

> *Orie,*
> *If you've gotten here, you need to finish the job that I started. The answer is in the question. You'll know what to do, given the time I was not allowed. Here are the pieces to the puzzle. Put it together.*
> *Jonny…(Dad)*

Orel stood up from the journal and the money and the deeds and the photos. His mind raced his feet as he quickly paced the room. There was still a chance to walk away from this thing. He could easily return to the life he had grown accustomed to in Canada. He owed his father nothing but the good upbringing he received when he was moved from the corruption of this place. He only needed to put the contents back into the bag, seal the stage and walk away.

Yet, he had sense that it was proper to carry out his father's wishes. It was a sense of legacy and commitment instilled by the relatives who raised him. If the rumors he heard about his father while growing up were true, he certainly owed it to him to try to finish the job.

Orel dropped the notebook paper back into the manila envelope and stuffed the contents into the gym bag. He quickly gathered the tongue and groove pieces of wood and, board by board, reassembled the section of the stage he had ripped up. Before long, the floor was complete. He swept dust into the grooves until the main spot shone on the stage once again looking as undisturbed as it had been an hour earlier.

Then he stood up and walked away—with the Boston Celtics gym bag by his side.

Chapter 8

Lucy watched the ripples touch each other after she got done throwing the crabs back into the water. As the circles intersected one another, she could not help but think of the things that Orel had told her. She wanted to live her life like this but was not sure how to start.

"Loose!" came a yell from the parking lot of the tavern.

This was the second straight week of Rudy having left her to work with his father and Orel. In a way, Lucy felt like she was missing out on the fun. While she had spent most of her days with Rudy as a companion, she was now primarily alone. Many times she just stayed around the motel helping Joyce fold towels.

"Loose! You should have seen what we did today," Rudy called out as he ran across the sandy lot.

"Oh, goodie. Another 'what we did today' story," Lucy whispered under her breath.

"Hey," Rudy gasped, as he came up to her. "Dad was able to get the change box of the Ball Four game open. We got into the coins and found eighteen bucks in there. Of course, a lot of it was ours, but still, it was eighteen bucks, and we ate lunch on it. And Dad gave me five bucks spending money out of it, too." He rambled on, not waiting for Lucy to answer. "And the best part is—Orel figured out how to rig it so we don't have to pay to play it anymore."

"Well, that's far out, Rude," Lucy responded, indifferently.

"Yeah, it's great, never having to worry about quarters. I can play all day if Dad says it's okay."

Lucy looked at Rudy and smiled. Deep down she was happy that he was finally able to spend some time with his father.

"Right before lunch, Orel found a yardstick and a rubber ball, and we played stickball on the dance floor till it was time to go home."

"Sounds like you guys are doing more playing there than working. I'm sure that makes your dad very happy."

"Nah, he's okay with it. As long as we get our 'threshold work-load' done by the time we start playing, we can do whatever we want."

Lucy looked at the diminishing circles in the water as she struggled with Rudy and his "threshold." She noticed that the water was almost flat again. Then she heard a far-away splash.

Over her shoulder she saw Orel, standing in a rock-throwing follow through pose. "You catching anything this fine afternoon?" he called out to them.

"Hey, Orel," she answered. "As a matter of fact, I am."

"Glad to hear it," Orel said as he rubbed his chest and belly through a dingy, white T-shirt. "I think I'm ready for a glass of ale and a game of billiards."

"Sounds good to me," Rudy agreed. "Well, the billiards part at least."

"Yeah, me too," Lucy said, quickly gathering together her fishing gear.

Time and alcohol were doing their best to soften the emotions Dorothy had gone through since the days of Winston's sudden death. She still would have crying jags about her friend when she got into the Scotch too heavily. But even they were happening less often with each passing night.

Dorothy's face creased in a grin at the sight of Orel and his entourage approaching the bar. She deliberately sucked on her cigarette when he stopped in front of her.

He looked at her warmly. "Well, my day just got better, ma'am."

"Mine too, sweetie," she whispered flirtatiously, as her cheeks reddened and her eyes glowed a lighter brown.

"Wally, I'll have a large draft and a coupla root beers for my partners," Orel said. "An' for you, ma'am?"

"I'm fine now, sweetie," Dorothy drawled. "I don't ever recall seeing you drink a beer before, Orel. What's the occasion?"

"Well, a hard day's work, I suppose."

Dorothy smiled as Orel handed the root beers to his young friends. She marveled at how easily he seemed to get along with everyone, especially children.

"Rack 'em, Rudy. I'll break. Lucyball gets the winner."

Lucy watched as Orel got himself comfortable on a barstool near the pool table. His arms seemed to have gotten bigger since he was working with Rudy's dad. She loved how his chest stuck out past his flat stomach while his jeans hung on his hips.

"Is this seat taken?" whispered an angelic voice.

"Use ta be," answered Dorothy without looking up from her cigarette.

"Is it okay if I sit here?"

Dorothy turned and saw a young woman in her early twenties with large blue eyes and pigtails. She was wearing a yellow dress and was barefooted. When Dorothy nodded her approval, she climbed onto Winston's former stool, unaware that she was only the second person to settle there in more than a decade.

"Hi. I'm Susan," she whispered.

"Dorothy," came the raspy reply along with a wrinkly, bony hand to shake.

At the pool table, Rudy barked, "Three up high," looking to make his first rail shot of the evening.

"Okay," answered Orel, distracted by the new stranger. He made his way to where Lucy was sitting and gave her his cue stick. "Here, you take my turn, Lucyball. I gotta go ask your dad something."

As Orel walked to where Bill and Gene were talking outside, he took in the fresh smell of the young woman. Glancing over his shoulder, he snuck a quick peek at the simple beauty of her face. He savored her pretty smile and continued on his way.

"There's the sonofabitch who's costing me all this money," bellowed Bill.

Orel smiled modestly and stole another glance at the lady in yellow.

Gene patted Orel on the shoulder, proud of the help he was giving his friend. "You know, I don't think Bill could have handled this job on his own." He winked in Bill's direction. "You've really lit a fire under his ass to get him going on this project."

Orel continued smiling and eventually positioned himself at an angle where he could get a good look at the young woman over Bill's shoulder.

"'Another Man's Treasure,' too," Gene continued. "Damn clever. Bill needed a name on his business for years. More of a reason to get his ass out of bed."

Bill smiled in acknowledgement that he was happy with the new name as well.

"Too bad you two couldn't do something with that old joint," Gene said, shaking his head. "Always loved it there. Hate to see them knock the thing down. Was some talk of it being an historical monument. Not sure how easy it'll be for them to demolish it."

He continued, showing off his experience with the city fathers and the Chamber of Commerce, "The city council is not the brightest collection of folks in the world, but surely they wouldn't let a landmark like the Nearvana turn into a parking lot overnight. I'm sure they wouldn't want another motel either."

"Kronis'll get his way," mumbled Bill into his beer. "Always does."

Orel tore his stare away from the lady in yellow for a moment. "Well, what do you have in mind, Mr. Lewis?"

"I don't...I don't know," answered Gene. "Just a shame, them getting rid of such a nice old place with so many memories. Shame you two couldn't find a way to get in there and make a new joint of it. Bill's always saying 'asses put asses in the seats.' How he'd always wanted to open the biggest and best joint on the beach. Hell, that place is ready to go."

"Takes money though, Gene," said Bill. "And that's one thing I ain't got."

He returned to his familiar leaning pose on the bar and took a long sip of his flat beer.

Orel checked back on the lady in yellow. She and Dorothy appeared to be engaged in a pretty good conversation.

"Yeah, money," he agreed. "'Root of all evil,' my Uncle Lou used to say. 'And it's especially evil if you don't have none.'"

Bill's body shook as if he really got the joke and was laughing to himself.

"So this Nearvana was something, eh?" Orel continued.

"Hideaway for the rich and famous," Gene said. "In the 1920s, guys like Capone would winter down here, and that would be where they'd go for entertainment. Sinatra ducked in there a time or two. They say President Kennedy stopped in there once. For Ybor cigars and brandy, no doubt."

"Ahh, I remember Brandy. Very nice girl," Bill said, laughing. Gene cackled loudly.

Orel remained preoccupied. "I'll talk to you fellows in a little while," he said. "I'm in the middle of a pool game with Rudy right now." He patted Gene on the chest and walked back into the tavern.

Dorothy was on a roll, enjoying herself, though the night was young. It had been quite awhile since she'd had a fresh audience. "Well, Winston was such a kind man. Never a bad word out of his mouth. Just a little lonely is all," she said.

"Take me up on the drink now, Dorothy?" Orel asked as he walked up to where the two women were sitting.

"Well, sure, honey," she answered through a veneer of white smoke. "Meet my friend, Susan. She just got into town today. From Minnesota."

Orel shook her soft, pale hand. "Orel Hughes."

"Nice to meet you, Mr. Hughes," Susan replied.

"Gosh. Mr. Hughes? Please, Orel. We're ah-boot the same age."

"Your accent, Orel?" asked Susan.

"Canada," he answered almost short of breath. "Toronto."

"Well, we're both from the north then."

"Yes, and funny to meet down here in sunny Florida, eh? Can I buy you a drink?"

"Well, sure. As long as Dorothy joins us," Susan said. "Red wine would be great."

They held their drinks high as they navigated a tangle of bentwood chairs and settled for a square table by a window.

From the pool table Lucy called out harshly, "Eight! Corner!" quite aware of the romance in the air.

Distracted by the threesome, she struck the cue ball badly, causing it to English in a direction far from the black ball.

"Wow, you usually make that shot," said Rudy, laughing. Though he seemed sympathetic, he was really happy he would not be losing so quickly tonight.

As Lucy rosined her cue, she watched the young woman critically. The breeze off the bay was blowing through the window, making Susan's silky, blond hair flap off her neck, then lie back lightly against her cheek. Lucy's grip tightened on the chalk each time the newcomer threw her head back with a contrived laugh.

"Your turn," Rudy said.

Lucy's stomach knotted. She pulled the cue stick closer to her face and worked the blue chalk harder on the felt tip. Her breath caught as the blonde lightly touched the top of Orel's hand on the table. The lilting laugh and head toss this time was punctuated with a slow sip of a long stemmed glass of wine.

"Loose," Rudy called impatiently.

Dorothy got up from the table to assume her normal position at her barstool. Lucy's eyes narrowed to tiny slits when Orel joined the blonde on her side of the table. His arm draped the round back of her chair and he smiled as he leaned in close to her.

"Loose. You're up!" Rudy finally shouted, snapping Lucy out of her trance.

The shrill thud of a pool stick bouncing off the slate pool table shocked Rudy. His eyes widened as the stick rolled off the table onto the floor causing another series of pings. Lucy pushed him out of the way and ran past him.

"I'm not playing this stupid game anymore," she shouted, scampering out the back door of the tavern and into the darkness of the night. A few patrons turned their heads toward the commotion. Rudy stood by the pool table awkwardly.

The couple by the breezy window noticed nothing.

The sun rose slowly giving off an orange hue, which was parted by the fan-shaped palm fronds around the pool. Seagull screams pierced the silence of the bluely tinted courtyard.

The sunlight made the different colored blond streaks in her hair more noticeable. While she seemed concerned about her morning appearance, she could not take her eyes off the finely molded body of her friend.

"So, you're new in town?" Barbie asked, running her fingers through her hair.

"Yes," Ken answered stiffly, prone to few words.

His eyes gave off the blank stare she had seen before. His perfectly formed hair accentuated his chiseled features.

"Well, since you're new in town," she said, pouting her stiff lips, "why don't you let me show you around?"

"Okay," he answered in a forced, overly masculine voice.

She made her way closer to him and her leg gave off that familiar pop.

"But first, why don't you come over here and kiss me like a woman should be kissed?" she panted, moving a stiff arm down her shapely leg.

"Okay, that sounds good to me." Ken's voice was too manly and sounded rehearsed.

The two did their best to get their arms around each other and became lost in their passion.

"Ohhh, baby," she moaned. "Ohhh, babeee!"

"Ahh, Barbie!" came a deep voice from behind her.

Lucy whipped her head around to see Orel standing over her. Blushing, she quickly pulled the dolls onto her lap under the table. Her heart throbbed from embarrassment.

"Always enjoyed playing with Ken and Barbie myself," he said.

"Ohhh, oh, this," Lucy stammered. "No. Just found these old things from when I was little."

Orel sat down on the dew-dampened bench next to Lucy. "I was always more fond of Skipper myself, though, eh? Never was much for the Miss America type. Ya know? 'Mah dream is world peace, vanilla ice cream and cats and dogs living together,'" he mimicked in his best beauty-queen voice.

A grin spread over Lucy's face.

"And Ken? C'mon. How many guys you know have stomach muscles like that?"

"You," giggled Lucy, not looking up from the concrete and tile table.

"Yeah, sure, Lucyball. Me."

Lucy felt uncomfortable with how awkwardly she'd blurted out a comment about Orel's body. "So'd you kiss her?" she asked, not sure she wanted to hear his reply.

"Kiss her? Who?" said Orel, his blue eyes shimmering with the reflection of the pool's water.

"That girl from last night. Suuu-zen."

"Kiss? No. We just talked for a while, then I came back home. She was a little spacey. Sort of a free spirit. I've got too much other stuff to worry about to have someone like that around."

Lucy kept drawing circles around a red tile on the table. Her finger moved more rapidly as the circles became ever larger. It was obvious that she had something on her mind.

"Remember the other day when we were by the pool and you talked about making waves?" Lucy started. "Did you—"

"Oh, Lucyball, darling," he interrupted, laughing. "Making waves is one thing. I don't think you should run around making waves. I believe I put it, 'ripple the pond.'"

"Waves, ripples, whatever, yeah," she continued, giggling nervously.

Orel bit his lip to hold back a grin so as not to hurt her feelings.

Lucy looked up at him from the table, "If you're out there 'rippling' everyone else's, who's rippling yours?"

Orel broke into a half smile while he leaned back to ponder the question. His eyes caught a swaying palm frond. The moment was quiet enough to hear the gentle breeze turning the aluminum umbrella in the hole at the center of the concrete and tile table.

"Who ripples mine?" he resumed. "What's funny is that sometimes you're paying so much attention to rippling others' ponds that you don't pay attention to who's rippling yours. Good question, Lucyball. I suppose I've had so many people influence my life, it's hard to say who had the most effect on me."

Their eyes locked briefly, but Orel looked away when he sensed Lucy was asking him for something more than he wanted to give.

"I'll have to get back to you on that one. Listen, I'm gonna be late for the route. I better get a move on, Skipper."

He winked at her as he rose and made his way toward the street.

Lucy was surprised by Orel's reaction and smiled as she looked after him. *He called me Skipper!*

The whinny of the starter sounded promising.

"One more time, Son!" shouted Bill from under the truck.

Rudy turned the ignition while he pushed the clutch with all his might. The knuckles of one hand were white points on top of the steering wheel. If he popped the clutch he'd have to hear his father yell again. Or worse. It would make the truck leap forward and run the risk of crushing his father.

He slowly turned the key.

Pop! Pop! Chug!

He thought of how it reminded him of *Chitty Chitty Bang Bang*. If only this were *Chitty Chitty Bang Bang*.

Chug! Pop pop pop...vroom vroom.

Rudy pushed gently on the gas pedal.

"That's it!" Bill shouted. "That's it!"

Rudy's head twitched. Then he realized it was a good shout.

"That's it, Son!" Bill shouted again. We did it! We got this old girl running the way she's supposed to."

We did it? Rudy slowly unwrapped his sweaty, cramping hand from the old, sticky steering wheel. He thought again. *We did it.* This was perhaps the first time his dad had considered him and Rudy as we.

"Got old Melba purring like a kitten, boss?" came a voice from the street.

Rudy turned to see Orel walking up the parking lot.

Bill pushed himself along the sandy ground from under the truck. He sat back leaning on his elbows and looked up at Orel.

"Yep, followed your lead. Since she had new plugs, I thought a clutch adjustment might be the next step. Of course, that led to a new muffler. Like a poker game, once you're in, you better ante up."

Orel nodded in agreement and then greeted Rudy with a four-fingered wave.

"You ready to hit the road?"

"Absolutely," answered Orel as he hopped in the cab of the truck.

"Me too, Dad?" asked an excited Rudy.

"Sure, Son. Might need my assistant mechanic again on the road."

Rudy jumped into the back of the pickup. He sat with his back to the cab and pulled his ball cap over his sweaty face to conceal his smile.

As Bill got into the truck, he gave one last wipe to the new logo on the driver's side door.

"Rides even smoother than before," complimented Orel. He looked toward the duplex where the curtains were barely parted by three bony fingers and then flopped closed.

"Yeah, huh?" Bill agreed with enthusiasm. "So I figure we concentrate on the main dance floor area today. Work on getting all the electrical fixtures and crap out. Then move on to the kitchen."

"Yes, sir."

"Nearvana. Hard to believe that place won't be around anymore. If only...Nah." Bill stopped himself. He shook his head with a smile, then a frown.

"If only?" asked Orel.

"Hah?"

"You said, 'if only.' If only what?"

"I dunno. If only. If only in another world I had some money. If only there was a way I could get them to sell me the joint instead of knocking it down. If only I didn't get into this stinking business years ago. If only. If only someone would take me seriously. I think

I could run a joint. Best joint on the beach. Girls in short shorts. Belly buttons. Big chests. Nice asses. Asses put asses in the seats, I tell ya."

"So you'd go in competition with the tavern?" asked Orel.

Bill kept his eyes on the road. "No. Not in competition. In conjunction. Tavern's usually good up till sunset, then it thins out 'cept for the regulars. My place would be more of a nightclub. Place you go after you hit the Tavern. You know, go to the Sunset Tavern till sunset then stumble over to my place when it gets dark."

Orel held his thumb to his mouth and listened. It was obvious that Bill had this conversation more than once.

"What would you call it?"

Bill looked over at Orel blankly. "Ya know, in all the years I've thought this out, that's the one thing I never thought about. Usually I tell people about this over beers, so that's probably why."

Orel returned a sympathetic smile.

"Ahh, shit. It's really just a waste of brainpower anyway. Without the cash, you can't accomplish your dreams. I'm down to my bottom dollar as it is," Bill mumbled, his enthusiasm deflated.

"Bottom dollar," laughed Orel. "You betcha bottom dollar."

Bill looked at Orel and then away again. He found no humor in the situation.

"That's it! I've got it!" Orel suddenly yelled, "DOLLAR BILL'S!" The name was punctuated with two slaps at the air as if to stamp the words in front of him.

"What, what the hell is that?"

"That's the name of your joint. DOLLAR BILL'S!" repeated Orel.

"Dollar Bills, huh? That's not bad. Now if I just had a few dollar bills we might be in business."

The truck bounced along the bumpy surface of Palm Way and then Sunset Boulevard in silence for a while. Not an uncomfortable silence. More of a thoughtful one.

Then Orel pulled out a yellow, rectangular box of candy and popped a few in his mouth. "I came into a few dollar bills recently," he slurred, his mouth full.

He rattled the box of candy in Bill's direction. "Joo Thee?"

Bill looked at it and then at Orel, blankly.

"I found these in the gift shop on the boulevard. Jujyfruits," Orel said. "I especially love the black ones. Licorice, I believe."

Bill looked back at the road. "Not sure how they taste, but they sure smell like hell."

Orel giggled. He pulled himself onto the passenger door, stuck his head out of the window and reached to the back of the pickup. "Jujee, Rudy?"

"Got any reds?" Rudy shouted.

"I like the red ones almost as much as the black ones, Rudy."

"Black ones? Ew, how can you eat those nasty, stanky things? I throw them out the minute I see them."

The Canadian fished around in the yellow box until he found a sizable offering of the red candies. He deposited them in Rudy's palm without a word and slid back into the passenger seat.

Lucy walked into the office of the motel and brushed off her T-shirt, dusting away the remnants from emptying the ashtrays around the pool. The job had scored enough butts to keep her and Rudy supplied for a solid day of fishing.

"Thanks for cleaning up around the pool," Gene greeted her warmly.

Lucy pushed her bangs away from her eyes. "Welcome."

"I was wondering if you couldn't do me one more huge favor this morning," he started almost apologetically. "Joyce is down with the flu today and won't be in. Would you mind dropping fresh towels to all the rooms?"

Lucy exhaled with a pre-teen attitude.

"I gotta run to Ace and get some parts for the deck light timer," her father pleaded. "Don't want Mrs. Hanson tripping on anything again."

Lucy relented. "Sure, Dad. Lemme go wash my hands first."

"Thanks, sweetie," he said and gave her a peck on her cheek. "Need anything while I'm out, honey?"

Lucy was about to say, "a mother," but stopped herself. The last time she had made that "joking" remark, she'd watched her father grow very sad. "How about some mint chocolate chip ice cream?" she said instead.

"You got it, sweetie," Gene said. He grabbed a big hunk of keys, pushed his way out of the office door and bounded down the walkway with a spring in his step, exchanging waves and happy banter with the guests around the pool.

Lucy wondered how any woman would have left a man who seemed to be so full of life. A half-smile formed on her face when she saw him trip slightly on a crack in the walkway. She giggled as he stopped to inspect the problem, pointed and gave another wave and chuckle to the guests before he disappeared behind a clump of hibiscus bushes that bordered the sidewalk.

Then she sighed and decided to get the chore of changing towels done.

Mrs. Hanson's room smelled of air-conditioned smoke and coconut suntan lotion. For some reason, this was a comfort smell for Lucy, one she had grown accustomed to know as home.

Mrs. Hanson was a "six-monther," a snowbird. Since she had been coming to the motel long before Gene owned it, he had essentially inherited her along with her demanding ways.

The number 16 unit was hers and her husband's for six months out of the year. They would spend the cold months in Florida and then head back to Long Island when the weather warmed up, right after the Mets were done with spring training. This year she had extended her stay indefinitely, due to the passing of her husband.

Although Lucy acted annoyed to have to change the towels in the guests' rooms, deep down she enjoyed doing it, because it gave her a chance to be nosy. A lot could be learned about people by poking through their medicine cabinets or thumbing through their magazines. Over the years of visiting her room, Lucy had come to know Mrs. Hanson's peculiarities quite well.

The busy season had the motel almost at full capacity and Lucy had done the rounds of all the rooms except for number 17. She had saved that one for last. It was one of the smaller rooms. Unlike Mrs. Hanson's efficiency, which had a living room, a kitchen and a bedroom with two double beds, number 17 had only a bed and a bathroom.

Lucy hesitated when she got to the orange door. Although she had seen Orel leave earlier, she stopped and knocked gently, as was common courtesy when doing any maintenance in a guest's room.

"Orr...," she started, but her voice cracked and would not allow her to finish. She tried again with a different approach. "Mr. Hughes? Housekeeping!"

When no answer came, Lucy inserted the master key into the doorknob. The lock gave way smoothly. She pushed it gently ajar.

A waft of cologne and soapy air tickled her nostrils and a rush of excitement and nervousness flushed through her body as she realized she was about to be alone in Orel's room.

Remembering why she was there, she grabbed two bath towels, two hand towels and a bath mat from the maid's cart. She pushed the door open further and leaned her head inside to make sure no one was sleeping on the bed. When she saw that the room was empty, she crossed the threshold and stepped inside.

The room was dark except for a light that was left on in the bathroom. Lucy was surprised that the bed was neatly made with nothing on top of it. Most guests became slobs the moment they got on vacation. A pair of dress shoes lay on the floor side by side half underneath the bed with the bedspread barely covering the laces.

Lucy took her time to absorb all the aspects of the room. As she approached the bathroom, she could make out the pungent whiff of Listerine. She picked up a tube of hair tonic, which quickly erased the antiseptic mouthwash odor from her mind.

A black comb lay flat on the sink. Placing the towels on the closed toilet seat, she grabbed it and inspected the teeth, running her thumb and forefinger across them. She brought her hand to her nose and inhaled the essence left behind by the mixture of hair and tonic. Then she placed the comb next to her cheek and started to sway, imagining herself dancing with Orel like in one of the old movies she watched when her dad let her stay up late on the weekend.

A slamming door a few rooms away snapped Lucy back to why she was there in the first place. Since there was a special way to hang the towels, Lucy thought it best to finish the job before looking around any further.

First the bath towels had to be folded end over end and then in half again and placed on the rack. Then the hand towels had to be arranged, the bottoms folded back upon themselves to form a cupped cuff. The bath mat had to be draped over the left side of the bathtub with one edge folded in a triangle back over the top of the tub. The final touch was to place a piece of wrapped soap in the folded triangle. This was standard operating procedure that had been handed down to Gene by the previous owner.

When she was done, Lucy gathered up all the used towels in a pile and made her way to the bedroom area. The soggy bath mat fell at her side and dragged lazily behind her. Normally an arm full of damp, smelly towels was the worst part of this job, but on this occasion Lucy did not mind.

Just before she got to the door she felt a tug. Looking over her shoulder she could see that a wet towel had gotten snagged on the chair in front of the dresser. She yanked at it. Then, she noticed that it was wrapped around more than the chair. She gave the towel another pull but it did not budge. Finally, with one fast yank, it came free, recoiled and smacked her in the face with a wet slap. Then she heard a loud "clunk," followed by a "thunk" and then another "clunk."

"Oh no!" Lucy mumbled. "What'd I do?"

She slowly pulled the musty towel from her face. Next to the overturned chair lay a gym bag and more money than she had ever seen all spilled on the floor right up to where she was standing. In the middle lay a brown leather book with "The Journal of Jonny Hughes" on the cover.

Lucy scurried to get all of the wrapped bills back inside the gym bag. She placed it on the uprighted chair, unsure of how it had been arranged. She was worried that she would get caught, and considered leaving the room, but then curiosity won out. She picked up the book and slowly opened it to a scribble on the first page.

> *…to my Son Orel,*
> *Sins of the father were in the name of the Son…*
> *please forgive me. I simply played the hand I was*
> *dealt.*

Lucy touched her mouth knowing that this was not simply going through someone's medicine cabinet but delving into his privacy, his innermost thoughts. Yet, she could not help herself. Her heart pounding, she flipped forward a few pages and, squinting at the fine handwriting, began to read.

> *5/29/51*
>
> *The most beautiful lady was sitting at the bar*
> *watching me play. Most crystal blue eyes I've ever*
> *seen. I walked past her on one of my breaks. She*
> *smelled like the lady with the perfume at the*
> *department store. I really need to ask her out.*
> *What would we do? A drink maybe.*
>
> *5/29/51 cont'd*
>
> *…Okay it's really the thirtieth but does the date*
> *really change when you stay up all night drinking.*
> *Really a beautiful sunrise today.*
>
> *Day off. Not sure what to do. Walk the beach maybe.*
> *Drink some more?*

Lucy's breath quickened. She found the man's innocence and thoughtfulness attractive. Flipping forward a few more pages, she found something of a verse he had written.

Oh yonder orb
of glowing love
you come, you go
still all above…

The burn you bring
feels bad and good
still on we ask
for more, we should.

Without all you
would be we lost
the point we be
for nothing most.

Arrive with hope
all possible thee
you leave behind,
all dark and me.
                    j. hughes

A jingling of keys snapped Lucy's concentration.

"Omigod," she whispered.

Trying to control her rapid breathing and pounding heart, she went to the window and looked out between the gap in the curtains. It was Mrs. Hanson coming home and letting herself into her unit. A rush of adrenalin made Lucy weak in the knees. She suddenly felt guilty for invading Orel's privacy.

Quickly she pulled herself together and arranged the gym bag once more, praying it was close enough to the way it was before she knocked it over. A scan around the place to ensure her tracks were covered, and she picked up the pile of towels and ran out of room 17.

Chapter 9

MARS 4 LAUNCH SET
SOVIETS SCRAMBLE TO BEAT VIKING MISSION

The headline looked big and scary. There had been Mars probes launched a few years earlier, but there was something strange every time the name of the red planet ended up on the front page.

"We're not gonna be happy till we find some goddamned green men running around up there," Wally complained, slapping the newspaper on the bar.

Dorothy, seated on her familiar chair next to the now empty one, brought a cigarette to her lips as she continued to stare in the direction of the water. Just watching her gracefully smoke made even a nonsmoker crave the comfort and serenity of a cigarette.

"Nutha one, Dot?"

"Yes, a little more, Wally dear."

"Waste of time and money," he muttered, pouring coffee into her cup.

Dorothy smiled as smoke enveloped her free hand and she took a slow sip. Her deliberate attention and pleasure in her coffee and cigarette gave an indication how little she cared about the topic.

"HELLO, FANS!" a familiar voice interrupted the calmness of the quiet morning.

"Oh, Christ. Speaking of goddamned aliens."

"Good morning, Wally," said Orel, ignoring the jibe. "And how are you this glorious day?"

"Day to day and customer to customer," Wally said irritably.

"I love the morning," Orel continued expansively. "New start. Kinda like shaking up one of those Etch A Sketch things. If you didn't like the picture you painted the previous day, just shake it up and paint another one."

"Friggin' lunatic," Wally mumbled as he turned and made his way back to wash the morning dishes.

"Mars, eh?" said Orel picking up the newspaper.

"Buncha shit," yelled Wally through a wall of steam rising from the sink full of dishes. "CIA is screwing around again. Happened back in the '40s. They just can't leave well enough alone. Joe D. told me they even got into his shit along the way, too."

Orel glanced in Dorothy's direction with a half-smile and a raised eyebrow.

"They had ideas that he was from outer space. Nobody should be able to play baseball that well. Had to be a friggin' Martian," Wally rambled on.

"I think it's interesting. Space travel, that is," Orel said, making sure Wally was aware which story he was endorsing. "It's a tribute to the character of mankind that we go beyond our limits in search of something better. Nobody seems to do that like the Americans, either, eh?"

Wally nodded without looking up from the soapy dishes.

"And it's also nice to see rockets going up peacefully for a change, too," continued Orel.

The smile on Wally's face soured, changing to the more familiar, bitter twist.

Orel adjusted quickly. "Well, I just think it's nice that something productive is being done with American rocket technology for a change."

"A change of what? Don't tell me you're one of those goddamned pansy hippie sonsabitches, burning flags, bitching and moaning about killing babies and shit."

Orel stood up straight, realizing he had chafed one of Wally's nerves.

"Canada? You take an' hide those pussies afraid of serving their country. That kinda shit didn't happen in my day when men were goddamned men. Joe D., Ted Williams. These guys were Americans," Wally shouted, his face flushing and a white pastiness forming in the corners of his mouth. "They weren't the goddamned pussies like that sonofabitch Cassius Clay Mohammed, or whatever the hell his name is."

Dorothy coughed from a puff. She had sat through Wally's tirades before, but this one looked to be special. Slowly she sat back on her stool and positioned herself in the middle of the two men to get a better view.

"Well, sir, I understand where you are coming from," Orel said, still taken aback by Wally's comments.

"Where I'm coming from? You have no idea where I'm coming from, you goddamned Canadian hippie sonofabitch. Your type wanders through here every so often and I gotta listen to this shit. I tell you what. Leave your tourist dollar at the door and go the hell back to waving that Maple Leaf piece of shit you call a flag."

Dorothy dabbed out her cigarette vigorously in the ashtray, obviously unhappy with how far Wally was pushing things. Just as she was about to put a halt to the proceedings, Orel stepped up.

"You don't see a lot of Canucks floating around in space suits, do ya?" he challenged. "Know why?"

A silence hung in the air. Dorothy's eyes darted back and forth between the two men.

"There's no fish in space," he added quickly.

Dorothy's hacking laugh produced a puff of smoke from her nostrils. This kid was the first to stop Wally in his tracks without batting an eye.

Orel's joke seemed to have a soothing effect on Wally.

"That's goddamned right. Nobody does it better than the Americans," he muttered. "If it wasn't for us, the rest of the world phhh dhh haa…" The final portion of his comment was muffled when he turned his face back toward the steaming sink.

Once it became clear that Wally was safely preoccupied again doing his dishes, Orel pulled up a chair across from Dorothy. The two exchanged knowing smirks, but Orel remained quiet, a tad more miffed than he'd let on.

After a long silence, Dorothy's face lit up. "You 'bout ready to shake up that Etchy Sketch a yours yet, son?" she joked, digging for another smoke in the bottom of a crumbled pack.

Orel rewarded her with a smile. "Nah. Hey, he's passionate about what he believes in. I admire that," he said. "I'd much rather you yell your piece at me, than sit there and be wishy washy. Say nothing to my face and a mouthful to my back."

Dorothy nodded in agreement. Her eyes squinted as she exhaled and coughed her way to another sip of coffee.

Orel looked at the bar and studied a vase that was placed next to the newspaper. "What's that?" he asked.

"More of a 'who' actually," she answered with a grin.

A puzzled look formed on Orel's face.

"It's Winston. Or what's left of him. Funny—all the ashes we sprinkled over this bar from our butts over the years—that he'd be joining them one day."

Orel put his hand to his mouth in thought. "I've never seen ashes before. You think he'd mind if I took a look?"

"I'm sure he'd be okay with it, son. In fact," she started looking around to see if anyone was paying attention, "the day I got them, I ran my fingers through them just to see what it was like. Of course, it was just like sticking your hand in an ashtray, so I don't know what the hell I expected."

About to lean forward, Orel pulled his head back. "I'm not sure I wanna take it that far. Just a look should suffice."

With a long slender hand, Dorothy grabbed the base of the urn and pulled off the top carefully. She then slowly tilted the open jar toward Orel and watched him inspect the contents like a young boy seeing a naked woman for the first time.

"Hard to believe you can shrink a whole human life down to a tiny jar. Makes it seem a bit insignificant, doesn't it?" offered Dorothy sympathetically.

"Why do you have them?"

"Winston had nobody. So I became the next of kin by virtue of proximity—the proximity of my barstool to his for the last fifteen years," Dorothy quipped through another veil of smoke.

"Did you know him that well?" asked Orel.

"I knew he was an electrician. I knew he drank Miller and smoked Marlboros, which never made sense to me, since his name was Winston. I guess a lot of things never made sense to me about Winston. But he kept to himself and chuckled at my jokes every now and then. So I guess he was just a good companion here at the tavern." Dorothy's words took on the tone of a eulogy the more she spoke. "He did some work for Eisenrad and Kronis toward the end and always seemed a little nervous about that."

"Ahh, I can see that. Sam does have a bit of an edge to him."

Orel turned his back to the bar and looked at a pair of pelicans gliding inches over the wavy salt water in the distance. "Never met this Kronis fellow, although I keep hearing his name. Done a little bit of reading about him lately, too."

"Well, Winston would get nervous if his beer didn't foam the right way. So there's no telling what was wrong with him."

"I understand he hung himself. Was there any reason why he would do such a thing?" Orel asked.

"If there was, he never told me. Last day I talked to him, he was just hunched over the bar in his normal spot. Only thing I found odd was that he died of electrocution. Electrician electrocuting himself is one thing. Hanging himself, too, is another. Whole thing seems very strange to me. Bucket of water, piano wire, rope. Didn't know he was capable of that type of thing. "

"Piano wire?" Orel whispered, his eyes going blank for a moment.

Dorothy nodded.

"Well, what are you planning to do with the ashes?" he asked.

"I haven't decided yet," she said, turning her head in the direction of the bay. "Wally, can you get me a Scotch?"

The low-pitched mumbling from the area where Wally was working made it clear that he was still stewing.

Orel stood up and pushed himself away from the bar. "Excuse me," he said politely.

Then he walked to the outside porch of the tavern. The bay's current seemed really strong. The seagulls weathering the stiff breeze seemed to be suspended from invisible wires above the rippling waves.

A low rumbling from inland grew until it eventually drowned out the cries of the seagulls. Orel looked over his shoulder. The noise belonged to Einstein's beat up Falcon. As he pulled up in front of the tavern, the brakes gave off a whiny squeal, which turned into a metal-on-metal churning. The driver's side door opened slowly and Einstein's dusty boot emerged, followed by his lanky frame. Though the car had been turned off for a few seconds, the engine knocked and sputtered clumsily before giving up the fight.

"Engine run on," Orel yelled, standing with his hands in his pockets.

"Yep. She's like a good woman. Can't stop her once you get her warmed up," Einstein joked while he reached in the backseat and pulled out the long stick.

Orel slowly walked toward the car to get a better view. Einstein handled this task methodically, as if he had done it a thousand times. No one at the bar paid any attention, though. The novelty of the odd process seemed to have worn off a long time ago.

"Gauge down?" asked Orel when he got close enough to speak in normal tones.

"Hmmmm?"

"Your petrol gauge broken?" he persisted.

"Yeeeeah, something I've been meaning to fix but never get around to," Einstein answered. As he swung around, his hair swayed like the feathered head of a cockatiel.

"Does that method work as well?" asked Orel pointing to the wooden, gas-stained stick.

"Within a half gallon, I'd say," Einstein professed proudly.

"Well as my Uncle Hank used to say: 'If it ain't broke, I can't afford it.' "

The old painter grinned in appreciation. "Looks like enuff to git home ta'night," he said. "I realize it's before noon, but on a Saturday, it's gotta be noon somewhere in the world. Right, son? And if it's past noon, it's past time to start drinking."

He winked at Orel and headed to the tavern, surrounded by a cloud of musky odor.

"What's the word?" barked Wally.

"Thunderbird!" came the ritual response.

At the back of the parking lot, the old red truck was chugging its way through the powdery sand. Orel glanced at his watch and noticed that Bill was late. Although Bill had many faults, tardiness was not one of them.

When the truck pulled to a stop next to Orel, Bill leaned out of the window and said, "Sorry I'm late, kid. Had some thinking to do. Hop in. I got something ta talk to ya about."

Orel began to walk around to the passenger side of the truck.

"No! No, you drive," Bill said, stopping him in his tracks. "I need to concentrate, so I'd like you to drive."

Cocking his head sideways for a moment, Orel climbed into the truck as Bill slid to the passenger side. Orel plopped himself into the seat worn to the exact curvature of Bill's backside. He could feel the springs poke up from below. The worn fabric exuded Bill's body odor, which was not altogether pleasing to the senses. Orel grabbed the steering wheel. Caked with years of accumulated grease and grime, it was sticky to the touch.

As he got settled, Bill offered him a hand to shake. This was very uncharacteristic and gave Orel pause. When he saw Bill's sincere expression, he finally laid his right hand on top.

"Ya know," Bill started. "You've got me to thinking over the past few weeks or so. Your little quips and lines from your relatives have made me look at things differently. I've watched you and my boy. He sees something in you. Respects you. He gives you looks I have never seen him give me. And I appreciate that."

The seriousness of Bill's tone made Orel stiffen uncomfortably.

Bill noticed the tension in his partner. He pointed to the windshield and said, "Drive."

"Where are we going?" asked Orel.

"Crazy!" laughed Bill. "Cray-zee...," he repeated, trailing off at the end when it became apparent that Orel was not enjoying the same joke. "Just drive to the end of the jetty so we can watch the water."

Bill worked at a piece of gum he had stuck in his mouth just prior to picking up Orel. He chewed it vigorously in anticipation of the pending conversation.

The truck jerked with an unfamiliar foot pushing its clutch. Second gear was hard to find and third gear balked. By the time Orel finally got a rhythm for the truck's transmission, they had reached the end of the pier. He pulled the truck to the edge of the water, turned off the engine and asked, "What are you trying not to say, Bill?"

Pausing in mid-chew, Bill looked obliquely in the Canadian's direction and started nervously. "You said you...you had money."

Orel remained silent.

"Said you came into some 'bills' recently," Bill ventured.

The heat on the hood from the engine made the water in the background look like a distorted, shimmering mosaic. Sunset Island seemed to liquefy as it rose into the sky off the red truck. A palm tree bent from its trunk to its fronds with each passing stream of heat.

In the far distance, a parachute moved across the horizon effortlessly behind a boat.

"I said that," answered Orel after a long, thoughtful pause. "I did indeed say that."

"Well, is it true?"

"Yes, it's true." Orel looked at his index fingernail before he put it into his mouth and continued. "Few hundred."

Bill let out a sigh of disappointment. "Few hundred?"

"Thousand. Few hundred thousand."

Bill's eyebrows rose so high that they nearly met his receding hairline. He wiped his upper lip with the palm of his hand and stared at the floor for a second.

"A few? What's a few?" he asked trying to regain his composure.

"I always considered a few more than a couple but not quite several," Orel mocked, seemingly back on top of his game.

The piece of gum in Bill's mouth was once again getting a workout. His eyes danced left and right, though he maintained his focus on the floor of the truck.

"Earned it the old fashioned way—inherited it," Orel said. "Lost some family not long ago who seemed concerned about my well being."

"Sorry about that," Bill said and allowed a moment of silence before continuing. "Would you be interested in a business proposal?" he asked slowly, moving his hand to his chin and turning his head and eyes sideways. "We talked about the bar thing. Remember, women in short shorts, asses, big tits."

Orel nodded slowly, still enjoying the view of the parachute over the Gulf.

"How'd you like to be an investor in the project? I say we even give it the name you thought up: Dollar Bill's. Catchy! I like it."

Orel paid close attention to his thumbnail, doing his best to bite off its tip. "What do we know about running a place?"

"How's it any different from the junk game? Buy right, sell right. Rest takes care of itself," Bill responded.

"Where's it gonna be? Where are we gonna open it?"

"The site," Bill answered. "Nearvana's. Just gotta get Eisenrad's seal of approval. Gotta convince him that a tenant might make more sense in the short run. Maybe the city council can give me a hand. Put in a good word about an historical landmark."

"Is that possible? He seemed pretty sure that he needed the placed gutted and ready for demolition by the end of the month."

"Sam's a goddamned Jew. You wave a little cash under their big noses and they tend to see things completely different than before," Bill explained, imitating Wally's voice.

"You're starting to sound like a bar owner already, Bill," Orel kidded.

"So I have your commitment as an investor then?"

"Let me think about it. I'll let you know by the end of the night."

Bill nodded, then shrugged.

"What's that?" Orel asked, changing the subject abruptly.

"What?"

"What do they call that thing behind the boat? The parachute."

"Parasailing," answered Bill somewhat irritated. "These crazy tourists plunk down twenty bucks to let some burnout surfer pull them around behind their fishing boat for fifteen minutes. It's amazing what people will pay for."

"Parasailing, eh? I'm gonna get out and watch this for a bit. You mind?"

"No, not at all. Take your time and think. I'm gonna go by the site. Think things over. I'm gonna go by Sam's tomorrow and see what he thinks of the idea."

Orel got out of the pickup and stayed at the end of the jetty while Bill drove off, leaving a haze of dusty sand in his wake.

"Parasailing," Orel repeated, intrigued by the concept.

Sam rubbed the top of his balding head, trying to remain patient with his boss. Staying cool and composed was very important when dealing with a man as impetuous as Lawrence Kronis. Sam had seen the man dress down a barber for improperly trimming his sideburns. Rumors were that his dissatisfaction had reached the point where Kronis had the man beaten to a pulp.

It was probably Sam's deft ability to deal with Kronis' impulses that kept him in the good graces of his employer. "Things are going smoothly. Connor's got the place in pretty good shape. Electric fixtures pulled. Sheetrock stripped. Almost all gutted but the large appliances," he recited, as if ticking off a checklist.

Kronis studied a painting on the wall of his office, a portrait of a woman in her twenties with long black hair. The blueness of her eyes was either an artist's rendering or the work of a higher power. Her skin was smooth and her neck had the look of a porcelain doll.

"Ever lose something?" he started.

Sam looked up from his notes with an inquisitive look. "Sir?"

Kronis kept his gaze on the portrait. "Ever lose something?" he repeated, causing the question to become more cryptic.

Sam slowly exhaled through his nostrils hoping this conversation somehow related to the demolition of the Nearvana.

"Love? Money? Both?" Kronis turned to Sam whose mouth was agape.

He decided to treat the questions seriously, "Sir, I've been happily married for the better part of thirty-five years. Love is one thing I have not lost. As far as money is concerned, I watch the pennies very closely, as I'm sure you're aware."

"You're a lucky man, Sam. Over the years I have not been as fortunate," Kronis said as he searched a crinkled pack for a cigarette. "Met the love of my life back in the early '50s and lost her twice. First time was to a man. Second time…"

Sam decided it was best to say nothing.

"Who's the kid?" Kronis fired out of nowhere.

"Kid, sir?"

"Connor's help. Who is he? What's his story?"

"He's a Canadian who is staying at Gene Lewis' place. Helping Connor out to make a little money, I suppose."

Kronis popped a sulfur hiss onto a cigarette that was dangling from his lips. He said nothing as he inhaled the smoke.

Saturday night was probably the best night of the week at Sunset Tavern. That was when the most interesting mix of characters showed up. There were those who had been fishing and were finishing off their day with a few beers. There were the people dressed up for a night on the town who were at their first stop. And then, of course, there were the regulars. The combination turned the tavern into a fine blend of looks and smells.

Rudy was at the pool table chasing the same ball for several shots. Lucy sat on a barstool nearby, annoyed at Rudy's behavior. Dorothy was in the same seat since her morning conversation with Orel and Wally. She looked remarkably lucid for a woman who had a belly full of Scotch. Winston's remains occupied the exact same place on the bar as in the morning, too.

Outside, Gene and Einstein were discussing the latest news about Nixon's Watergate problems. To the right of the two men, Orel sat and listened as they debated "H.R. Haldeman this" and "Bebe Rebozo that." As far as Orel was concerned, there was no difference between H.R. Haldeman and H.R. Puff 'n Stuff. Bebe Rebozo, for that matter, sounded like the name of a kid's clown.

Though he had quietly observed the tavern before, Orel was seeing it in a new light this Saturday evening. He sipped his draft and watched the dressed up people full of energy on their way to a wonderful evening. The fishing crowd seemed to glow with the day's sunburn. It was hard to tell who had a good day fishing and who had a bad day. Orel was unsure if there was such a thing as a "bad day fishing."

The regulars did not seem to notice the dressy visitors or the fishing people. They were merely décor, filling in the spaces of the normally empty seats. But in comparison to the guests, the regulars seemed sadder. The observation troubled Orel. Why were they so unhappy? Why were they so different from the others? Would these be the people coming to his and Bill's place?

And what about the money? He had gotten it so easily, it did not even seem like it belonged to him. His grandpa Rufus had always told him, "Nothing unearned is nothing worth keeping." Was this money his to invest? And where did his father get it? How? There were so many questions he wanted to have answered, but none bigger than his father's request to "put the pieces of the puzzle together."

Orel grabbed his glass and walked inside. "Hello there, Dorothy. Did you have a good day?" he asked politely.

"I sure did, hon."

"Are you up for an adventure?"

"Why? What do yoo haff in mine, my hahhnsome friend?" Dorothy slurred, her tongue thick from Scotch.

"Something very exciting. You up for it? It won't happen till tomorrow."

Dorothy ratcheted her head toward Orel with turned a down mouth and a pair lazy eyes. Slowly she nodded. "What the hell. I'm not doin' anythin' tomorrow."

"Excellent! Meet me at the north beach at 10 a.m. And don't forget to bring our friend."

He pointed at the urn. When Dorothy nodded again, he patted her on the back. Then he left with a wave to the children at the pool table.

"See ya t'morrow then," Dorothy called after him as he disappeared into the darkness.

Chapter 10

Lucy pushed aside the shade that covered the jalousie windows of the motel office. She had been waiting for roughly forty-five minutes when finally she saw him emerge from his room. Orel locked the door and checked his watch before heading off, a bounce in his step.

She knew what she was planning to do was wrong, but curiosity got the better of her. She quietly grabbed the master key from the hook by the door in the office and slinked into the laundry room to gather some clean towels.

Doing her best to look normal, although she felt anything but, she walked to Mrs. Hanson's room. Three tentative knocks and the elderly lady opened the door and looked down at Lucy.

"Your towels, Mrs. Hanson," the young girl chimed with a smile and an offer of crisp, white towels.

"Sunday service?" Mrs. Hanson asked.

"Yes ma'am. Just trying to help Miss Joyce stay ahead of things."

"No, my dear. Shouldn't you be at Sunday Service?"

"Yes, ma'am. Your towels," Lucy said, ignoring the question.

The ensuing silence and judgmental look on Mrs. Hanson's face made her feel uncomfortable.

"I'll just put them on this chair for now," she offered and dropped the towels on a pool chair near the front step.

Backing away onto the sidewalk and toward number 17, she said, "Have a nice day."

Mrs. Hanson stared after Lucy as she made her approach to Orel's room. "He's not in, dear," she called out to her. "Saw him leave a few minutes ago."

"That's okay. I have a master key," Lucy answered as she continued to the door of room 17. She let out a nervous sigh, annoyed with the nosiness of the old lady. The key slid smoothly into the lock and it popped easily. The door opened and the room gave off the familiar smell of cologne and soap.

Lucy dropped two towels onto the couch and searched the room for the gym bag. Her heart pounded the longer she looked and the worry of getting caught gave her a rumbling feeling in her gut. Finally, she saw it on the floor under the bed.

She knelt down and pulled it in front of her. Opening the zipper exposed the cloth that covered the journal. Hurriedly, she removed it and thumbed to the place in the book she had last read. Her mouth whispered the words as she read them.

6/9/51

I talked to her for the first time. Wasn't easy. She was watching me play real close, though. During a break I just decided I'd just say hello. Little clumsy at first. I think I said, "Hey you doing." I could have done better than "Hey you doing," but it got her attention. She looked around. Pulled her hand and cigarette to her chest.

Lucy's pulse quickened with excitement. A real love story was unfolding. Entranced, she thought she heard a noise outside. She jumped up quickly and ran to the window, but she saw no one in the courtyard.

She scooted back to the gym bag, picked up the journal and continued with the story.

6/23/51

Finally did it! Asked her out. And she said that would be nice. Veronica. What a beautiful name. She is so elegant. She's like a porcelain doll, but so regular. Before I asked her out, she watched me play. It wasn't me playing. I felt it coming through me.

6/24/51

When she speaks she has the most lovely southern twang to her voice. The most crystal blues eyes. I watched her walk in the moonlight. Her body has the most perfect lines and curves. I want to stop time. Paint it maybe. I have never met anyone like this. I have never felt anything like this.

Lucy sighed and put her hand on her chest. As she continued to read, she relaxed a bit twirling her hair with two fingers.

7/4/51

I kissed Veronica. It was unbelievable. We took a walk down the beach. Her laugh makes her more beautiful. We stopped for a while and sat on some rocks by the seawall for a short time. I told her my dreams. I've never told anyone stuff like that. I want to be a piano player for something big. I told her maybe Carnegie Hall or Broadway. Who knows? She listened and really seemed to care about me doing it. The moon hit her eyes. I took a chance and leaned toward her. Her lips were so soft. My stomach burned when I kissed her. A good burn. Fireworks are so

*beautiful when they reflect off the bay. I can't wait to
see Veronica again.*

Lucy's eyes had glazed over into a faraway stare when a slamming door snapped her back to the present. "Oh, my gosh," she whispered, her heart pounding. "I've been in here too long."

In a nervous panic, she put the journal back under the cloth, zipped the gym bag and pushed it under the bed. Grabbing some wet towels from the bathroom, she dashed from room 17.

As she walked back toward the laundry room, Lucy noticed Mrs. Hanson watching her from behind the window of her room. She nodded politely in her direction and picked up the wet towels the old lady had left for her on the chair in front of room 16. Her breath quickened as she passed by, feeling as if the cold stare poked holes in her back.

The darkness in the living room made a stark contrast compared with the beautiful Sunday dawn. The lone light in the room pierced the blackness while the television droned on—two men in dark suits discussing the possibility of the president being impeached.

"This is unprecedented territory for Congress," said the one wearing glasses.

"Nixon will need a hell of a Checker's speech to slither out of this one," added the other.

Days old dishes soaked in a slime of once soapy water. The lime green counter top, peppered with syrup, milk and coffee stains, was littered with pots and pans that would not fit in the murky liquid.

An ashtray filled with cigarette butts lay on an ironing board that stood in the middle of the kitchen, cluttered with wrinkled clothes. Another ashtray was dumped upside down in the middle of the carpet in the living room, its contents spilling under the couch.

Lillian's narrow nose and chin created a black silhouette against the white flickering of the television. A cloud of smoke hung heavy in the air, which grew thicker with each exhale. Her tired eyes stared straight ahead into the darkness, the bags beneath them telling the tale of many sleepless nights. Exhausted from those restless nights, Lillian's days were long blurry episodes filled with fear and worry.

"Heeeeeeellow?" A loud greeting accompanied the knock on the front door. "Heeeeellow?"

Lillian, startled by the yells, jumped to her feet and stamped out her cigarette. With her free hand, she pulled her housecoat closed and loosely tied it in one motion.

"Just…just a minute," she answered weakly as she made her way to the front door. "Who's it?"

"It's Orel," said the voice from the other side of the door.

"Orel?"

"Yes, Orel Hughes, ma'am."

"Bill's help? The Canadian fella?"

"Yes, ma'am. I was stopping by to have a talk with Mr. Connor. We had some business to discuss, and I thought I'd like to get it done before I started my day."

Lillian placed a bony forefinger on the doorknob while she unlocked the deadbolt with her other hand. Momentarily, her robe fell open, revealing a tattered T-shirt underneath. She quickly pulled it closed again and started to work at undoing the chain on the old brown door.

Orel could hear the noises of the locks turning and looked around the front porch nervously. The peeling paint on the door jiggled with each methodical movement on the other side. When all the noise had ceased, he saw that the door began to open slowly.

Lillian's dark, stringy hair covered one eye as she allowed a glimmer from the outside to enter her self-inflicted prison.

A white hot, vertical line of light pushed its way into the dark foyer. Dust particles danced in circles around each other in the beam. Lillian's crusty eyes squinted to make out the slender, yet muscular figure of the young man standing on her porch.

Orel pushed his face closer to get a look at the woman on the other side of the big, heavy door.

"Hahh," Lillian said, with a scratchy voice. "Haarrmm, hello, Orel? I'm Lillian. Bill's talked about you a lot."

"Good things, I hope."

Lillian's tired eyes smiled momentarily. "Bill doesn't say many good things," she started. "But when he does, I hear them."

Orel nodded with a sympathetic smile as he studied the face framed by the door and wall, black fatigue lines descending from her puffy eyes. He could see the beauty that once graced Lillian's face and wondered why it had faded at such an early age.

"Are you expecting him back soon?" he asked.

"As far as I understand, he decided to go on his route today and had some talking to do with an Eyes on Rat."

"Yes, Sam." Orel chuckled at the surprising cleverness of Bill's intentional mangling of Eisenrad's name. "He's the fella we're doing some work for right now. Interesting that he'd be working on a beautiful Sunday, though."

"Bill's always working. But somehow we're always broke. Not sure how that works," Lillian said, looking past Orel's shoulder to see what other activity was going on in the street. "Better be careful. You stay around him much longer, he might break you, too."

Orel bit his lip as he looked deeper into the wandering eyes of the sad lady. There was fear in them. The same fear he had seen when a deer stumbled into his fishing area back in Canada. They flickered with a sense that something was about to happen. Something bad.

"I wasn't always broke...ken. I worked once," Lillian stammered. Her attention was still distracted by whatever was going on past Orel's shoulder. "Worked real well," she continued with a sad, sobbing laugh.

Orel was getting uncomfortable. "Well, ma'am, would you mind telling him I stopped by and I'll catch up with him later?" he said.

"Very well," she replied. "I worked...very well."

Orel stretched out his hand to give a farewell shake, but when Lillian seemed oblivious to the gesture, he turned it upward and waved. "Good day, ma'am. Gonna be a good day."

He turned and walked down the pathway from the duplex, occasionally stealing a look over his shoulder. Lillian remained frozen in the doorway like a statue, her stare locked.

"Who was that, Mom?" came a voice from behind her.

"Whaa?" The voice startled Lillian back to life. "Ohh...that was some young man that is helping your father."

"Orel? Orel was here? Darn, I wanted to see what he was up to today." Rudy sounded disappointed. "Did he say where he was going? What's he doing today?"

Lillian swung her head slowly back into the duplex and shut the door behind her. Rudy was still in his Superman pajamas from the night before. After making sure each lock was back in its secure position, she pulled together her robe and walked over to her son.

"Is that blood?" she asked, pointing to a small dot just above the S in Superman. "And why are you so sweaty?"

Rudy looked at his mother and then down at his pajamas. "Nah, probably just some jelly, Mom. I was bouncing on my bed, too."

"Oh." Lillian fixed on Rudy's pajamas, seemingly lost in thought.

The long silence made Rudy nervous. He fidgeted and stole glances at the TV.

Then Lillian said, as if no time had passed. "Just make sure you brush your teeth, honey. Jelly'll rot 'em in a hurry."

Rudy scampered off without an answer, leaving his mom with nothing to stare at but the dingy gray carpet, littered by the over-turned ashtray in the darkness of her living room.

The colors of the big parachute danced in the sunlight. The red seemed paler, but the blue really stood out with the yellow orb providing momentary backlight. The white provided a wonderful contrast to the colors.

The cloth rolled with the wind like a jellyfish in the water. Sometimes it bounced on the sand and other times it would float and twist the heavy ropes which the men were holding with all their might. With each gusty breeze, the men would jump at the whim of the big chute.

When viewed from far away, it all seemed so poetic, as if it happened in slow motion. But close up, it seemed a bit more violent and out of control.

"Sorry I'm late!" Orel called.

Dorothy turned to see him trudging through the heavy, powdery sand.

"Had a meeting," he continued as he came up to her, "Great to see you. I was hoping you wouldn't change your mind. Did you bring our friend?"

Dorothy proudly held up the vase with what was left of Winston. "Yeees, ahh did," she mocked. "Now what did you have in mind for 'our friend'?"

Orel's face lit up. "That!" he said, pointing toward the red, white and blue parachute.

"That? That what?"

"I thought we'd give Winston a proper burial."

"In that?" she asked pointedly.

His smile grew. "Well, not in that," he said, admiring the graceful tango of the chute and the four men. "On that. From that."

"You're crazy," Dorothy laughed. "You're outta your mind."

Orel nodded smugly. "Perhaps I am, but why not? Winston probably never did anything this exciting in his life, so why not let him do something 'out of his mind' in his death?"

The wind blew Dorothy's thin hair forward across her face and caused a straight-lined part to form on the back of her head. She continued to watch the men do their best to tame the wayward dance of the colorful nylon cloth.

"An' what are we gonna do once't we get up there?"

The crease on Orel's cheek turned into an even bigger smile. "Well, we'll fly around there for awhile, maybe see the sights. Then set ol' Winston free. You in?"

Setting the vase down in the soft sand, Dorothy started digging in her purse vigorously. She pushed her way past old tissues, makeup and finally found a crumbled pack of Marlboros.

"Well, hell yea, I'm in. Lemme smoke a cigarette first. If I'm gonna die, I might as well have one last smoke."

Fifteen minutes later, after signing papers, getting briefed on safety and learning how to hang properly in a parachute, the two were ready to take Winston for one last ride.

Dorothy stood a few feet away, watching one of the men buckle Orel into the harness. His arms were muscular, strong from wrestling the wind and sail. He clicked a ratchet strap over Orel's shoulder and one between his legs and pulled them taut.

Then it was Dorothy's turn.

"Are you sure about this shit?" she asked one last time, allowing a rare bit of profanity slip out from fear.

"Sure? Why not?" Orel answered confidently.

Dorothy reluctantly stamped out her last cigarette and moved into position. "It just doesn't seem natural," she said as the man lowered the harness over her shoulders.

"Natural?" Orel asked, laughing. "What's more natural than hanging a hundred feet in midair on a piece of cloth while a speeding boat pulls you at forty-five miles an hour across a body of water filled with sharks and God knows what else?"

Dorothy grew pale, but perked up as the burly harness man pulled the strap between her legs and gave it a friendly tug.

"Easy there, sailor," she drawled. "That girl's been in dry dock for some time now. Treat her nicely."

Accustomed to dealing with squeamish patrons, the man continued without acknowledging the remark.

When all the straps were tight and the two had eye goggles snugly in place, the muscular man handed Orel the vase containing Winston's remains.

"You two realize that this type of thing is against city ordinance. It's also frowned upon by the beach patrol, but we'll just let it be our little secret," he advised, smiling. "You two have a wonderful ride and do your best to let the contents of that jar go downwind."

Orel gave a thumbs-up. Dorothy could only muster a nod since her hands were locked around the two harness lines so tightly her knuckles were turning white.

"You ready?" the man asked one last time.

"Let's go!" Orel yelled excitedly.

"Let's get this shit over with," Dorothy said, allowing another expletive to slip out with a nervous grin.

The motor of the boat roared in the distance as the towline slowly gave up its slack. Orel and Dorothy exchanged worried looks, realizing it was too late to turn back. The towline rippled in the sugary sand and snaked its way to the T-bar, which joined the harness straps. A gentle tug dragged the parasail into the air, causing their upper torsos to jolt forward in unison until their feet left the ground. With each tug, the beach got smaller and smaller.

Dorothy looked over her shoulder. The brawny man dwarfed into a small ant-like figure waving at them.

"Woooooohoooo!" Orel roared, taking in the spectacular view. "Hey, there's the tavern!"

Stiffly, Dorothy managed to catch a bird's eye view of her bar hangout but did not utter a word.

"Betcha Winston's never seen it from this high up," Orel yelled.

Across the inlet, Sunset Island grew wider than either of them had imagined. The trees, which seemed to line the coast of the island, actually covered the entire interior in a dark green carpet surrounded by a border of snow-white beaches.

The new perspective seemed to ease Dorothy's fears. "This is unbelievably beautiful, isn't it, dahling?" she drawled happily. "Ahh mean, ah never saw anything lahke this."

The late morning sun made the water clear, and the two took turns pointing at the fish they could see. Manta rays, stingrays and porpoises seemed to be the most abundant.

When it looked like that the boat was turning back toward the parasail launch site, Orel glanced at Dorothy. "I guess we should get about the business of why we did all this in the first place," he said.

"Yes hon, ahh would say it's about time," she agreed.

Orel carefully pushed the urn toward Dorothy. She looked at him and then at her wrinkled hands clasping the harness line. Slowly she peeled them off and took the container from Orel. Her numb hands felt sore against the porcelain vase.

As she pulled off its top, the lid jumped out of her hand and tumbled into the expanse of water below.

"Ohhh…oh no," she yelled. Her growing sense of disappointment faded when her flying partner merely shrugged.

"Well, it's not like ahh was gonna use the jar for canning peaches or anything," she giggled.

She stuck her forefinger in her mouth to wet it. Then, she moved it around in a circle to find which way the wind was blowing. At that altitude, it seemed to have a mind of its own and direction seemed of no consequence.

Realizing the wind was not going to be predictable, Dorothy started with a eulogy for her former drinking buddy. "Winston, you were a great friend, and an occasional confidant," she intoned as if she'd had clergy training somewhere during her sixty-two years. "Ahh wish't you'da had more fun in this life, and here's ta hoping you have fun in tha next."

Orel looked on as if he were only one of a member of a large congregation. He watched as Dorothy put the urn upside down and shook it between her knees, spilling the contents out over the vast, beautiful inlet in front of the Sunset Tavern. This would be Winston's new seat at the tavern. After the urn was empty, she gave it one last shake and threw it into the water.

"You did great Dorothy," Orel said. "I think Winston appreciates what you did." He rubbed her shoulder as tears welled up in her eyes. "You did great," he insisted.

Dorothy gave her flying partner a sad smile and put her head on his shoulder as the parasail traced a colorful path across the deep blue horizon.

"Nothing out of the ordinary. Just a run down dump, a bunch of cobwebs and some exposed electrical wires."

A woodpecker tapping rattled the office door. Sam Eisenrad covered the mouthpiece of the phone to muffle the noise. The tap grew louder.

"Yeah!" he shouted.

Slowly the door opened and Bill poked his face through the small opening. Sam motioned with his hand for him to come in and have a seat at his desk.

"Yes, I think it would be the best course of action at this juncture," Sam mumbled into the phone. "Yes sir. You too, sir. Thank you."

He hung up the phone and stuck a wet cigar in his tobacco-stained mouth. He looked at Bill's humble expression. It was a look he had never witnessed on him before.

"Clients can be a real pain in da ass, if ya let 'em," Sam slobbered through the cigar. "Howsth da clean-out coming?"

"The site's comin' along just fine, but that's not what I am here to talk about," Bill said. "Mr. Eisenrad, I've worked for you a lot over the years and…"

A smile grew on Sam's face. "Mister? Whenever anyone calls me 'mister,' I grab my wallet. Especially you," he joked. "Jew or kike I expect...but not 'mister'."

Bill bit his lip, ignoring Sam's comments, and continued. The rhythms of his rehearsed speech were stilted and stiff.

"I have worked for you a lot over these many years, and in that time I think I have earned your trust," he said. "What I am getting at is, I would like to open up the Nearvana again."

Sam's smile shrunk into a tiny circle as he pulled the cigar from his lips and plopped it into a pristine ashtray.

"Did you find somethin'?" he asked fiercely.

Bill looked puzzled. "What I'd like to do is put girls in short shorts. Asses put asses in the seats," he stammered.

"What'd you find?"

"Dollar Bill's," he answered.

Sam swiped his cigar from the ashtray and leapt to his feet. "You found dollar bills? You found...money?"

Again Bill appeared puzzled, trying to understand what Sam was asking him. "We're thinking of calling the place...we're thinking of calling the place, Dollar Bill's."

"We're? Who's we're?!"

Bill fidgeted in his seat like a young child being chastised by an angry parent. "I've got an investor lined up who might be interested in backing me," he answered.

Sam pulled his cigar from his mouth and looked at it sideways without saying a word.

The Sunday afternoon crowd trickled in slowly but steadily after the late morning Mass had finished. The tavern proved to be a great place to reflect on one of Monsignor McKnight's sermons.

Orel and Dorothy were already at the bar.

"So that was some kinda rush, eh, ma'am?" he called out to her, after taking a long sip from a frosty mug of beer.

Dorothy's grin had not left her face in hours. Her skin was still ruddy from the morning's activity. Her white fluffy hair kept the shape the wind had given it, streaked back over her scalp.

"Hell yeeyah, it was," she said excitedly. "What's next? Skah divin'?"

Orel looked at Dorothy, his lip still covered with white suds. "Skah?"

"Yeeyah, skah," affirmed Dorothy, adding mockingly, "Aye!"

Orel grinned and was about to take another sip from his mug when he saw the rumpled figure of Bill striding across the sandy parking lot. The August heat caused air above the ground to ripple with steam and gave Bill's body an even sloppier appearance than usual. When he got to the door, Bill motioned to Orel to the back of the tavern.

Orel finished his sip and placed his glass back on the bar. He rose from his barstool, nodded politely to Dorothy and went over to Bill.

"I need…I need to talk to you, son."

"Sure, Bill. What can I do for you?"

"Not here. In the back."

They made their way to the back of the tavern where a long-haired man had just finished playing pool. When he left, Bill looked around to see if anyone was near enough to listen.

"You never got back to me," he started.

"Back to you?"

"Yeah, you said you'd get back. Back to me about the idea. Dollar Bill's."

"Ahhh, back to you about Dollar Bill's," Orel mused. "Well, I did stop by your home and met your lovely wife, but you weren't home."

Bill's face seemed to sink into itself.

Orel continued, "Yes, I have done some thinking about that."

"And...?"

"And, I will do it," Orel said. "But I will do it only if you let me do one thing."

Bill's face lit up in expectation. "Anything. You...you name it!" he said, unable to contain his enthusiasm.

Orel leaned back on a barstool and fiddled with a cue stick and some chalk. "Well, it seems this would be a partnership of sorts. So, as partners, we would both have some say in what kind of place it would be, right?"

"YES! Absolutely. I wouldn't have it any other way!"

"You can have your 'asses' and your short shorts, but I want one thing." Orel paused while he put the finishing touches of blue chalk on the cloth tip of the stick. "I want..."

Bill's eyes were fixed on Orel's lips.

"We keep the stage!"

The seconds of silence seemed to hang in the air a lot longer. Bill mouthed the words "keep the stage" inaudibly as his eyes drifted slowly back and forth.

Then he said, "The stage? For what? Like a band? We're gonna have a band?"

"Well, perhaps. But I was thinking more of a stage for our customers."

"Our customers? Our customers are gonna be on stage? And what the hell are they gonna be doing on the stage?" Bill's curiosity was giving way to frustration.

"They will be doing whatever it is they do," Orel said

"Singing?"

"Sure—singing, music, harmonica, spoons. Who cares? Whatever they're good at."

"So you're telling me that Dollar Bill's is gonna be an amateur joint?" Bill asked, shaking his head.

"Well, more of a place where the regular people can be the stars. Everybody, deep down, thinks they're special. We give them a chance. Let 'em be a star for just once in their life," Orel said, gently finessing the six ball toward the side pocket. "You'll still get your asses, and I'll finance it as long as I get my stage."

Bill followed the ball with his eyes as it fell into the pocket.

"You've got a deal. The stage is all yours!" Bill chortled and gave Wally a wave for some drinks to celebrate.

Chapter 11

What had seemed so taboo not too long ago was now becoming a daily routine for Lucy. She would wait by the office window till Orel left, grab some towels and head back to room number 17. Master key into the lock, waft of cologne and soap as the door opened, and she was back next to the bed to read more of her steamy romance novel.

There was the obligatory banter with Mrs. Hanson, which got easier with each go round. And of course, the chance of getting caught made each morning visit more thrilling.

The courtship of Veronica and Jonny had progressed to a point where they went boating…were expecting a child…and had decided to get married. Lucy found it cute how in each of the journal entries about Veronica, Jonny would refer to her as Ronnie.

> *9/8/51*
>
> *I don't think I've ever been so happy. It's coming out of my piano more. My heart is warm when I play. My hands don't feel like they're connected. My heart feels like it's connected. I'm connected. Connected to something. Something good.*

Lucy smiled as she leafed past a few blank pages until she found another entry, dated over a month later.

10/21/51

*Strange things happening at the Nearvana. Harry's
always got someone in his office talking. Mr. Kronis
is there a lot, too. Angry looking faces always asking
"Where's Larry?" Nights are getting to be long. I'm
not sure if it's because Ronnie has to stay home and
rest. I miss not being around her.*

Lucy frowned, disappointed at the change of subject. She
turned over another group of blank pages filled with doodles before she found the next entry, written more than three months later. A door slammed somewhere outside, but Lucy did not flinch.

1/25/52

*Doctor told Ronnie to take it easy. He was a little
concerned about how she was progressing. Ronnie
didn't seem too worried about it. "It's a doc's job to
worry," she told me. We talked about baby names at
the ice cream parlor. Jonny Junior? Nah. Ronnie Junior. Hah. Nah. Girl? Elizabeth? Sarah? Boy? Rocky
Road? Billy? Howard? Howard Hughes wouldn't
work. There's one of those already. Ronnie giggled a
lot when we talked about names. She has the prettiest
little dimple on her cheek when she laughs. Ronnie
likes the name Orel. She had a cousin by that name.*

Her heart hurt for a moment, as did her lungs, when she realized
that she was reading a true story. It didn't help that Lucy was reading
it sitting on the bedroom floor of one of the main characters.

4/2/52

*Made my third trip to Tampa. The fellas at the Co-
lumbia seem a little more comfortable with me now.
Good way to make extra money. Baby on the way.*

That made Lucy smile again—*Baby on the way.* Another door slamming went unnoticed, as did a jangling of keys. Lucy's eyes darted across the pages in anticipation of the announcement of a newborn baby.

> *6/1/52*
>
> *Ronnie had to go to the hospital this morning. Happens a lot during a pregnancy the doctor explained. She was feeling weak. Nothing to worry about doctor said.*
>
> *6/5/52*
>
> *Ronnie is excited to get out of the hospital with our baby. Due date in five days. Can't wait. Big gig tonight. Supposed to be a Senator stopping by to watch a show.*
>
> *6/10/52*
>
> *I had a son today! Orel Benjamin Hughes. 6 pounds 2 ounces. I have never been so happy and proud. I feel like the sky's the limit. Though there were minor complications during labor, Ronnie and baby seem to be doing fine.*

Another door slamming, a jangling of keys and a lock popping close by snapped Lucy back to reality.

"Ha ha, it's always something," Orel called back from a half opened door. "Sometimes I think I'd forget my head if it wasn't attached to my shoulders, Mrs. Hanson."

For a moment, the room spun as all of the oxygen drained from Lucy's head. Panicking, she scrambled to squeeze under the bed along with the journal and gym bag. Pushing and pulling, she repositioned the gym bag in its normal spot with her head just behind it. Though the quarters were tight, she was able to slide the journal inside, back to its usual resting place.

Lucy's heart pounded so hard she was afraid Orel would hear it from under the bed. She bit her tongue in lieu of screaming out in surrender. To be invisible was her only defense at this point.

Hearing him reach for a bottle in a cooler reassured her a bit, but all efforts to regain her composure were quickly lost when she noticed the cloth which always covered the journal still lying in the middle of the floor next to the night stand. She squelched her impulse to grab it when she saw Orel's foot appear next to the bed.

The length of this pause was excruciating for Lucy. It was only lengthened when Orel put his bottle of Yoo-hoo down next to the gray cloth. He hunkered down in a catcher's squat, reached under the bed, and pulled at the gym bag that was hiding Lucy's face. She gnawed at her lip as she watched the smiling man with the basketball spinning on his finger slide away from her.

Orel unzipped the bag, swooped up the gray cloth and reached into the gym bag. Wrapping the journal in the cloth, he placed it neatly on the floor under the bed inches from Lucy's face. Then he reached into the bag again and retrieved the manila envelope. He emptied its contents of photos and deeds on the floor.

Lucy's eyes widened when one of the black and white photos spun her way and she saw the younger version of someone familiar to her. On the bottom she could make out the name James Rose scrawled in red magic marker.

Orel pulled out two stacks of wrapped bills and placed them among the other items on the floor. He took a moment to push the photos around, fanning them out as he inspected them.

As the adrenalin rush wore off, Lucy's body began to feel limp. Her pounding heart steadied into a regular beat.

Orel seemed satisfied with his viewing of the photographs. He collected them one by one and put them back into the manila envelope along with the legal documents. With deliberate care he placed them and the journal back into the gym bag. The smiling man with the basketball spinning on his finger advanced toward Lucy, hiding her face.

Without a further glance at his surroundings, Orel picked up the two stacks, grabbed his Yoo-hoo and walked out of the room. A bottle clinking on the counter, a jingling of keys, a door slamming, and he was gone.

Spent from the experience, Lucy relished the security of being under the bed for some time. Although she didn't want to leave the spot till she felt completely settled, the urge of curiosity gnawing at her gut won out. Against her better judgment, she pulled at the zipper of the gym bag and removed the cloth-covered journal.

She examined the way Orel had wrapped it so that she could reproduce the exact look. Carefully, she uncovered the book and thumbed her way to the last journal entry she had read. She placed the book squarely on the floor and wiped her hand over it to flatten its page. She whispered the date and then read on silently.

6/11/52

To hell with them all. What the hell do they know? They don't know shit…God help me. It was worse than they were telling me. I can't do this. Hem or ridge. I don't even know if that's how you spell it. She's got internal bleeding is what it amounts to.

6/12/52

She's not responding to treatment.

Lucy's eyes welled with tears and her nose began to run. The difficult emotions of the journal and the near miss with Orel were taking their toll. Her face twisted in a grimace as she read the last entry.

6/13/52

Ronnie passed away today.

Lucy squeezed her eyes shut. She pushed her face down on the carpet beneath the bed and sobbed.

Chapter 12

Several weeks had passed since Orel and Bill had sealed their deal in the back of the tavern. The old Nearvana was abuzz with the bustle of renovation. Electricians, carpenters, plumbers and other tradesmen were working here and there. The smell of fresh cut wood enveloped the sawdust that floated in the air.

Bill walked into the office where Orel was repairing a large hole in the wall with a piece of sheetrock. Cigarette in hand, he waved a fistful of papers. "You wouldn't believe some of the broads that are applying!" he exclaimed. "Definitely asses. Nice ones, too! Asses put asses in the seats, I tell ya."

Orel nodded to his partner and returned to skillfully buttering a glob of plaster on the wall with a wide silver trowel.

"This hole always bothered me for some reason," he said, catching a piece of wet plaster with his trowel before it hit the ground. He worked his way to his feet, stretching his cramped legs until he felt comfortable standing.

"Start interviewing tomorrow," Bill continued as if the wall discussion hadn't occurred. "Blondes. Gotta have a few blondes. I don't care if they're dumber than a hubcap. Gotta have a few blondes."

"DELIVERY!" came a ringing voice from the foyer of the bar area. "DELIVERY!"

"It's here!" Orel exclaimed.

Bill looked at Orel whose delight was palpable. They made their way through the office door to find a man in uniform brandishing delivery papers.

Orel looked closely at them to make sure he had gotten what he ordered. "Perfect," he said and signed on the appropriate line.

"So bring it in, then?" asked the deliveryman.

"Yes, yes…please, Stan?" Orel said, reading the man's name tag. "Right here next to the stage, if you would."

Bill peered over his eyeglasses at his partner hurrying to the entrance door, unsure of what surprise Orel had in store for them this time. He followed him outside and made a face as he saw Orel's gait turning from a skip into a gallop on the way to the truck.

"Christ, I'm going into business with a goddamned ballerina," Bill mumbled.

Inside the dark cargo hold of the box truck, Stan repositioned his load until he got to the large, white crate that matched the number on his paperwork. Stan's helper grabbed a pallet jack from the side of the truck and helped pull the big white crate to the tailgate of the truck.

"It's bigger than I remembered," Orel noticed. "Never saw them delivered before."

Bill came up next to him and took a puff of his cigarette. "Them? There's more than one?" he asked.

"No," Orel answered, his eyes still fixed on the crate. "There's only one."

The two men in the truck huffed and grunted as they worked the load down the ramp and onto the pavement.

"I need to get paid by the pound on these," Stan joked as he handed Orel a second piece of paperwork. "Gimme your Johnny H-cock on the dotted line. First initial, last name printed next to it."

"My what?" Orel looked up at Bill, unsure of what Stan wanted him to do. Bill motioned a signature with his hand, and Orel nodded in understanding.

Stan's helper grabbed a crowbar and began to pry the top and sides off the crate. Orel shoved the paper into Stan's stomach and ran over to him.

"Please be careful," he said. "Don't wanna scratch it."

Stan's helper stopped and looked up at Orel. "You wanna do it?" he challenged with a thick New York accent.

"Uh, no, eh. Just…just please be careful."

The man gave Orel a long stare and then returned to pulling at the nails, which held the crate shut. One by one the panels came off revealing a maroon cloth covering. After the last panel fell away, Orel pulled the covering off, exposing a dark, wooden piece of furniture.

"What'd ya get, a desk?" scoffed Bill. "We already gotta desk in da office. That's where I'm gonna be doing my interviews tomarra."

"Not a desk, Bill," Orel said, pulling the remainder of the covering away to reveal a baby grand piano. He ran one long hand over the smooth, polished wood while the other gently plinked the white and black keys. "It's an instrument, Bill. My father's. He was…a virtuoso."

Bill looked blankly at Orel. "If he was a virtuoso, how'd the hell did he have you?"

Orel returned a vacant stare, then repressed a grin. As he resumed, he seemed to be looking through the piano, as if revisiting the memories of his father's playing.

"He was a pianist. He played marvelously. Large venues and small clubs," Orel said. "I was very young. But I remember it well. They didn't normally let kids go to the concerts or get in the clubs. You know, for fear that they would cause a disruption. But my dad pulled some strings, eh?"

He laughed happily at his accidental pun before adding, "And he was able to get me backstage at some of them."

Bill shoved his cigarette between his lips and sat down on an empty overturned pickle bucket.

Orel continued, "I watched as he played one night. His body was glowing from the spotlight. Shiny. I remember everything was shiny. The black and white piano. Him. Especially him. He played Canon in D...my favorite. His hands moved over the keys so effortlessly. It was like he was connected. Connected to the piano. Connected to the audience. Connected to God. Connected..." He laughed and added, as if in afterthought, "My father was connected!"

He emerged from his trance to find Lucy staring at him. "How long have you been there, honey?" he asked.

"Virtuoso," she answered simply.

The orange five ball lay tight against the green rail a few inches from the corner pocket. Only the 15 added an extra obstacle, but not enough to matter. Rudy's thumb and forefinger held the cue stick loose enough for easy movement. Pulling it slowly back and forth, Rudy inched closer to the cue ball. With one strong swipe, he slammed the blue tip of the stick into the cue ball, causing it to violently smack into the five. The cue ball banged two or three times off the five, leaving the two to come to a slow standstill.

"Double kissed it," Einstein smugly observed.

"Ahhhh, it's a stupid game anyway," Rudy yelled, threw his stick onto the table and stormed into the bathroom.

"Boy's gotta lotta issues," Einstein said, looking up at the television behind the bar above Wally's head.

A weatherman announced, "Small craft advisories in effect until 7 p.m., with isolated thunderstorms for the beaches and a light chop." He recited his message with a nonchalance common to that line of work. Since the storms were a regular part of the Florida summer, the announcement was repeated three times a day over a 90-day period. Even for the newer meteorologists, it quickly became second nature.

Einstein looked away from the television. "She's out there for sure," he said, stroking his brass-colored mustache.

Sometimes, the storms would approach quickly, pelting the beach with wind and water and be over in a matter of minutes. At other times, they stalled out in the Gulf, built up strength and then beat the bay with a fury. In either case, it gave the spectators on shore a sporting opportunity to speculate.

"Yep, should be nasty later. Not sure how much longer I'll be able to leave the back porch open tonight. Gonna be goddamed bad for business," Wally said, as he leaned further out on the exterior bar to take a look at the approaching squall line.

A cloud of dust at the rear of the parking lot caught his attention. When he saw Bill's red truck emerge from it, he grimaced in disgust.

"Speaking of bad for business...," he groused. "And what the hell does a junk man know about running a bar? I'd love to see his ass go belly up and watch him go crawling back into the dumpsters with that Canadian, where he belongs."

The red truck came to a halt with a slow slide on the sandy surface. The driver side door opened with a faint creak. Wally noticed the logo on the side of the door just above an emerging leg.

"'Another Man's Treasure?' Who the hell are they kidding? They wouldn't know a goddamned treasure if it came up and pissed in their Cheerios," Wally bitterly spewed, looking to Einstein for support.

Orel and Bill slowly made their way through the heavy sand to the outside bar. "Gotta beauty building up there on the horizon, eh?" Orel commented.

Einstein gave a snort and returned his eyes to the television, which now was broadcasting the sports segment of the news. As he did, he ignored Orel's attempt at a handshake.

Orel smiled. The awkwardness of the moment did not bother him. He called to Wally, "Two beers. One for me and one for the boss."

"Da boss," Wally mumbled. "Boss a trash is what he is."

"So, how's that gas gauge working out for ya?" Orel said in another attempt to reconnect with the old painter.

"Stick's still working fine."

Sensing the tension, Bill motioned with his eyes to move inside. "The air's a little thick out here, son," he said. What say we get in the air condition for a bit?"

The storm rumbled louder on the horizon. The dark gray clouds rolled closer, chased by gusts of wind, causing the water to turn a steel blue color.

Inside, Bill pulled up a barstool and settled with the sigh of someone who felt satisfied with a full day's work. He tapped a fresh pack of cigarettes on the bar and looked around the tavern.

"Kinda slow tonight, Wally?"

"Weather," came the terse reply.

"Weather or not, looks like we'll be in the same business before long," Bill said.

"What's going on with your reclamation project anyway?" yelled Einstein from the wind-whipped outside bar.

"Coming along nicely. Got the woodwork done today. Some appliances. Tables."

"And a piano," Orel piped up from the pool table.

"Pee-ah-na? Who'z gonna be playing that?" Einstein shouted, becoming engulfed in a sea of wind and debris.

Bill took a sip from his beer and looked up, foam garnishing his upper lip. "The kid says he knows how," he yelled back.

He got up, walked over to the pool table and gave his son a one-armed hug.

"Roodee."

"Working on my rail shot, Dad."

Einstein smirked at the boy while fighting off the wet wind.

"Rail shot? Whatta you know about a rail shot?" Bill joked, sliding his arm over Rudy's head before allowing him to break free and join Orel at the pool table.

Einstein came inside and plopped down in the stool next to Bill's. "So you're bringing back the Nearvana?" he addressed Bill and Orel. "Nearvana? What kind of name is that anyway?"

"A state of perfect bliss," remarked Orel who was powdering his stick for the next shot. "Well, that's what nirvana is. A Buddhist term. Buddhists believe that through right thinking and right living you achieve nirvana."

Bill stared straight into the weather while Einstein turned around in his barstool to watch the young man continue with his speech.

"So our idea of nirvana would be heaven. Based on the name of the old place, Near-vana.... I suppose the owner considered it Almost Heaven," he concluded.

"Goddamned hippie freaks," rambled Wally from his spot beside the register. "So I guess it's your job to get the friggin' heaven back into the Nearvana. Is that right, junk man? And what are you gonna call it? Almost Nearvana? Near Nearvana? Goddamned Heaven, that's what you should call it!" Wally's face reddened as he continued. "And Covington. Christ, if that guy's anywhere near heaven, I should be the goddamned pope. When he ran that place, he had more shady dealings than you could shake that pool stick at."

"Dollar Bill's," answered Bill, exhaling a smoky air of satisfaction. "Dollar Bill's," he repeated, tilting his head back and slapping an imaginary sign in the air with a dirty hand.

"Sounds like a goddamned titty bar," Wally grumbled and stalked back into the kitchen.

The wind slammed the door that led to the outside bar. A light plastic chair danced in circles on one leg, as sideway sheets of rain bounced off the awning.

Rudy eyed the red ball on the table as it rested against the green felt. He pushed the stick slowly through his fingers and made contact with the white cue ball. It struck the red ball too hard, causing it to skip away from the rail and around the pocket. Rudy collapsed on the table, turned his head to one side in disgust and released the stick, which fell to the floor with a high-pitched ping.

"Dang, why is this so hard?"

"Keep trying, Rudy," Orel consoled. "You gotta just keep trying. Remember, hit a lotta rail and some of the ball. One day, the light bulb will go on and you'll wonder how you were never able to do this before."

Chapter 13

Sam's fingertips were black from rubbing the newspaper's morning headline.

BEACH LANDMARK REOPENING
HOPES TO RECAPTURE GLORIED PAST

"This is not necessarily a bad thing," he ventured, balancing a cup of coffee in his hand and the paper on his lap.

Kronis sucked in his top lip. His chin rested on a triangle of forearms and folded hands. His elbows provided the foundations on a pristine desk whose top was empty except for a letter opener, a fountain pen and a pair of nose hair clippers.

"We pull in rent from the property. We get the place renovated with none of our capital. And the property increases in value," Sam continued cautiously.

Silence hung in the air for a few seconds before Kronis rose from his high-back cushioned chair. He straightened his vest and strode across the room.

"A man tells the truth when he's in severe pain," he whispered in Sam's ear as he wandered by the couch to the picture window overlooking a shallow pond. "I learned this over the years. If you want information, it's always best to beat it out of them. Other guys always want them dead."

He stopped to watch a spider crawling on the interior marble windowsill, walking sideways away from one corner. He seemed fascinated by the creature's behavior.

"It creates an air of respect in a relationship after it's over, too," he started again halfheartedly, still engaged in watching the walking patterns of the arachnid.

Sam kept his eyes on the newspaper without reading anything in particular.

"He left a map," Kronis started out of nowhere.

"A map...Sir?"

"Truth begat of a beating."

Sam thought it best to let well enough alone.

"Like a fucking pirate. Son of a bitch steals my money and property," Kronis said, his forefinger teasing the spider in circles. He smiled as he watched it dance in fear. Pulling back for a moment, still leaning on the windowsill, he glanced in Sam's direction. "Then he has the balls to tell me, as he's suffocating on his own blood, I can have it back...if...I can find it. Guy had an incredible pair."

Straightening, Kronis walked over to his desk and searched in the top drawer until he located a cigar cutter and a gold-colored torch lighter. He took a long, brown cigar from a wooden box with the words "Romeo y Julieta Piramides" emblazoned on the lid and held it under his nose. "Churchill smoked these," he commented with his eyes closed in satisfaction.

Not sure how to respond, Sam took a sip from his coffee cup.

"A hidden treasure. Isn't that romantic?" Kronis started again as he walked back to see how the spider was doing. It had inched closer to the corner and stood still as if waiting. Sliding his flat palm over the marble sill, Kronis noticed a web in the opposite corner. He found it interesting that the spider had ventured so far from its home, especially with the treatment he had just given it. "A hidden treasure and no map," he mused.

He rolled the cigar between his forefinger and thumb and pulled the cutter out of his vest pocket. "Not a fair fight, really. I know my money is out there. I just have to find it. Without a map."

He slid the shoulder of the cigar through the cutter and guillotined the tip, which fell gently to the floor. Turning the cigar around, he ignited the torch and toasted its foot until a hint of tobacco aroma filled the air. A few slow drags with the torch still flaming in front, a veil of white smoke enveloped his head.

Sam watched with discomfort as we watched the methodical process. The fire danced and illuminated Kronis' face. The measured pace of the conversation made him feel uneasy, too.

Kronis stared at the smolder on the end of the cigar. He turned and found the location of the spider on the windowsill again.

Another long puff inflamed a cherry red bloom on its end. Kronis pushed his face close to the windowsill within inches of the spider. He positioned one hand in front of the web and the other, which held the cigar, to the right of the spider. He curled his tongue in his mouth and slowly brought his hands closer together. The spider jittered between them.

"There was…one thing I loved about that man. That Jonny Hughes," Kronis rasped through another exhale of smoke.

His left hand was now right next to the spider. The cigar was just as close on the other side. The heat from the smolder made the creature twitch nervously. With a deliberate push, Kronis forced the burning ember against the spindly legs of the creature. One by one, they melted and spun in odd directions. The bulbous body shook wildly and popped as the torturer paused.

A moment to feel the pain was allowed. Allowed too long. Kronis forced the burning cigar and spider into the palm of his left hand. A closed-eye shiver and wince accompanied the action. When the pain subsided he pulled the cigar from his hand and inspected it closely as the remnants of the creature hung loosely on its charred end.

"His wife," he released through a clenched jaw.

"MARCO!" a female voice called out.

"Polo," came back in a whisper.

Rudy stepped lightly into the shallow end of the pool where Lucy was blindly searching with her eyes shut tight. Little giggles slipped out under his breath as he got close enough to smell her lip gloss.

"MARCO!" she called again.

Rudy kept his face inches from Lucy's.

"MARCO!"

Barely able to fight back the giggles, he kept quiet for a few seconds longer.

Lucy fought the urge to open an eye and felt perhaps it was time to play the "fish out of water" card. Instead she tried one more time. "MARCO!"

"POLO!!" Rudy screamed, a mere inch from Lucy's face.

"AHHHHHHH! God, I hate when you do that," she scolded as she swam to the deep end of the pool.

Rudy had expected her reaction. She always withdrew after he screamed "Polo" at her from point-blank range. But the urge to do it was just too great. He knew that it was best to let her stew for a few minutes and then ask if she wanted to play a different game. She usually came around.

After some time had passed, Rudy pushed off the wall and backstroked otter-like to the deep end where Lucy was pouting.

"Hey, Loose," he started. "Wanna play something else?"

Lucy stared straight ahead, her chin lying on her folded arms. Her blonde hair was beginning to dry, slick yet stiff like straw. Rudy crept up beside her and made funny faces to get her to laugh. He started blowing bubbles and darting his eyes back and forth in his best imitation of a crab. The laughter never came.

"Orel's mom died," she said out of nowhere.

Rudy stopped blowing bubbles, pulled himself out of the water and sat on the side of the pool. "How'd you find that out?"

"Overheard a couple of conversations," Lucy fibbed. "She had Orel and a few days later, she died."

The splashing ripples from the pool pump return were the only sound as Rudy struggled for something to say.

"From what, though?" he finally managed.

"Having babies doesn't always work out the way it's supposed to, I guess."

"Must have been hard growing up without a mom," Rudy began and suddenly stopped, realizing he might have hurt Lucy's feelings. He quickly pushed off and floated backwards in the water with a beach ball against his chest. "My dad's place is opening tonight."

Lucy rubbed a cuticle whose surrounding skin had cauliflowered from too much time in the pool. "Yeah, I heard."

"Dad said I'll get to drink all the free soda I want. As long as I wipe up tables."

"Parents always find a way to bribe you to do work, don't they?"

Their exchange was interrupted by Gene yelling from the laundry room, "Loosie! Loosie!"

"See. Joyce probably needs help folding towels. I'll see you later," Lucy said.

Gene stepped out of the door and waved. "Bring Rudy with you!" he called. "He might be able to help out."

Lucy looked back at Rudy with a turned-down mouth. "Guess you're getting bribed, too."

It had been a matter of controversy between the partners and even among the city council members, but Bill finally won the argument and got his way on the design for the bar's signage. A big green single dollar with Bill's face in place of George Washington's was on top. Underneath was his name next to a dollar sign, the two split by an apostrophe: DOLLAR BILL'$. Orel had hoped for something more classy. The city council had preferred something "less gaudy."

"Beeeuteeful, ain't she?" Bill grinned as he flipped the switch to light up the sign for the first night of business.

Orel looked on from a tall ladder. He was finishing the job of hanging the shiny white Grand Opening sign over the front entrance. His sour smile conveyed plenty as he completed weeks of preparation and hard work with one last tie of a knot.

As Bill stood back and took in all of what he and Orel had brought to fruition, he felt melancholy. The best part of the dream is sometimes the dream itself. The reality of seeing it come true can sometimes bring a bit of a letdown.

"You know," he started, "I have been thinking of this for years. Talking about it to friends. Working out the details every day on the route. Wondering how I'd act if I ever got successful." He took out his handkerchief and wiped his nose and mouth. "I never thought it through to this point. I never thought it'd happen. Now what?"

Orel slid down the ladder without touching a rung and gave his partner a pat on the back. "Open the doors and see what happens, I guess."

Bill walked slowly to the front door to unlock the deadbolt. Before he got it fully turned he laid his head against the heavy wooden door and stared down at the floor for a moment. On his feet he still wore the shoes he had always worn when riding the route. He turned to look back at Orel to see if it mattered, but he was busy getting the waitstaff into position. With a deliberate turn, Bill finished unlocking the door. He pulled it open slowly.

As Bill stepped onto the sidewalk that led to the front door, he realized he was a bar owner. But somehow he did not feel any different. It felt the same as seconds before. He turned back to the parking lot, which was empty except for his red pickup off to one side. His eyes caught the logo Orel had painted on the truck door months earlier.

"Another Man's Treasure…," he whispered and looked up at the cartoon image of his face on the sign with big dollar signs in the eyes. "Once a junk man, always a junk man," he mumbled with a quiet laugh and went inside.

Orel was giving a last minute pep talk to the assembled waitresses. "Okay now, remember—these people don't have to come here. There are tons of places on the beach they can go and have fun. We have to be better than that. We have to make this an experience they bring back home and think about."

"That's right, girls" Bill said, joining the conversation. He winked at Orel and cupped both of his hands on his once muscular chest and pushed upward. "Don't be afraid to show them who you are."

Orel went to the stage to do some last minute checks. He ran his fingers over the white keys of the piano, causing some of the waitresses to giggle. A few taps on the microphone he grabbed from the piano created some feedback, which turned the giggles to shrieks.

"Sorry," he calmly announced. He then looked around the room with the mike in one hand while doing his best to make eye contact with each person in the room. "Ladies and Gentlemen," he started. "I would like to introduce to you—DOLLAR BILL'S!"

"SURPRISE!" came a roar from the front door.

Every eye turned to a group of people dressed in jester masks spilling in from outside. Gene was leading the way with a bottle of champagne and a hand full of confetti, which he dispersed with each step. The rest of the crowd spread out to the empty tables, which were neatly adorned with "Grand Opening" signs, condiments and fancy glasses.

"Congratulations, my friend!" Gene yelled when he finally reached Bill. "Here's to long success and happiness." Dorothy came behind him and gave Bill a peck on the cheek. With the dab of a tissue, she quickly wiped off the lipstick left behind. Lucy and Rudy ran to the piano and took turns plunking out no particular song.

Bill looked around in shock. "Where did all these people come from?"

"I...I knew you were opening tonight, so I walked around the pool and told all of my guests I'd give them a free night if they came by and checked out my buddy's new place," Gene explained.

"You did that?" Bill asked in astonishment. "And the masks?"

"Ahh, just leftovers from a Mardi Gras promotion I did one year at the motel that didn't really go anywhere."

Bill found one of the waitresses and proclaimed, "This man drinks free all night!" He threw his arm around Gene, gave him a good look and hard squeeze, and laughed.

Gene glanced down toward the floor. "If you're gonna be a successful bar owner, you might think about getting a new pair of shoes, pal," he teased.

They were interrupted by the *whrrrrrr* noise of microphone feedback, as Orel got ready to address the crowd. "Ladies and gentlemen, if I could have your attention once again," he said. "One of the features at Dollar Bill's that we're proud of, besides our lovely waitstaff, is the opportunity for our customers to become the entertainers. If you believe you have a talent that you want to share with us, please fill out this card, and you will get the opportunity to perform before the evening is finished."

The group responded with a mixture of "ohhs," laughter, and nervous giggles, which led to gentle ribbing by friends.

"Since this idea might be a little hard for most people to swallow right away, I thought I'd get things started off," Orel said as he sat down at the piano.

Bill released his grip on Gene and made his way behind the bar to help serve some of the customers. Gene walked over to his guests, dispensing handshakes along the way. Dorothy dug around in her purse for another tissue as she ordered her first drink of the night. Rudy moved to the back of the bar so he could see the whole place. Lucy finally found the table closest to the piano, sat properly with her hands folded on it and waited for Orel to start.

Orel got comfortable at the piano and looked around the room. He saw Lucy and gave her a special smile. As the audience began to quiet down, he pulled the microphone close.

"I think we all have something in us, and it's just a matter of finding a way of getting it out of us. There's a fella who does this song on the radio who I think encompasses the feeling I'm trying to convey. It's called *Drift Away*."

A sense of expectation grew over the crowd as he hit the first notes. Lucy's eyes sparkled when she saw the way Orel took command of the piano. His fingers maneuvered the keys with strength and ease. The baby grand sounded richer with each stroke.

He sang with more soul than anyone had expected and a tone deeper than that of his speaking voice.

Bill stopped what he was doing behind the bar. His mouth dropped when he realized the talent his partner possessed. Gene nodded in rhythm and smiled at his guests. Dorothy wiped her eyes. Rudy watched the people watching. Lucy stared at Orel. Thoughts of Ronnie and Jonny ran through her head.

The stage light hit Orel from behind and made him glow. His passion flowed from his fingers and his voice touched everyone in the place. With each passing verse, more people became riveted by his performance.

Gene did his best to get Bill's attention. When he finally did, he mouthed, "This guy's good."

Bill simply nodded and shrugged as if he knew it all along.

The crowed clapped in time as Orel worked into a crescendo.

"And drift awayayayayay!"

Applause punctuated the finale. Orel stood and beamed a wide smile, a hand in the air. The spotlight caused him to squint as he thanked the crowd.

"That's all there is to it, folks," he said with a nod toward Lucy. "Who's next?"

Bill's eyes scanned the crowd. He found his son who was clapping and laughing. He saw Gene yucking it up with his guests. He watched as Orel took his bows. "This guy's got something," he thought as he pulled his hands out of his pockets and joined in the applause.

Chapter 14

The leaves found their way down the pool deck on a single stream of water till they gently eased into the soft St. Augustine grass border. The sun sparkled off the stream, bringing out the vibrant colors of everything in the surrounding area.

Orel sipped his coffee, admiring how Gene worked the garden hose like a technician, surgically freeing the pool area of the debris left from the storm the night before. From the look on Gene's face, it seemed to have a therapeutic effect on his mental state as well.

"You're quite adept at that," Orel said, nodding in the direction of the line of water.

"It's amazing what you'll get good at if you do it enough times," Gene answered without looking up. He smiled to himself as he continued working.

The late September morning sun was making its way over one of the palm trees, throwing an angular shadow on the motel courtyard. The blue pool rippled in contrast to the swaying red, yellow and green vegetation.

"Yes, repetition seems to have its rewards," Orel agreed.

Gene put down the hose and walked over to where his Canadian guest was seated. He indicated toward an empty chair. "May I?"

"Well, sir, it is your establishment, after all. I don't think you're required to ask," Orel politely responded.

"Speaking of establishment, you and Bill seem to have something quite unique going. Been several weeks, and I hear my guests are having the time of their lives at Dollar Bill's."

"Yes, it is amazing," Orel concurred. "People sure do love getting up on stage and performing. I suppose there's a star deep down in each one of us just aching to get out." Orel looked down at his tomato juice and then back at Gene. "We just give them that chance, I suppose."

"I gotta tell ya, I really get a kick out of that Chinese fella."

"Oh, you mean Joe."

"Yes, Joe, that's him. Funny guy. Those poor Asian fellas have the hardest times saying their r's, too."

Orel rubbed the condensation on his glass. After a long, awkward silence, he looked at Gene and said, "Joe tells me he's a picker. Picks fruits and vegetables? Tells me that anyone can do it for a charge."

"Oh yeah? Sounds like he's a produce guy."

"Produce guy," Orel said, perplexed.

"Picks fruit from the farms and then sells it on the side of the road. I understand it's a pretty good business, though I never really wanted to get my hands that dirty," Gene said, laughing.

"And it's true that anybody can do this?"

"Sure, all you need is a truck and some hands."

"Morning!" interrupted a girl's raspy voice.

The men swung their heads around to see Lucy in her pajamas rubbing sleep and sunshine from her eyes.

"Gonna meet Rudy today for some crabbing," she said, stifling a yawn.

She perked up when she realized that Orel was at the table with her father.

"Yep, gotta take advantage of these Saturdays, now that you're back in school," Gene said.

"Gotta go get dressed," she said, shy about being seen in her pajamas.

"I'll walk you down to the tavern in a bit, if you'd like, Lucyball," Orel said, craning his neck to keep her attention.

A wave was all he got as she walked back to the door and went inside.

A 20-minute shower provided plenty of steam to fog up the bathroom mirror. Orel stared at it thinking while toweling off his head. His father had written that the answer was in the question. His dilemma was that he did not even know the question.

He strolled barefoot to the bed and looked down at the collection of pictures from the manila envelope. After months of studying the tattered black-and-white photos, he had come to know the cast of characters as well as the regulars at the tavern. James Rose was the only man in the pictures he had met personally.

There was a handwritten description on the back of each photo explaining the involvement of that person in the Kronis organization. Rose was simply listed as a thug.

Orel went back to the bathroom and drew a small circle in the center of the steamed-up mirror. He added another small circle to the top left corner, and one to the top right and bottom left. Before long the mirror was dotted with circles with only the steam holding them together.

After he scrawled the initials of each person in the photo next to a specific circle, Orel drew a line from one circle to the next, marking a relationship between them. When he was finished, he could see how the spokes of the organization fit together.

He gave his creation one more look before he strolled back to the gym bag and pulled out the plain white envelope with Lawrence Kronis' name and address on the front. Orel knew this was a big piece of the puzzle, but was hesitant to examine it further until he met the man for himself.

The fall breeze made it one of the most comfortable times of the year. The brisk air made her open pores tingle. Her wet hair felt cool against her skin as she walked down the street.

"Lucyball! Lucyball."

At first, she pretended not to notice that she heard the far off voice. It was something she had always seen in movies and had wanted to try herself.

"Lucyball," said Orel, breathing hard when he finally caught up to her.

"Oh, I didn't see you coming," she said disingenuously. "I was just on my way to the tavern to do some crabbing with Rudy."

"Yes…yes. I know that," Orel said still doing his best to catch his breath. "I was hoping to catch you."

"Catch me?"

"Yes. I heard that there's a place where you can go and pick your own vegeta…," he started but left off, unsure of how to finish.

"Vegeta?" she asked with a giggle. "What's a vegeta?"

"Vegetables, actually," he corrected. "I was looking for the word your dad used but couldn't think of it…. PRODUCE! That's it. Produce."

Lucy scrutinized Orel inquisitively.

"Your dad told me there's some places down in Ruskin where, for a fee, they will let you go and pick your own vegetables and fruit. Most men sell the stuff they get on the side of the road. But,

I think I would just like to do it for the fun of it. Maybe put it out for the people at Dollar Bill's to snack on."

"Why not just go to the store?" Lucy asked.

"It'll be fun. A day out. We'll bring Rudy, too."

When they got to the edge of the walkway to Rudy's house, they could see one side of the window curtains swing closed quickly.

"Rudy's mom is kinda weird," Lucy offered. "I've never seen her outside of the house. Just a bunch of times through that window."

"Yes. I met her once. Very nice lady."

Lucy looked strangely at Orel as he tapped gently on the front door. The two could hear movement on the inside, but there was no acknowledgment of the knock. Orel tapped again, this time a little harder.

The door opened slightly and four fingers emerged, wrapping around the outside edge, and remained there for a few seconds. Then finally, the door opened quickly as Rudy leapt outside with a laugh.

"Look out, blue crabs, here we come! See ya, Mom!" he shouted happily.

Both Lucy and Orel leaned back, startled by his sudden appearance. Then they saw Lillian standing in the hallway. The shadows made it difficult to see what she looked like, but Orel got close to the door for a quick word.

"Ma'am, I was wondering if it would be okay if Rudy went vegetable picking with Miss Lucy and me tomorrow morning?" he asked, not entirely sure whether she was paying attention. "I'll talk it over with your husband as well, but I thought it was always polite to go through the proper 'channels of Mom' first. Mr. Lewis said that Ruskin is a wonderful place to do this."

After a brief silence, Orel was about to repeat his request, when Lillian said, "That'd be fine. Just please be careful down there." Her eyes developed a far away look. "I understand there can be some weirdos in those fields."

Orel nodded and started to walk back down the sidewalk, but something made him stop and turn around. He told Lucy to go on, then went back and knocked on the door again.

This time the door opened more quickly. The light that came from the inside even seemed a little brighter and the shadows somewhat diminished.

"Yes?" asked Lillian in a whisper. "Forget something?"

"Uh, no. Well, um, yeah," Orel stammered. His eyes studied the lines in Lillian's face. Her powdery skin paled with the additional light. "I was wondering if you were interested in–"

He stopped short, reflecting on the appropriateness of his comment. "I was wondering…well, if you had any interest in coming to Dollar Bill's tonight."

Orel exhaled. He grinned, considering the silliness of his behavior. His only goal was to get to know his partner's wife better. And maybe have his partner get to know his wife better in the process.

Lillian responded by staring at the floor and laughing quietly. Smiles were exchanged, and Orel walked off to join the children.

Saturday nights were becoming the times of the best business. A full day of fishing and sunset at the tavern would give way to drinking, singing and laughing at Dollar Bill's. While everything was going well, it was the singing and the opportunity to be a star that were putting "asses in the seats." Either way, Bill did not care, since it was putting money in his pocket.

Usually Orel went to Dollar Bill's a few hours early to help the waitstaff set up the tables with silver and glasses. Occasionally, he wandered through the kitchen to see if the cook needed anything cut or cleaned. This evening, since he had spent most of the day crabbing with Lucy and Rudy, he arrived later than normal with the children by his side.

"Helllllooooo, fans!" he shouted as he walked through the foyer.

"Orel!" just about everyone at Dollar Bill's responded in harmony. Lucy noted how the entire place stopped as the workers admired their boss. The men greeted Orel with back slaps and handshakes, while the female staff broke into smiles and giggles. Orel's charisma was not wasted on these folks.

Rudy wandered from the crowd back to the office, while Lucy sauntered over to the piano and began plunking keys. When Orel heard the sound, he broke away from the friendly group that surrounded him and went over to sit down next to her.

"She's pretty, eh?" said Orel pointing to the piano.

"Why is everything a 'she' with you men?" Lucy asked pointedly.

"Well…" he said, running his fingers over the keys, "I think 'we men' find beauty in things. So when we see something beautiful, we call it 'she,' I guess. Besides, what would you think of me if I came up to you and said 'He's pretty,' eh?"

"I guess you have a point," Lucy said, unable to hold back a smile.

Orel's face changed as he moved his hands across the piano. The pace of his breathing slowed and his eyes squinted. A melody developing, he worked his way to the higher keys, which made a tinkling sound. Eventually, they turned into one long chord as he held his foot on the pedal and lifted his hands.

"I love the piano," he said with his eyes still closed, enjoying the note to the very end.

As the tone dissolved, he slowly lifted his foot off the pedal and looked at Lucy. A moment passed, until she realized she was staring into the most beautiful blue eyes she had ever seen.

"It's all here," he continued. "Every song ever written. It's all here, right in front of us. It's just a matter of figuring out the combination. That's the beauty of the piano. She knows all the answers. All you have to do is be a musical safe cracker."

Orel began picking out another tune.

"What's that?" Lucy asked, watching his long fingers dance over the black and white keys.

"Not sure yet. Making something up, I think."

"Making it up? That sounds like a finished song," said Lucy.

"You think?" He looked at the ceiling for more inspiration. "I play it by ear mostly. What if we do this?" He slowly changed the melody, giving his simple song a new twist.

Lucy looked on in amazement at the ease with which Orel improvised. It was if he had this beautiful music in his soul and was pouring it out through his fingers for her to hear and see.

"Here—you try," he said, pulling his hands off the shiny ivory keys.

"Me? I can't write. Music."

"Sure you can," Orel reassured, his eyes catching a sparkle from a ceiling light. "We all can. It's just a matter of telling ourselves we can do something and then letting it happen.

Orel gently placed Lucy's hands on the piano. Then, he moved each of her fingers, one by one, till they were positioned exactly as he wanted. Lucy noticed how his meticulously manicured fingernails extended from his finely shaped fingers. Her hands tingled under the warmth of his guidance. He then put his hands in his lap and smiled at his young 'student.'

"Middle C," he said. "Your thumb is on what we call Middle C. I always go to Middle C to start. It's a comfortable place for me. Kinda like home."

Lucy wanted to look at Orel's face, but she was too busy watching her hands on the keys and trying to follow what he was talking about.

"Just like home, it's a great place to start and a wonderful place to return," Orel elaborated.

Lucy's eyes moved from her left hand to her right. She had never learned to play a musical instrument. Paralyzed by fear of failure, her hands locked in half-moons over the piano.

"To play well, it's important to relax," Orel said, sensing Lucy's tension. "You can't play well when you're trying to be too careful or worrying about making a mistake. That's why they call it *playing* the piano. If it was meant to be hard, they'd call it *working* the piano, right?"

Lucy giggled nervously as she loosened her hands and placed them gingerly on the instrument.

"Give it a shot. Go ahead. Play!" he said with enthusiasm.

Staring at her thumb, Lucy pushed on the Middle C key. At first she produced a thin, light sound. And then after some time, she hit it with more ease and courage. When she felt brave, she hit the C and the key next to it with her index finger. Before long, she made the leap to others. She glanced up at Orel with a nervous smile when her pinky danced back and forth between two adjacent keys.

"Now you're playing," Orel said, laughing. "Nothing to this nonsense, eh?"

"No," Lucy said tersely. Her hands had stopped when she spoke, and she quickly returned to playing.

"Okay let's jazz this up a bit." The tip of Orel's tongue protruded from his lips as he positioned himself alongside Lucy. "Let's start at C, dance around a bit and then return home."

Lucy's eyes widened as he smoothly wiggled his right hand, imitated her melody and then played the exact opposite, which sounded similar, yet different.

"It's kind of like life," he commented. "Once you go out and find out that there's nothing better than home after all, you end up bringing the whole thing full circle."

Playing the original portion of the tune, he danced around a bit more before returning to Middle C. "See," he said, smiling. "Back home where we belong."

The lesson was interrupted by a shout from the kitchen. "Orel! Need your help."

"Okay. Be right there!" Orel smiled at Lucy and patted her on the shoulder. "You play around with that a little bit and see what you come up with."

Lucy watched his lean figure pass through the darkness of the dance floor and into the white light of the kitchen. Then she returned to the piano keys, trying to find the tune Orel had helped her write moments earlier.

"Man," she whispered to herself, amazed that she was picking up the song. "I am playing."

Then, with one swift motion, she dragged her middle finger all the way down the length of the keyboard just like she had seen Liberace do on television. It made the most beautiful tinkling noise. All the keys plinged in succession except for one note.

The lowest C made no sound.

Chapter 15

It had taken some persuasion, but Gene finally gave in to Orel's wishes to take Lucy along for produce picking in Ruskin. While he trusted his daughter's judgement, he had only known Orel for a little over two months. So Gene went along for the ride.

Bill stayed behind to cover Dollar Bill's in case of an emergency. Problems were rare and usually limited to dealing with an inebriated tourist. The responsibility made him feel like he was in charge of something for the first time in his life.

The morning air was thin and the rising sun was beginning to burn off the mist which hung over the grass by the red truck. The bags under Rudy's eyes were a reminder of a poor night's sleep due to his excitement of the coming day. He nodded at Lucy who looked equally tired. The two climbed into the bed of the truck and settled in between boxes of gloves and tools.

Orel and Gene climbed into the cab of the pickup. The old truck was slow to start but eventually rumbled on its way. A right turn down Gulf Boulevard and a left turn toward the causeway had the four heading in the direction of the Sunshine Skyway Bridge, which spanned the mouth of Tampa Bay.

"So, what's it gonna be first, eh? Peppers? Tomatoes?" Orel asked enthusiastically. His face lit up as he drove the red truck toward the big bridge.

"You know, we could just as easily run down to the market and you could pick out anything you want," Gene said dryly. "Squash, cukes, tomatoes. It would take you only about fifteen minutes and you'd be back home."

Orel flashed Gene a wry smile in return for his simple, yet effective comment. Then he put one of his knees against the steering wheel and started to strum an invisible guitar in time with the song on the am radio. Gene gave his motel guest a long look and thought he may have been smart to tag along on this harvesting trip.

For Lucy and Rudy, riding in back of the pickup was nothing new. But at 45 miles an hour, the wind really hurt. A straight line part in the back of their hair and some spit flying out of their mouths was par for the course.

Lucy pulled the *Mad Magazine* out of her back pocket. She normally struggled trying to make sense of the back page. The fold-in always seemed clever. She knew there was a joke when the page came together to make a new image and the words spelled out a new line. But she came to the conclusion this time that it was adult humor she was not quite ready for yet.

Pushing herself toward the driver's window, Lucy handed Orel the fluttering magazine, overcoming the wind's effort to jerk it out of her hand.

"I never understand these things," she shouted through the muffling breeze and the grinding of the old truck engine. "Do you get it?"

Orel took the magazine and placed it on his lap. "I'll take a look at it later when we stop driving, sweetie," he yelled back out the window.

Lucy returned his smile in the rearview mirror and plopped herself back into the truck bed.

"Whatta you think we'll pick first, Loose? Oranges?" Rudy asked.

"Strawberries. I hope there are strawberries there. I love strawberries."

The two bantered about favorite fruits and vegetables, exchanging laughs as the little red truck struggled toward the incline of the large bridge.

"Welcome to the Sunshine Skyway!" exclaimed Orel, reading the sign that spanned the road. "Sounds like a beautiful thing, doesn't it, Mr. Lewis? Two wonderful things. Sunshine and skyway."

He watched cars drive up the steep concrete incline ahead like ants climbing up a hill. "It's funny how things from faraway seem to move so slow, eh?"

"Sure is," Gene agreed, admiring the newcomer's appreciation of the bridge he himself had traversed countless times. "Ships are the best to watch in that regard."

Orel followed Gene's pointing finger and saw a large tanker approaching the bridge in the distance. It rocked against the waves with an unexpected nimbleness for a vessel so bulky and large. Although it seemed serene from afar and graceful in its movements, one could only assume the men on deck were working hard to keep it stable and unwavering against the rough waters of Tampa Bay.

"How far are we from the top, you think?" asked Orel.

Gene looked over his shoulder at the tollbooth they had passed moments earlier and then back again toward the approaching bridge.

"Well, the entire thing is about five and a half miles long. We travel this causeway part for about two, I guess. About a mile... mile and a half, I suppose. Why?"

Orel put a thumb to his lips and his eyes became thoughtful. "We used to play a game back home," he said, a reminiscing smile forming on his lips.

Gene stared at the dried sap on the windshield.

"Rudy!" Orel yelled out the driver's side window. "You wanna play a game?"

Startled, Rudy jumped and then got his face close to the window. "What'd you say?"

"A game. You want to play a game I played as a youngster?"

"Sure," answered Rudy with wiry curls flying in every direction. "What kinda game?"

"Torpedo," Orel said and extended his left arm toward the water. "You see that ship?"

Rudy nodded, but his answer was blown inaudibly away by the wind.

Orel continued to shout, poking his head halfway out the window. "Whenever we would see an approaching boat getting ready to go under a bridge, my friends and I would ride our bikes as fast as we could. Well, sometimes not as fast, too, depending on the speed of the approaching boat. The goal was to be a torpedo and sink the ship as it passed underneath."

"Sink the ship?" Rudy yelled back.

Gene sucked in a long breath and looked at Orel.

"Well...not literally sink it. Just get to the top right when it was underneath. Sometimes we would throw something down onto the ship, just to prove we did it."

Rudy's eyes widened as a mischievous grin blossomed on his face. He looked at Orel in the rearview mirror and then back again at the approaching ship. "Think we can do it?"

"Sure, it's all about timing. Timing is everything."

"Whatta we got to throw?" Rudy asked looking excitedly around the bed of the pickup.

"You'd have to think there'd be something on a junk truck," Orel yelled and pulled his head back into the cab of the vehicle.

"You realize throwing objects from your car is not only dangerous, but can bring a fine up to two hundred dollars," Gene scolded. "Now, I realize you're not familiar with our laws down here, but I am not interested in shelling out a coupla hundred bucks to play a silly kid's game. Especially on a ride to go and pick my own damned food."

Surprised by Gene's sudden passion and disapproving look, Orel sat quietly for a few seconds. Then he reached his head back out the window. "Find anything, Rudy?"

Gene turned his head toward the water on his side in a huff.

"A piece of plastic fabric and some string is all," Rudy announced.

"Hmmm," Orel responded.

"Wait!" Rudy yelled. "Wait, I know."

He reached in his pocket and pulled out a green army figure who was crawling forward while pushing a rifle in front of him. He looked at the three objects in his hand and then at Lucy.

"Parachute Guy?" Lucy asked, with a knowing smile.

"Parachute Guy," Rudy concurred.

The approaching ship lost some of its graceful appearance as it labored toward the spans of the Skyway Bridge. Whitecaps lapped against its side like milk on a kitten's whiskers. Innocently, the ship closed the gap separating it from its meeting with the 'torpedo.'

"So what'd you come up with?" Orel yelled out the window.

"Parachute Guy!" came the chorus from the children, yelling skyward against the noise of the wind.

"Parachute Guy," Orel mumbled to himself. He looked at the ship and then at the speedometer. "Well, this may call for some fancy maneuvering by the torpedo then, won't it?"

He looked at Gene who seemed resigned to the idea of throwing litter at a passing ship.

The truck was now leaving the flat causeway portion of the bridge and began the steep climb to the top. The wavy water appeared flatter as the truck slowly got higher and higher.

"How tall's this baby anyway?" Orel asked.

"Supposed to be one hundred and fifty feet at its peak. Favorite place for the suicidal to call it quits," Gene answered.

"One-fifty. I need to factor that into the equation. We'll need velocity and accuracy." He gripped the steering wheel tighter and yelled, "FULL SPEED AHEAD!"

Lucy got on her knees facing forward and pushed her head into the passenger side window. "This is fun, huh?" she said with an excited giggle.

Gene acknowledged his daughter's enthusiasm with a single nod.

The ship was now in plain view just off the portside of the 'torpedo' truck and the bridge. It looked much larger and more details were visible—the gray deck, blue railings and deep black smokestacks.

The old red truck sputtered as the incline of the bridge tested its mettle.

"She's still got a slight miss. Bad points probably," Orel said, apologizing for the bumpy performance of the vehicle.

Gene sat up uncomfortably, his mechanical prowess being tested again. Relying on his last experience with Orel regarding engineering, he worked up a self deprecating jab.

"Maybe it's a seat," joked Gene, as he exhaled and turned his attention back to the ship.

Orel smiled and then gauged the distance of the approaching ship. "It won't be long now, eh?"

The large ship continued its plunge through the water. What had seemed graceful now appeared violent—water crashed over the bow and sent the crew scurrying. Thick, black smoke billowed from the stacks as it muscled its way closer to the bridge.

"Say when!" Rudy yelled, pushing his face close to Orel's.

"Not yet. Not yet."

Orel's eyes were focused on the vessel. Gene sat forward with a hand firmly pushed against the cracked dashboard. He looked back and forth from the ship to the latticed-steel overhead supports that adorned the top of the Sunshine Skyway Bridge.

Rudy's hand was sweaty from holding tightly onto the red plastic fabric encasing Parachute Guy. His heart raced in expectation of the moment Orel would give him the go ahead. His eyes darted nervously between the ship and the cars on the causeway behind them.

"Almost. Almost," Orel drummed his hands on the steering wheel.

The ship lumbered beneath. The truck huffed and puffed. They were moments away from destiny.

"Ready, Rudy?" Orel shouted.

"Ready!"

Rudy cocked his arm, ready for launch.

"Aim!" Orel yelled.

The tip of the tanker had reached the edge of the northbound span of the bridge. The gap between the two spans would make the ship easier to see. There was a long whir as the truck's tires glided across the metal grid at the apex of the bridge. The pickup weaved on the irregular surface, causing Rudy to sway precariously.

Lucy put her hands around his lower body to steady him.

Gene gripped the dashboard tighter.

"Fire!" Orel commanded.

Rudy flung Parachute Guy with all his might into the nothingness that was the space between the two spans of the Sunshine Skyway Bridge. At first, the ball of red plastic hung together and spun in the air like a poorly thrown football. After a few seconds, the wind unfurled the plastic, allowing Parachute Guy to free himself from the entanglement. His body descended quickly until the plastic opened with a pop to slow his momentum.

Lucy's face lit up with excitement and she expelled a breath.

The ship was now well under the two spans and moving faster than any of them had anticipated. Its mammoth hulk was gray and ugly.

"He's almost there," rooted Orel, looking through the mesh of steel in the bridge, not paying much attention to driving.

Gene's mouth was open in expectation as he did his best to keep his eyes both on the parachute and the road ahead.

The children were both leaning over the same side of the truck, watching the ship pass underneath. The first stack was now under the middle of the bridge moving quickly, with the second stack shortly behind.

Parachute Guy was falling, dancing at the whim of the wind. It was sure to be a direct hit on the ship.

"Beauty, eh?" Orel said to Gene who now seemed to be enjoying the action wholeheartedly.

The first part of the second stack was now visible. Black smoke rose from its darkness. Parachute Guy was so close. Feet away, maybe. The second stack was now half way through the gap. Parachute Guy was even closer…and closer…

With the second stack fully under the two spans of the bridge, the red plastic melted into the nasty black smoke and withered in its heat.

"Direct hit!" Orel yelled.

"Woohoo!" screamed Rudy.

"Oh my gosh," Lucy yelped.

Gene, caught up in uncontrollable laughter, slapped Orel on the back.

The ship lumbered from under the bridge out into the Gulf of Mexico, unaware of its new stowaway.

As Lucy watched it fade into the whitening expanse of water, she was interrupted by Rudy's laughter turning into a violent cough.

"Man, too many cigarettes for you or what?" she whispered under the wind.

Rudy was still leaning over the side of the red pickup when he finally regained his composure. Slowly he righted himself and sat down next to Lucy. He exhaled deeply and looked at her. "That was great," he said with shining eyes.

"What's that?" she asked, excitedly pointing toward his lips.

"What?"

"That," she continued and wiped fresh, dark red blood from his lower lip. Her face became as white as his. "You're bleeding!"

Rudy stalled as if searching for an answer. "Musta bit my lip," he finally mumbled.

Lucy sat speechless for a moment.

"Don't tell my dad," Rudy pleaded calmly as he finished wiping the rest of the blood from his lip and tongue with the back of his hand.

Another half hour passed before the truck finally arrived in Ruskin and at the entrance of the first produce field.

Orel pushed his chest onto the steering wheel and looked straight up at the sign overhead. "Yew Pickum Yew Boughtum," he said in a feigned southern accent.

Gene glanced apologetically at Orel. "Sometimes we Floridians take our dialect a bit too far," he mumbled.

"No, that's great, eh," Orel responded. "That's what gives places flavor. The way the people who live there talk, eh?"

"I just think it makes us look like we jumped right out of 'Hee Haw' sometimes, is all," Gene said.

As the truck pulled under the sign, Orel's eyes widened at the sprawl of land in front of him. Rows upon rows of black plastic lined the ground, with green shoots sprouting out in all directions. Large green, red and orange tomatoes dotted the vines.

"Pretty, eh? It's truly amazing how neatly it's all cut," he marveled.

Gene nodded. "Yes, they have men working around the clock maintaining things."

"No. No. I'm talking about the world," Orel said. "It's cut so perfectly. Things live, things die, they rot and make it all grow again."

Gene nodded again, slowly, but this time without enthusiasm.

"FAR OUT!" yelled Rudy, leaning over the side of the truck and pushing his head into the truck cab to get Orel's attention. "How many can we pick? Is there a rule on how many we can pick?"

Orel's face exploded into a grin. "Yew Pickum Yew Boughtum," he drawled.

"It's beautiful, isn't it?" Lucy said toward the passenger side of the truck, gazing at the unending lines of ripening vegetables.

"Yes honey, it is. It really is beautiful," said Gene.

The red truck chugged its way past the entrance and cut an imperfect, dusty trail through the symmetrical rows.

It was late afternoon and they had been picking for several hours. The dark orange sun started to burn shiny squares on the tomatoes and vegetables through the lattice of the cardboard boxes.

Orel and Gene continued to toil, doing their best to make the trip worth the distance they had traveled. A few rows over, Rudy lay against one of the tomato plants, his shirt stained dark red. Next to him, Lucy sat upright still wiping the red off her shirt. A tomato fight earlier in the day had left its mark on their clothing.

"Why'd you go to the Outta Sight Shop that day, Loose?" Rudy said without warning, swatting the no-see-ums that darted around his tomato-juiced face. "What was the real reason?"

"Why was there blood in your mouth?" she asked back.

Rudy flapped his hands in the air in agitation. "I asked you first," he persisted.

Lucy worked at a piece of dirt that was bothering the corner of her eye. "You miss your mom?"

Rudy gave her a puzzled look.

"You know, since she lost it?" she continued. "I mean she used to be normal and then she kinda just wasn't anymore."

"Lost it? What's this got to do with?"

"I miss mine. I mean, at least yours is still there. At least you can still see her and talk to her. Mine—mine just left. She didn't give me a reason. Just left." Lucy tilted her head back as she looked over the rows of vegetables. "Dad said she wasn't happy with us. She had to go figure out some things. Figure out who she was."

Rudy looked sympathetically in Lucy's direction. Nervously, he twirled a long strand of sweaty hair at the back of his neck and brought the other hand to his mouth and began to chew on the side of his thumb.

"So, what's that got to do with the Outta Sight Shop?"

"I don't know. The smells. I think my mom used to take me there…for candles and incense. Dad hated it. I remember him always saying in arguments. 'You're not the person I married!'"

A long silence ensued, with the two taking turns kicking at the farm dirt.

Then Rudy asked, "Where is she now?"

"California, I think. She hitchhiked. I think that's the last place my dad said he got a postcard from." Lucy's face twisted into a scowl. "Imagine her sending the family she left, a postcard. A stupid one, too. It was a picture of a jail. Al-ca-traz…I think was the name. I looked at it not long ago in my dad's jewelry box. It said, 'Get out of jail free. Collect two hundred dollars. Love, Nancy.'"

"Like Monopoly?"

"Yeah, I guess. Dad grinned when he first told me what it said." She mimicked in a feigned masculine voice, "That Nance always had a sense of humor," and added, "I didn't get the joke, though."

"Hmm." Rudy shook his head in agreement. "Me neither. Must be some adult thing."

He gave up twirling his hair began to work at removing the stains from his shirt. "You mad at her?"

"You mad at your mom?"

"Why should I be mad at my mom? She got sick. She didn't leave me!"

"Well, maybe my mom got sick, too. Maybe she just didn't want to stay around and let me see her be that way," Lucy said, reddening. Then a smile briefly grew on her face and disappeared just as quickly. "Yes. I get mad at her sometimes," she continued. "But sometimes I feel sorry for her. She left a good guy—my dad. And I'm not so bad either. I wonder sometimes if she met someone new. If she's happy."

Rudy flashed a quick smile of his own.

Lucy's long sigh sounded liked she had been crying inside for sometime. She looked down at the dirt and searched it for courage. "So," she started through teary eyes, "why don't you want your dad knowing about a bloody lip?"

Rudy's thumb immediately went back into his mouth and his other hand reached for a curly hair to twirl. His face got white as if all the blood had been drained from it, and his thin lips disappeared into the whiteness.

Lucy did her best to lighten the tension. "C'mon. It can't be worse than getting postcards from California prisons, can it?"

Some of the color came back to Rudy's face and he laughed nervously as he struggled to find the right words. "My dad thinks I'm tough. So I am. I mean, I have to be."

Lucy looked at the dirt at her feet and kicked at an ant that was exploring the remnants of a crushed tomato.

"I don't know what it is. I mean, I get up almost every morning…," Rudy started mundanely. "I get up every morning and have to throw up."

"Like the flu?"

"Well, I thought that at first, but then it never went away. A lot of times I puke, and blood comes out. I get cramps real bad, too. One time I peed blood," he continued.

"Rude, you gotta go to a doctor!"

Rudy shook his head vigorously. "No!"

Across the green, leafy space of the farm, Orel and Gene were still toiling to fill up the remaining empty boxes spread out in the dirt road. Gene was slow and methodical while Orel moved with a frenzied, yet fluid motion, as if his picking was being timed against a stopwatch.

"This is it," Orel exclaimed, wiping a brown soiled forearm against his sweaty brow. "This is what it's all about. It's the process that is the fun part. Sure, going to the store and shopping for your fruits and vegetables is a process. But this is as it was meant to be."

"Process schmoshess. This is a lot of work," Gene said, flashing a grin.

"You do a fine job."

"Well, not bad for my first time, I guess," Gene answered.

"No, I mean you do a fine job with your daughter. I'm sure it's not easy to be a parent by yourself. You're raising a wonderful person in Lucy."

Orel looked in the children's direction. He reached into his back pocket and pulled out the *Mad Magazine* Lucy had given him earlier. He stared at the back fold-in, which was worn with three creases. "It's a hard enough job for two people, let alone one," he offered as a compliment.

Gene cupped his hand around a shiny red tomato and pulled it from the vine with the same gentle twist he had learned hours earlier from the migrant worker who had been picking next to them. He sat down in the moist black dirt with his back against a clump of bushes and stared at the tomato.

"You think they'll notice?"

"Hmm?" asked Orel, engrossed in the *Mad Magazine*.

"You think they'll notice if I snuck a try of just one?"

Orel's face broke into a large, toothy grin when he got the magazine joke. "No. I'm sure it happens all the time."

"Yes, it was…IS…hard," Gene started, with a juicy line of tomato seeds streaming down his chin. "You know that feeling when you're about to jump into freezing cold water?"

Orel's eyes gleamed. "I'm from Canada, my friend. That's a birthright."

"Well, when you're staring at the water, you know it's going to be freezing. You keep staring. Somehow, after awhile, you work up the courage. And then you finally jump in. Sure, it's shocking at first. After you get used to it, it's really not that bad. That's how it went for me."

Orel picked up a tomato and bit into it, listening sympathetically.

"When Nance left, she took half my soul. She also left a whole human," Gene said, laughing, while he studied his tomato. "A human that I was solely responsible for. I remember staring at that little four-year-old for hours. The innocent child didn't know. She just slept in the bed that Nance and I had gotten her the year before. She had no idea what happened. Her mother decided to walk out of her life. I just kept staring."

The ensuing silence was shattered by a distant yell. Gene and Orel leapt to their feet and looked at the children down the row.

Rudy lay in a ball, his shirt stained bright red.

Lucy stood over him.

"You suck!" Rudy screamed as he jumped to his feet and returned fire. He hurled a beefsteak tomato that hit Lucy in the side of the leg. "We're even."

"Okay, kids!" Gene commanded. "It's time to wrap it up."

The children both ignored Gene's orders, like a couple of young puppies at play, and continued to pummel each other with tomatoes.

"After all the tomatoes they're wasting over there, we're in the clear over the two we ate," Orel quipped as he picked up the remaining produce that had missed his basket.

Dusting dirt off his jeans, he walked over to the children. He stood over them for a moment until Lucy felt she was being watched.

"Time to load up the truck and get a move on," he said and extended a hand toward the young girl. "Here's your magazine back."

She nodded a polite thank you as she took it and returned it to her back pocket.

"It's adult humor. It's even a little over my head, sweetie," he said gently. "Maybe one day we'll both be smart enough to get the joke."

When they had loaded the truck with a bounty of fruits and vegetables, the four pickers headed home. The men rode in the cab in silence, fatigued from the day's labor. The orange-streaked sky made a pastel background for the approaching Skyway Bridge, which looked much taller and darker than it had during the mid-day hours.

The ride had rocked Rudy to sleep in his small niche among the cardboard boxes. Lucy watched her friend. He looked so peaceful. He looked so weak, but inside must be so strong. Her gaze swept across the approaching bay. It was so large. She wondered how many bays and bodies of water there were between here and the jail on the postcard her mom had sent.

In the cab of the truck, an AM radio station played music past the growing static.

"I don't think I coulda done it," said Gene all of a sudden.

Orel squinted at Gene against the setting sun. "Done it?"

"Been so generous," Gene continued. "I mean, Bill's a nice guy and all. And he's come to me many times with ideas about doing things. Doing things just like the two of you are doing with Dollar Bill's. I mean, I had enough money to get into something like that with him, but I just wasn't sure…wasn't sure he was the type of guy to follow through. Someone to put his…well, his or someone else's money where his mouth is. He's always been a schemer. A dreamer. Wasn't sure he was a doer. Maybe it took a stranger like yourself to push him over the hump."

Orel turned his face back to the road. He tilted his head and smiled, the corners of his mouth uneven.

"You've lit a light in Bill I've never seen him have," Gene continued. "He walks differently, talks differently, acts differently. He even dresses better."

Uneasily, Orel moved his grip on the steering wheel.

"I mean, you've done all this for Bill. My only question, I suppose, is…"

Orel drew a breath and held it for a moment. His eyes were now firmly fixed on the Skyway Bridge growing in front of them.

"What's in it for you?" Gene asked. "What's your angle?"

Orel slowly exhaled as one inevitable question was finally asked while another was not. *What was the source of the money?* He did his best to keep control of his emotions. His eyes roved over the dashboard as if looking for an appropriate answer there.

Gene noticed Orel's discomfort and turned his attention to his daughter in the back of the truck. Her blonde hair blew in the wind.

Music and static filled the cab. Miles went by without a word when the truck's tires finally rolled onto the pavement of the bridge.

"Pond rippling," Orel said out of nowhere.

Gene looked at him, befuddled.

"Pond rippling," Orel said again. "That's my angle. And successful revenge."

Gene did not answer as the truck climbed the long, high bridge while the dark sun melted to an orange glob into the Gulf of Mexico.

Chapter 16

"Morning, Mrs. Hanson."

"Young lady. Been a while since you've done linen." The old lady's mouth turned downward in disapproval. Her eyes tightened to a squint. "Too busy mutilating crabs?"

Lucy bit her tongue. Sometimes the arguments that are won are the ones not made. She smiled politely and placed the towels down on the pool chair in front of number 16 without replying.

"You were spending a terribly long time in Mr. Hughes' room there for awhile," Mrs. Hanson continued. "Started to worry that you might be rifling through his private property."

"No, ma'am. Just refreshing his towels and some minor cleaning and straightening. He asked me if I wouldn't mind making his room more homey and comfortable."

Mrs. Hanson's chin rose slightly and a small grin grew across her wrinkly face.

"Have a nice day," said Lucy, nodding, and moved on to the next unit. Balancing a pile of towels in one hand, she reached in her pocket with the other and produced the master key. The pop of the lock gained her access to Orel's room once again. No smell of cologne and soap met her this time.

She walked to the bathroom, placed the new towels on the rack and picked up the wet ones on the floor and tub. Balling them up, she returned to the hallway and noticed that the gym bag was in the same spot under the bed as the last time she had been in the room. She felt an itch of temptation when she saw the journal neatly placed on top of the manila envelope and gray cloth next to the bag.

Orel was spending most of his time between the tavern and Dollar Bill's. The chance of him coming home and catching her again seemed unlikely. Lucy sighed, placed the roll of dirty towels down in the hallway and walked to the edge of the bed.

For a moment she studied the positioning of each object. Pushing her cheek close to the shag carpet, she slid face first under the bed. She had gone undetected the last time in this spot and figured it might be safer than anywhere else in the room. The height of the bed from the floor was a large enough space for a twelve year old girl. A full grown adult would have been more challenged.

The sun peaking through the partially shaded window illuminated the room and spilled under the bed. This provided just enough light for reading.

Careful not to disturb the rest of the items, she reached for the journal. She looked for the strand of her hair she had placed between the last pages she had read and was pleased that, after all this time, it was still there. She opened the book and turned to the next page.

6/10/56

Orie is four today. I haven't written since Ronnie died. Haven't even opened it. Haven't had the heart.
Tomorrow is four years. Seems like yesterday. Moving Orie out of this mess. No place to raise a kid. He needs more attention than I can give him.

"Orel lived here," Lucy whispered to herself. She stopped reading for a moment to imagine where that might have been—somewhere on the beach. He never mentioned it. At four years old, he probably didn't remember. It was also odd that he was American by birth, yet seemed so Canadian.

Lucy listened for noises outside of the room but heard only ordinary, muffled sounds. Relieved, her eyes returned to the page.

> *Still working bolita games for Mr. Kronis. It's a lottery with 100 balls. Pick a number and if the ball with your number pops up, you win. I carry numbers and large sums of money back and forth to many bars.*
>
> *Gonna be hard to live without my boy around. It's going to be the best in the long run. Canada seems so far away, though. Least he'll be with family up there. It's for the best.*
>
> *7-15-56*
>
> *Don't know where to start. Can't even sort out my emotions. Kronis and I argued today.*
>
> *7-16-56*
>
> *Didn't sleep much last night. Did lot of thinking. Walk away or fight. Decided to fight.*

She turned the page and found it blank, as were the next five. There were smudges and squiggly lines but no words. One more turn and she came upon a page which was ripped down the middle but hung together at the bottom right edge. Lucy's eyes widened and her nose flared as she read the simple entry executed with poor penmanship and no date.

> *Kronis is a dead man. He slept with Veronica.*

Lucy pulled her hand to her mouth and sucked in a sad gasp. Her stomach turned as she thought of the ramifications of this new revelation. That was enough for today. She closed the journal and laid her head down on the shag carpet.

"My ass he is. My ass," rumbled Kronis into the tobacco-yellowed mouthpiece of the phone. The wet cigar between his fore and middle fingers wagged violently. "I am sick and goddamned tired of all this bullshit! Respect is out the goddamned…window!"

A slight knock at the office door stopped him in mid sentence. He stuck the cigar into his mouth and motioned with his arm.

"C'min!"

The door opened a crease, letting in a line of light and fresh air as Orel's angular profile slowly pushed its way into the smoky darkness of the room. Kronis' eyebrows shot up in surprise at the sight of his unexpected visitor. He eased back in his chair, allowing a long space of contemplative silence to fill the room. He exhaled a white cloud of smoke into the phone as he continued to listen.

Orel's normally light expression was stern and tight-lipped. The muscles in the back of his jaw bulged as he looked around the office.

Photographs of the real estate mogul with dignitaries and celebrities adorned the walls. Cigars and drinks. Actors and singers. Mayors and governors. Even one president. Various plaques and certificates offering accolades and honors hung among the pictures: Lawrence Kronis, Greater St. Petersburg Beach Chamber of Commerce Member. Lawrence Kronis, Board Chairman Development Council. Lawrence Kronis—in commendation of this and that.…

"Okay, you do that. Do what you can to get it handled," said Kronis all of a sudden.. "Okay…okay. You, too. Buh-bye."

He looked up at the back of his visitor with a feigned smile. "Yes, sir. What can I help you with today?"

Orel paused for a moment in his tour of the history of the man's self-importance. Then, realizing he was being addressed, he turned his head in acknowledgment. "You have quite the background here."

Kronis stood up, dabbed the ash of his cigar into a saucer on his desk, and stood next to the Canadian with his hands behind his back.

"Yes, yes, it is starting to pile up. I call it my collection of good friends," he said proudly.

"Not bad to have Mr. Kennedy as a good friend, I suppose. Shame he had to die so young," Orel commented.

Kronis' pursed lips turned into a smile as he looked askance at the man next to him, then back at the picture of himself with the president. "Larry Kronis," he said with an extended hand. "What is it I can help you with today?"

Orel looked for a moment at the hand. Hesitantly, he put his hand out to meet it. "Orel," he answered simply.

"Orel?"

"Hughes. Orel Hughes."

"Ahh, nice to meet you, Mr. Hughes. Hughes? I knew a couple of Hugheses. Of course, there was this one," he said, pointing to a picture of a younger version of himself standing next to a man in front of an airplane named the Spruce Goose. Orel maintained a blank expression as he looked at the photo of Howard Hughes.

"There was another who was a remarkable piano player, who worked for me every now and then," Kronis continued. "He knew how to play all the songs. If you were in the mood for Glenn Miller, he'd play it. Sinatra, you name it. We called him the Hit Man, since he knew all the hits," Kronis continued. "Any relation?"

Orel turned away from the pictures and watched as Kronis puffed smugly on his soggy cigar. The room filled with a gray, reeking haze.

Letting the silence settle, Orel continued to stare at Kronis without a response.

Finally, Kronis said, "So, what is the nature of your visit?"

"Check," Orel said quickly.

"Hmmm?"

"Mr. Eisenrad was tied up today. He suggested I bring a check directly to you."

"Rent?"

"Yes. I'm with Mr. Connor. We're partners in the Dollar Bill's project."

"Ahhh, old Bill. How's that pain-in-the-ass junkman doing these days?"

"Quite well. It seems he's found his calling."

A smile grew around Kronis' cigar. "Hith callin?" he lisped. "Dee onlee callin' Connor knowths is last callin' for alcohol."

"Actually, he's quite an astute businessman," Orel said. "Very keen mind for knowing what the public wants."

Removing the cigar from his lips, Kronis remarked, "So if he's the brains, you must be the bucks."

Orel did not answer.

"And if you don't mind my morbid curiosity," Kronis continued, "where does a young man like yourself get the kind of money to renovate an old dump like the Nearvana?"

"No, I don't mind." Orel responded blankly. "My family invested well. Looked out for my future. It has given me a lot freedom. Freedom to take some chances."

"Yes, indeed. Chances. Sometimes we have to be careful of the chances we take. Occasionally they have a way of coming back to haunt us."

Orel placed the rent check on the desk and took another glance at the wall filled with pictures of friends. "Why didn't the piano player make any of these pictures?"

"Accident," Kronis flatly responded.

"Oh?"

"Terrible accident. Collision." He squinted and bit his lip. "Very bad collision. Wasn't paying attention to what mattered. The Hit Man became incapacitated before he got a chance to be in my collection of good friends on the wall here." He punctuated his sad, yet sarcastic smile with a long drag from his dying cigar. "Accidents happen."

"That's a shame. Terrible waste," Orel said. "My father was a man of considerable talent."

He walked over to another wall to the painting of the young lady. He took time to relish the beauty of the art, the fine lines of the woman's figure contrasting with the rough edges of her surroundings.

Kronis noticed Orel's interest in the painting. "Lovely young lady there, wouldn't you agree?" he asked.

Orel kept his eyes locked on the painting as his jaw tightened. There were ten different things he wanted to say. None of them appropriate. His mind raced.

He almost blurted out, "My father didn't make the wall but my mother did?" He held his tongue.

"Yes, she was," he said and walked out of the room without a goodbye.

The eight ball remained untouched in the center of the table for almost the entire game. Despite the fact that all but three balls had caromed around and eventually knocked into the pockets, it never moved.

When Einstein played Rudy, it was for keeps. Usually a coke or a candy bar was the wager. But this time, the stakes were high. A chocolate shake from Dairy Queen.

"Son, I like my chances," Einstein bragged, stroking his gray mustache as he surveyed the scene. Rudy walked around the table, figuring all the angles and possibilities before settling on a shot. Thoughtfully, he coated his hand in white powder and dabbed some blue chalk on the end of his stick. Then he pointed with his cue toward the table.

"Five in the side."

With great finesse, he sharply tapped the cue ball. It struck the five, which rolled gently into the side pocket, and continued down the green, knocking the eight ball into the rail.

Einstein's mouth turned down at the corners, impressed. "Not bad. But where'ya gonna put the eight now son?" he said. "I've seen you miss this shot a hundred times."

His taunt went unanswered as Rudy calmly walked around the table, taking a close look at the eight ball, which firmly touched the rail. The cue ball was at the opposite end of the table in front of the corner pocket. He deliberately slowed his pace and thought about what Orel had told him: "One day the light bulb will go on and you'll wonder why you were never able to do this before." Determination showed on his solemn face.

Remember—hit a lotta rail and some of the ball. A lotta rail and some of the ball. A lotta rail... He slowly grabbed the blue chalk and ran it over the tip of the stick again as he continued to get himself into position, leaning over the table to make the shot.

A lotta rail...some of the ball...a lotta rail...some of the ball.

With a long and deliberate motion, Rudy pulled the stick back. White chalk fell slowly to the table with its forward motion and blue dust exploded off the tip as it struck cue ball, which rolled rapidly toward the eight ball and the rail.

Einstein watched as the white ball got closer to the eight, then hit "a lotta rail" and "some of the ball." The eight then gently rode the rail in a straight line until it teetered on the edge of the far side corner pocket before falling helplessly into the pocket. The cue ball came to a slow halt in the middle of the table.

"You did it!" Orel shouted from the back of the tavern.

"I did it!" Rudy yelled back, his voice rising to an excited pitch. "I did it!"

He ran around the tavern slapping fives and tens and brushing handshakes with the bystanders. He stopped in front of Orel and threw his arms around him in a big hug.

"Lotta rail some of the ball. Just like you said," he sputtered.

Realizing he was hugging Orel, he pulled back. But beside himself with joy and relief of accomplishing a much-anticipated goal, he hugged the Canadian again, hoping he would understand. He had finally overcome the challenge he had faced for years. "Lotta rail, some of the ball," he rambled on.

"Congratulations, son. I didn't think you'd have it in you," rasped Einstein, offering an oversized, paint-stained palm. "One out of a hundred and one tries. Not a bad average," he mocked as he walked into the shadows of the bar.

"Lotta rail," Rudy started again.

"Nice when the light bulb goes on, eh?" Orel said, laughing.

Chapter 17

Months passed since the light bulb went on, but Rudy had yet to collect on the Dairy Queen bet. Dollar Bill's was in full swing, and Bill was making money hand over fist.

It was business as usual at Sunset Tavern as well, a busy Saturday afternoon with a mixture of regulars, tourists and fisherman grabbing a quick drink in between dropping a line.

Einstein was holding court before an admiring audience. "So what's gonna happen, see, is…they're gonna git up there and once they're in Venus' gravity, they're gonna use that to slingshot the rocket right on to the next planet," he said slapping the counter and then flinging his hand toward the sky.

It was during these monologues that Einstein was in his element and truly lived up to his nickname. He had a knack for appearing to be an expert, able to assimilate recently learned information and convey it to the lesser educated folks at the tavern. He figured his audience was not as well versed as he.

"So, for a period of time, the rocket is actually gonna be fallin' from the sky into Venus," Einstein continued, stroking his mustache. He paused to let it sink in before nodding to Wally, "'Nother Cutty, if you don't mind."

"Gravity assist," came a voice from over his shoulder.

Einstein slowly turned.

"The technical term for it is *gravity assist*," Orel said again, but this time to Einstein's face. "It's kind of like a bank shot in billiards. You know billiards, right, Mr. Rose? And if I'm not mistaken, you still owe Rudy a chocolate shake from the game he won from you some weeks ago."

Einstein defiantly put his drink to his mouth and sipped his Cutty Sark. Wiping his upper lip, he said, "I'm good for it. I don't stiff on my bets. Just haven't gotten the chance to stop by the Dairy Queen with the boy."

Orel backed away and continued looking around the room at the men at the bar who had been listening to the painter's lecture on interplanetary travel. Some had gone back to leaning over their drinks when it seemed that a conflict was going to occur. Sensing their discomfort, Orel continued to steal Einstein's thunder.

"Actually, it's also referred to as the Hohmann Transfer," started Orel, pulling an empty beer glass from the bar. "This happens when one body takes the energy of another and uses it to become stronger." He started to arrange objects in front of him. "Say this glass is the sun. And this shot glass is Earth. This beer cap is Venus. And your glass, Mr. Rose," he said, taking Einstein's Cutty from his hand, "is Mercury."

Einstein breathed in gently and backed away as Orel placed the drink further down the counter.

"Gotta light, Wally?" Orel yelled across the bar.

After his usual mumbling and muttering, Wally tossed a matchbook in front of Orel, who picked it up with one hand and lit a single match from it with two fingers.

"Tonight's launch will originate here from Earth," he started, with the flame next to the empty, beer-stained glass. "It will gain velocity in order to get out of Earth's atmosphere." He passed the flame around the upside down beer cap. "Then the rocket will head for Venus."

The onlookers who had been leaning over their glasses sat up straight in anticipation.

"Using Venus' orbital energy, the rocket will get stronger because of it. And as a result will fly faster. Or, as Mr. Rose was saying, slingshot toward Mercury," Orel continued.

He moved the still burning match until it got next to the wet condensation of Einstein's glass. Glancing toward the painter, he gently touched it to the moisture. The match made a sizzling noise and turned into a smoking ball of sulfur.

"And the rocket will be able to penetrate Mercury's orbit," Orel concluded.

The group contemplated the lesson in silence. Then Einstein motioned for Orel to return the borrowed drink.

When the whiskey glass was firmly back in its rightful place, he lifted it in a toast. "Here's to Mercury. Eighty-eight days in a year. Thank God we don't live there, or we'd be a helluvah lot older."

He guzzled down the remainder of his scotch to the roar of the group.

"Okay, fans, my work here is done," Orel said.

He waved his hand as he walked toward the door. Then he stopped a moment for emphasis. "But when you get finished here, don't forget to stop by Dollar Bill's tonight for the Space Alien Costume Party and Rocket Blast. First prize to the best costume and the best performer!"

A cool breeze hit him in the face when he got outside into the parking lot of the tavern. Although the rest of the Floridians were bundled in windbreakers and heavy sweaters, Orel continued to wear a pair of flowery baggy shorts Rudy had bought him over the summer, plus a tank top and a pair of cheap sunglasses. How funny he must have looked to the bundled up natives. How much funnier he would look to his friends back in Canada.

When Orel got to Bill's house, he noticed the familiar upside down Santa in the front yard. Since it was November and Christmas was around the corner, it seemed only natural to straighten him up for another year of celebration.

"Just goes to show you—if you stay out of fashion long enough, old man, eventually you'll be back in fashion," he whispered as he stuck the Santa firmly into the orange-pebbled front yard and gave him a friendly punch across the shoulder. Stepping back, he admired his work for some time.

After deciding Santa was back where he belonged, Orel walked up to the door and gave it his signature "Shave and a Haircut" knock. Getting no response, he rang the bell. Still no answer. Figuring no one was home, he started back down the sidewalk.

As he passed the Santa at the end of the walkway, he was startled by a muffled voice.

"Hey."

Turning, he noticed that the front door was now slightly ajar and a head poked out.

"Hey, Orel," said the voice again. "How are you? Sorry it took me so long to get to the door, but I was in the bathroom."

"Ma'am," Orel returned, inspecting Lillian's face. "Been awhile. How have you been?"

"I've been fine," she said sheepishly. Her eyes seemed more in focus than the last time she and Orel had spoken. There was also a hint of a smile on her face. "I...," she started hesitantly. "I just want to let you know how happy you have made Bill. Since the time we were married, I have never seen him so positive."

Orel's eyes gleamed as he listened to the mellifluous voice he had never really heard before. The more Lillian spoke, he noticed how much Rudy resembled her features.

"Bill gets out of bed every morning with a purpose. He seems to have a reason to live. It's even improved our relationship," she said with an impish smile that exposed her perfect teeth.

Orel smiled back without a word. He seemed content to listen to Bill's wife string more than two sentences together for the first time since he had known her. He noticed how she opened the door farther, to expose a slender and well-formed figure. A tight pair of pedal pushers gathered just above her calf and accented finely sculpted legs. It was apparent that the effect on Bill was also having an affect on her. She flipped her hair slightly as she continued to speak, well aware of her newfound attractiveness. With each word, Orel could see why Bill had married her.

All of a sudden he realized that the conversation had stopped and he was still looking at Lillian. He had obviously stared too long.

Lillian noticed his discomfort. "So...," she started. "So..."

"I fixed your Santa," Orel blurted out uncomfortably.

"My? Santa?"

"Yeah, front yard," Orel stammered. "Upside down Santa."

Lillian leaned forward to see where Orel was pointing.

"I better go," Orel said to save himself from further embarrassment.

"Okay," she answered with a breathy tone. "Thanks for stopping by."

Orel backed down the sidewalk. As he turned to leave, he stopped dead in his tracks. "Are you coming tonight?" he asked.

But the door was closing already and gently shut. No doubt, she had missed his last question.

Orel laughed to himself and whispered, "Space Alien Costume Party and Rocket Blast! First prize to the best costume and perforrrrrmance."

"What do you think they look like?"

"Green. Definitely green. Or brown. Not like us."

"Well, what are we?" asked Lucy pulling at her skin.

"I think we're pink or tan," Rudy answered, looking at his own skin.

"So you think they lie out in the sun and get greener?" giggled Lucy. "You think the girl aliens look at the boy aliens and say, 'He's cute, but he needs a better green'?"

Lucy's bed was filled with construction paper, felt and plastic. A few bottles of glue and scissors lay on the long, blue shag carpeting among the clutter of cut material. Rudy was busy fashioning large eyes to paste on the plastic mask he had spent the day fitting to his head. Lucy opted for a more conventional alien look, with purple makeup and green eyeliner.

"Loose, you believe in Martians?"

"Martians? Sure, like *My Favorite Martian*. Why not? A guy with antennas coming out of his head. That'd be pretty cool," she answered.

Lucy applied the green eyeliner, making sure to open her mouth the way she had seen her mom do when she was little.

"My dad said that Martians crashed in New Mexico once," Rudy said as he attached one of the eyes to the mask. "Said they have the dead bodies in a warehouse."

Lucy looked at Rudy. Her eyes widened. "A warehouse?"

"Yeah, like a garage. A big place where they keep airplanes and stuff."

"This is pretty cool that your dad is having a party like this, huh?" Lucy said while fitting a triangle blouse to her chest. "Better than his old job. Hard to get people excited about the junk business."

Rudy pulled his alien mask over his head and looked at Lucy. "Boo…"

"Help! The one-eyed alien!" she yelled.

"Boy, with eyes this big, I bet alien moms are always telling their kids, *careful or you'll put an eye out*." Rudy laughed, looking at himself in the mirror. "Or, *your eyes are bigger than your stomach*," he continued, then looked at the protruding alien belly of his costume. "Or maybe not."

"Or, *don't roll your eyes at me, young lady*," Lucy quipped.

They kept trading jokes until the costumes were finished. Lucy's outfit made her look big and beautiful, while Rudy's was all head, eyes and belly.

"Did I ever tell you about the money?" Lucy asked out of nowhere.

Rudy turned his alien head sideways inquisitively. A moment of silence passed until he finally answered. "I'm not sure. What money?"

Lucy's voice became hushed and she looked out her bedroom door to see if her dad was around. Feeling reassured that they were alone, she started. "One day my dad asked me to clean the rooms. You know, change towels and stuff. So I ended up having to change the towels in Orel's room."

Rudy kept turning the alien head sideways with every sentence Lucy said. At first it was funny, but then it finally got on Lucy's nerves.

"Take that off and listen to me!"

Slowly Rudy pulled back the mask and revealed a mischievous smile.

"So, I'm cleaning his room," she started again, "and when I did, I accidentally tipped over a chair. It had a P.E. bag on it."

"P.E. bag?" asked Rudy, fixing his messed hair.

"Gym bag. Had a green guy spinning a basketball on it."

"Celtics. Boston Celtics," Rudy said.

"When the bag hit the floor, tons of money fell out of it."

"What's tons?"

"I don't know. Hundreds, thousands. Tons. A lot."

"Yeah, so? Maybe he's rich."

"I know, but it was like the kinda thing you see in the movies where the bad guy is always running around with a briefcase full of money," Lucy said. "I mean, if you're rich, don't you keep your money in the bank like our dads do?"

Rudy nodded thoughtfully, as he glued the second eye on his mask.

"There were some old pictures and other things," Lucy continued. "There was a book, too. A journal. I've been reading it. Orel's dad wrote a diary. Sounds like his dad got himself messed up in some bad stuff, too."

Rudy pulled his mask quickly over his face. "Orel's not a bad guy!" came his quick, yet muffled response as he fell back on the bed and stared with his two big alien eyes at the ceiling fan.

The late afternoon sky was a mix of burnt orange and purple. A cool, early winter breeze made the palm fronds rattle. Every now and then a gust would blow sand into a mini tornado across the beach. People were milling everywhere on the street. The sun was sinking slowly into the Gulf. Music spilled out of motel rooms and bars all along the boulevard. It was one of those moments that should be captured in a bottle, kept away in a closet and the glass broken only in case of emergency.

"Fallout continues after Nixon's top aide fires Special Prosecutor Archibald Cox," came a deejay's rambling voice from an AM radio on an empty beach chair. "The Mariner 10 is expected to lift off tonight at 10 p.m. And if you're lucky, you might be able to hitch a ride on the Kohoutek comet. It's gonna be quite a night to remember. Speaking of comets, here's a little Bill Hailey."

As the radio seamlessly segued into "Rock Around the Clock," the sun melted into the Gulf with faint applause coming from the far side of Sunset Beach.

"I like what you did there," Bill said, pointing to the sign above the door. "Rocket Blast, and you made a rocket taking off as an exclamation mark. Nice touch."

He was talking to a young blonde in tight shorts and a glittering space suit top. "Thank you, Mr. Connor. I hope to be in advertising one day," she answered, smiling back at her boss with bright innocent eyes.

"Great—that's great," he said, not really sure what she meant, though impressed by her ambition.

Bill walked through the door of Dollar Bill's and was greeted by an explosion of decorations. Space ships and alien heads hung from the ceiling. Planets and stars were pasted on the walls. Each table had its own particular rocket, which was actually a bottle of champagne in disguise. No expense had been spared. Bill saw this as a golden opportunity to cash in on the launch.

"Perfect. It's all perfect," he said as he tightened his tie and adjusted the pinky ring he had purchased earlier that day.

"I got something for you, Mr. Connor," said the young wannabe advertising waitress.

"Oh…what's that, Molly?" he asked, somewhat surprised.

The rest of the costumed waitresses in tight shorts and glittering tops gathered around.

"We all chipped in to get you something," Molly started. "It's not much, really. Just something to show you what a great boss you've been to us over the past few months."

She pulled out a medium-sized box with a card attached.

Bill took the box, looked around the room at his staff and smiled stiffly. Having never been in the position of being appreciated, he was unsure how to behave. His fat fingers worked to open the purple envelope covered with loose silver glitter and partially dried glue. His hands shook slightly when he took out the Hallmark greeting card and read the personal message aloud.

"To a Boss Who's Out of This World! Dear Mr. Connor, Thanks for taking the chance to live your dreams so that we can live ours. Love, the Dollar Bill's Crew."

Bill closed the card and put it back in the envelope, smiling uncomfortably. He turned to the package. "And a gift, too?" he said, exaggerating his surprise. Once again, his fat fingers dug at the rocket ship wrapping paper and glittery bow until he was able to get to the box inside. He opened it slowly to reveal an iridescent orange blazer. Under the jacket was a mask of Richard Nixon wearing antennas and space sunglasses.

Bill chuckled loudly and held up the blazer to read the words on the back. In his best Nixon impression he said, "I am not a Spook!" to the cheerful roar of the assembled crowd.

After offering handshakes and giving hugs to various members of his staff, he yelled loudly, "Let's light this rocket!"

With that, the party started.

It was by far the most electric night at Dollar Bill's up to that point. The place was packed to capacity with just about everyone decked out in some space garb or costume. Booze was flowing and the waitstaff hustled to keep the food coming from the kitchen. Gene sat at a large table surrounded by his motel guests, sharing laughs and cocktails.

Dressed in his bright orange jacket and Nixon mask, Bill looked on as Orel kept the performers moving on and off the stage. An eighty-year-old man played *Yankee Doodle Dandy* on the spoons. Frannie, the shuffleboard lady, whistled *Sweet Home Alabama*. And Robert, the jeweler, played something strange on the harmonica. Then Joe the Chinaman belted out *Bad, Bad Leroy Brown*, always a crowd favorite.

"I've just been handed a note," interrupted Orel huddled over the microphone at his piano. "Although it is getting close to the time for the rocket launch, we have one or two more acts to squeeze in. This next one is a complete surprise to me, as well as to a lot of others in the room. This lady is someone I met only a few months ago, but I've seen her grow over that short period of time. She's a wonderful mother, a wonderful wife and, as I'm sure we're about to hear, a wonderful singer. Please, everybody, give a warm Dollar Bill's welcome to Mrs. Lillian Connor."

Behind the bar, Bill looked on in disbelief from behind his Nixon mask. His wife was not only out of the house, but she was actually going up on stage to perform in front of a crowd of people. He froze in fear, expecting to be embarrassed by the outcome.

Lillian moved from behind the curtain over next to Orel at the piano.

"Hey, Orel," she said with her familiar breathy voice.

"Hello, Lillian. You look like a lovely space creature this evening," he said.

"Why, thank you. Why no costume for you tonight?" she asked, pointing at his simple purple flowered shirt and khaki pants.

Orel looked at his outfit and smiled briefly. "I've been the alien since I got here. So, I figured I'd let you guys see what it's like to be me," he quipped and took the piece of paper she handed him.

Bill's wife smiled kindly and gracefully walked up the steps to the stage as Orel introduced her. "Lillian's going to sing a Carpenters' favorite of mine, *Close to You.*"

The cold blue light reflected off Lillian's shiny silver space suit as she stared back at the faces that were staring at her. Glasses clinked quietly and chairs slid on the floor among a murmur of voices. Many in the crowd knew Bill had a wife, but this was the first time any of them had ever seen her face.

"I'd like to dedicate this song to my loving husband Bill, and to my beautiful son, Rudy," Lillian started in a barely audible voice, too far from the microphone to be heard by those in the back of the room.

Lucy looked at Rudy, who seemed dumbfounded, although the hint of a smile of admiration played over his lips.

Orel stepped away from the piano to help Lillian get the microphone adjusted to her height and speaking voice. Noticing the room's uneasiness, he introduced her again. "Ladies and gentlemen—Lillian Connor!"

A smattering of applause came from the crowd as Orel made his way back to the piano bench and played the opening of the song. As the introduction faded, Lillian began to sing.

"*Why...do...birds suddenly appear,*" she sang in a beautiful voice no one knew she possessed. Her eyes twinkled and she looked in Bill's direction after she finished the first line. Feeling more confident, she opened up a bit and moved around. Pointing to the decorations behind her on the stage, she started the next verse.

Bill pulled his Nixon mask onto his forehead to get a better view. In all the years they were married, this was a side of her he had never seen. He wanted to make sure he did not miss a moment.

Orel vamped on the piano to give Lillian enough time to get off the stage and walk into the audience. Just when she was about to start the next line, she found Rudy and gently pulled off his alien mask.

Lillian looked deeply into his eyes and sang the song to him. The words seemed appropriate about the day he was born and how the angels conspired to create such a wonderful person. Her smooth, soft voice revealed a sincerity that was palpable.

Looking to Lucy sitting next to him, Lillian continued singing about how all the girls would have no choice but to be drawn to this wonderful person. Her eyes twinkled as the she sang about feeling the same attraction. Her hand gently stroked her son's hair as she slowly finished the verse.

Elegantly, Lillian made her way back to the stage, repeating the chorus, which faded gently into the piano's background.

Dollar Bill's exploded with applause as people leapt to their feet to show their appreciation of the performance.

Bill ran up on stage and hugged his wife.

"Ladies and gentleman, MY wife, Mrs. Lillian Connor," he said proudly and kissed her on the lips.

"ROCKET LAUNCH!" yelled a voice over the applause.

Realizing it was getting close to launch time, the crowd quickly filed out of Dollar Bill's into the parking lot in order to get a good glimpse of the historical Mariner 10 liftoff. Bits of conversation about the space program and the fabulous performance by Bill's wife intermingled until a voice from a car radio someone had turned up announced that it was "T minus 10 seconds and counting."

Someone shouted, "9!"

Then the whole group chimed in, "8! 7! 6! 5! 4! 3! 2! ONE! Blast off!"

It was like New Year's Eve. Champagne corks popped and flew, strangers exchanged handshakes and husbands kissed their wives.

After several seconds, a brilliant light could be seen on the distant horizon in the east. It started as a long white flame that turned into a small ball that rose with a bloom of fire. It rose fast and straight into the sky. The crowd oohed and aahed. The night launches at Cape Canaveral were always a thing of beauty.

Gene hugged Lucy as the two watched the rocket ascend.

"I wonder if we can see the comet tonight, too," Lucy asked her dad. "What do you think, Rude?" Receiving no reply, she looked around but did not see her friend. "Rudy?" she called out anxiously, turning her head every which way.

Over by a dumpster, a crowd that had been watching the launch was huddled in a circle. Lucy ran to the group and pushed her way in to find a small alien on his back with two big, empty eyes staring at the stars.

Chapter 18

Lucy still had makeup on from the night before as she stared out the window of the hospital waiting room, studying the dark clouds that were forming over the buildings. One concern kept popping into her head for some reason. *What will the weather be like the day I die? Will it be sunny? Will it be raining? Which would I want it to be?* These are not questions a 12-year-old should have to ponder. If anything, they should be ordinary questions like: *What is my husband going to look like? Will he be tall and good-looking? How many kids will we have? Will we have a dog or a cat? Will we live in a big house? Will we be rich? What will my new last name be?*

Lucy looked at the tattered picture postcard of Alcatraz she had borrowed from her father's jewelry box. Turning it over, she studied the words carefully. *Get out of jail free.* Still, the five words yielded no answers.

"'Scuse me, Miss Lucy," came a large, gentle voice from the other side of the waiting room.

Startled from her reverie, Lucy turned quickly and when she was able to focus her eyes, noticed a tall black man holding a bouquet of flowers.

"Leroy," she said, surprised. "What are you…? How did you…?"

The questions were never finished, but Leroy somehow knew what she meant.

"It got through the grapevine. I think Miss Joyce from ya daddy's place got da word out in our church," Leroy said. "In our group, word tends to spread, Miss Lucy." He smiled kindly at the forlorn looking girl. "How is he?"

"We're not sure," Lucy said slowly. "He fell down last night at the party and hasn't woken up since."

"Is it cause a da pains, ya think?" Leroy said.

Lucy looked at him blankly.

"Ya know, da pains," Leroy continued. "He's had da belly pains fa long time. Usta fall down a lot when we'd fish. Sometimes he'd throw up. Other times he'd fight it off and keep on fishing. Tough nut. I kept tellin' him, Roo, you gotta go to da doc, but he jus' nevah listen."

"You knew he had a problem?" Lucy asked incredulously. "I just found out about a month or two ago. And we're best friends. I can't believe he told you before me."

"Well, Miss Lucy, wasn't much chance not ta tell. His actions speaks louda than words," Leroy confided. "It's hard not ta tell somebody somethin' when dey is coughing up blood all over next to ya."

"Lucy, who are you talking to?" interrupted Gene, entering the room.

"Oh, hi, Daddy. This is Leroy."

"Hello. Leroy?" Gene said hesitantly, extending a hand.

Leroy rearranged the flowers around his chest to free his right arm and swallow Gene's hand in a massive paw. It was the old fisherman's main tool for feeding his family.

"Leroy is a fishing buddy of Rudy's and came by to pay his respects," Lucy said slowly.

"Respects?" Gene snorted. "He's not dead. It's just a coma. There is no need to pay respects."

Lucy looked up at him with remorseful eyes. "I didn't...I didn't mean that he was dead. I'm sorry," she stammered.

"I'm sorry, too, honey. It's just been a long night. Nice to make your acquaintance, Mr. uhh...Leroy."

"Pleasure's mine, sir."

Gene looked down at Lucy, whose face was streaked with makeup from the drying of old tears, and gave her a sympathetic smile.

Far down the dark hallway, a doctor could be heard speaking to Bill. "We won't be sure until we perform some more tests, but preliminary indications are that this coma is induced by a condition referred to as hyperinsulinism." He rambled on in the face of Bill's blank expression. "His body, specifically his pancreas, produced an inordinate amount of insulin, which caused his system to have an adverse reaction and subsequently caused your son to slip into a coma."

Lucy eased her way past her dad to the door of Rudy's room, which was slightly ajar. The pale green walls made a stark contrast with the red lights of the monitoring equipment hooked up to the patient. Since Lucy was not accustomed to hospitals, she had a hard time looking at her motionless friend with various tubes and wires plugged into him. Her eyes wandered and she saw Lillian sitting in a chair, praying the rosary. She had never known his mom to be a religious person. Perhaps in moments of trauma God seemed a viable option.

Down the hall, Bill continued to listen stone-faced to the doctor. His mood changes were marked by inarticulate physical outbursts. At times he would be attentive, then he would walk away flailing his arms. Occasionally, he squatted down near the floor and pushed his hands through his hair.

"Ready to go, hon?"

Gene was at the door, nervously spinning his car keys around an index finger.

"Uh, yeah, Daddy," Lucy answered awkwardly.

She had not called him Daddy in years.

Paper napkins and bottles littered the tables. Ashtrays brimmed with burned out cigars and crushed cigarettes. The work lights of Dollar Bill's washed out the carnival atmosphere of the night before. Orel worked vigorously over the washbasin, cleaning a tray full of glasses.

The front door opened with a slow creak, causing Orel to stop what he was doing.

"We're closed for business," he yelled toward an elderly man shuffling into the bar.

The man did not respond at first. He moved his head slowly from side to side, looking around the room. Occasionally, he stopped, shook his head and muttered something to himself. His baggy clothes hung on him like a windless flag on a pole. His shoes were muddy and flat soled, seemingly accustomed to much walking.

Orel picked up a towel and dried his hands while the man settled down in the first booth he was able to find. "Sir?"

"If you pardon the hackneyed expression," the man started with a raspy whisper, which cleared when he eventually coughed, "I like what you've done with the place." His baggy eyelids drooped over a pair of sad eyes that took in the room nostalgically.

Orel came around from behind the bar and approached the man cautiously. "We're not open for business, my friend," he tried again.

The man seemed oblivious to Orel's comments. "You've done a fine job," he remarked, looking at the ceiling for an extended time. "Fine job. Those beams up there always were a nuisance. Termites. Bastards don't sleep. Just keep eating till one day it all comes crashing down."

Orel bent over so his head was eye level with the man and sighted up to find the beams in question. His mouth fell open the longer he held his head in that position.

"Yeah, eh?" was all he could muster.

The man pushed a powdery gray strand of hair off his forehead. "Pity about the heydays. You're too damned busy to pay attention to them when you're in them, and all you can do is think about them when they're gone. Probably one of God's best practical jokes," he said.

Following another raspy cough and a fading chuckle, he extended his hand to Orel. "Harry...Harry Covington. I used to own this joint. Used to be one of the most important sonsabitches around here. Used to be...ahh, used to be."

Orel straightened up, exhaled and extended his hand. "How you been, Uncle Harry?"

A slow smile grew across the man's face. His watery, bloodshot eyes glistened with a twinkle. "Orel! It's been years, my boy. Too many years. Nice to see you again. You were quite a youngster the last time."

"Yeah. You, too, Uncle Harry. Your name has popped up quite a bit in conversations around here."

"All good, I hope."

"All good. Especially where matters of veal are concerned, Everybody on the beach raves about what a great chef you were," Orel said with a wink.

Harry inserted a cigarette between his lips. "What brings you here and now? Well, besides your dad, rest his soul, of course," he said, patting his coat pocket for a light.

There was a popping sound as Orel lit a flame quickly with a bright green book of Dollar Bill's matches and pushed it in front of Harry's face. He offered no answer and flailed his hand to extinguish the match.

"Your old man did well to get you out of here. Too much crap for a boy. Children should be able to have a childhood. Enjoy life before it turns to shit like it always seems to in this line of work," Harry rambled on between long puffs. "Best damned piano player I ever heard though, your dad. The Hitman." He coughed with a melancholy laugh. "Smart, too. Quiet. Smart ones are always quiet. Dumb ones shoot off their mouths, removing all doubt."

Orel grinned in approval. "Yes, Daddy was a man of few words. Spoken ones at least."

"Stupid sonsabitches. If they'd only shut their own goddamned mouths, then there would have been no worries. But everybody's gotta run their mouth. There used to be honor. Damn used to *be* is a pain-in-the-ass word anymore, as far as I'm concerned," Harry said.

Orel sat with his elbows on the table looking for the man he had known as Uncle Harry when he was a boy. He searched in his present ruined state for signs of the quick wit and a razor sharp mind for business he'd once possessed. But all he could find was bitterness, which seemed to have eaten away at the core of what used to be a wonderful man.

Harry sat up straight in his chair when he noticed he had developed a slouch. As he pushed his chin upwards, a heavy bag of skin gathered tightly against his neck. He reached toward the ashtray in search of the cigarette he had placed there only seconds earlier. "These bastard make their deals, sell their real estate, talk their talks," he said, shaking his head slowly in disapproval. "They want their delicious meals while their live piano player tickles the keys in the background. Do they not expect that live piano player to have ears? To be a human."

"What'd…what'd Daddy hear?" Orel asked apprehensively. He was not sure he wanted to know the answer.

Harry looked up from the table into the deep blue eyes of his nephew. "I think, son, the question isn't what did he hear. More a question of what didn't he hear," he mumbled with a shake of his head.

Orel knew this conversation was inevitable. As a small boy, the stories of his dad's reputation seemed romantic and faraway when he overheard them at the neat, ample dinner table in Canada. But now he was about listen to a tired old man spill them out onto a messy table, cluttered with condensation rings of drinking glasses and cigarette butts.

"Your dad couldn't help it. He knew too much. After awhile, things pile up. Once you know things, you end up getting involved," Harry said.

Orel wiped at the table nervously.

The old man suddenly gathered himself and said with unexpected force, "That sonofabitch Kronis. Nothing but an errand boy for the Tampa gang. Helped run the bolita money in the '40s and '50s. Occasionally he'd be in on a hit here and there. After that, he comes to the beach, thinks he's gonna be the next Florida Boss. He's a petty crook with some good connections. And an ego bigger than his brain. Has his own way of doing things. Sometimes when bodies turn up, there's rumor that it was a Kronis job.

Always something about the hit that makes you wonder what the hell the guy was thinking. Kronis' Law they call it."

Orel's eyes were locked on the man's wrinkled, quivering lips as his uncle proceeded to wobble his way through one story after another.

"Your dad, Jonny, did a little work for them. Deliveries as far as I could tell. 'Hey Hitman, run this over to Tampa,' I'd hear them say a lot. Not sure why he got mixed up in all that nonsense. He was very talented. I think he got a little confused after your mother died. She was all he had in the world…and then you. He always told me how much he worried about you. Losing you. Moving you. From the looks of it, he made the right call."

Orel inhaled slowly and held his breath for a moment.

"Things got strange after a while. Goddamned president gets shot, bodies start turning up all over the place. Nobody comes in the joint without some bullshit breaking out. Jonny started to change, right along with it. Lotsa arguments."

While Orel expelled his breath, Harry looked around the room to make sure no one was listening. Then he continued, "Some money ended up missing and some titles were stolen. He made a fine living, why would…why…you know…from those bastards? Kronis would as soon eat his own son as kiss him. Your daddy knew these guys better than anyone. The whole thing doesn't make any sense. Anyway, nothing ever came of it…even after his accident. Rumors were all that he left behind. Even one that Jonny buried money on the beach somewhere. Can you believe that shit? Like a goddamned pirate!"

When he noticed Orel's perturbed expression. Harry softened his tone, "Well, son, I've probably said too much. But that's all an old man's got. His memories. His words."

"And what happened to you, Uncle Harry?" Orel started, his quivering voice rasped like sandpaper.

"Me...I just got tired. Sick...and tired."

Harry crushed out his cigarette and tried to get to his feet from the deep seat of the booth. Orel grabbed him by the elbow and helped him stand. Harry took Orel's arm and wrapped it around his shoulder. Orel followed with the other arm as the two embraced.

"You be careful with these guys, son. They're dangerous. They have no regard for human life," Harry whispered into Orel's ear. "It's all about money. I kinda get the idea you're like your old man, though. Smart, like Jonny."

When the two men separated, Harry pulled out a handkerchief and dabbed his eyes and nose.

"Don't be a stranger, Uncle Harry," Orel mumbled, doing his best to keep his composure. "Stop by here again."

Harry nodded as he put his handkerchief back in his pocket and headed for the door. Before he made it all the way out, he stopped. "Orel," he yelled, "don't let your heydays get away, kid!"

Then, the old man turned back toward the door, shuffled out and disappeared into the blinding white light of the day.

The church steeple loomed ahead as the car approached the building.

"Daddy, would it be okay if you dropped me off here and let me walk?" Lucy said, looking out the car window.

"Right here?" Gene asked, shooting her a questioning glance.

"Yeah. I'd like to walk and think."

"Okay, honey. But please don't be long. I'd like to have an early dinner in case Bill needs me for anything this evening."

Lucy nodded to her father, gave him a peck on the cheek and got out of the car. A cloud of dust twirled in a circle as Gene drove away. Lucy stood and watched to make sure he was out of sight before she walked up the steep steps of the church.

Her father had been a devout Catholic, but became less of one after her mother left. Lucy had tried to go to church by herself on occasion, but never seemed to make it a habit. For some reason, she was drawn toward it today as if compelled.

The glass door opened slowly and she walked inside, inhaling the musky odor and looking at the altar up ahead. The silence of the place always amazed her. Unlike other churches she had visited, the Catholic church always seemed to be very quiet. Whether it was almost empty or full of people, only a chair squeak or an occasional cough would break through the sense of serenity and peace.

Lucy walked halfway down the center aisle and sat in one of the pews. Pushing the heavy kneeler down made a bang that echoed off the terrazzo floor and all the way up to the vaulted, plastered ceiling. She knelt and clasped her hands as she looked up at the statue of Jesus hanging on a cross. *He must be in so much pain. How is he doing it? How long had he endured such pain? Why didn't he tell me?*

She bowed her head to pray. "God," she started, then giggled uncomfortably and grimaced. "Hi," she started again. "I know I don't come here as often as I should, but can you help me? My friend Rudy...well, of course you know Rudy. You know everything right? So, of course you know Rudy."

Lucy let out a frustrated sigh when she realized she was talking in circles. She gathered herself and suddenly pleaded in earnest, "He's just a kid. Please don't let him die. I...I need him.

He's my…he's my best friend. If I lose him, I don't know what I will do."

She shut her eyes, forcing herself to concentrate. "I tell you what, God. Let's make a deal. If you help him, I promise I'll come here every Sunday for a year. No, two."

Lucy opened her eyes when she heard the doors to the church open. The clicking of heels on the terrazzo church floor pierced the silence. A tall man walked past Lucy and made eye contact with her. She held his gaze for a long time as he passed. A nervous breath quivered in her lungs when she realized it was the man on the pictures in Orel's room—Lawrence Kronis.

Startled to see the man she had read about, she averted her eyes toward the kneeler.

Kronis continued down the aisle and settled in the second pew. Moments later, Lucy could see the silhouette of a familiar figure in the glare of a stained-glass window. He walked toward Kronis and joined him in the second pew.

Lucy peered through her praying hands and whispered, "Einstein."

Kronis seemed calm while Einstein appeared more animated in their discussion. The photographs she had found in the manila envelope hinted at some sort of wrongdoing. What was Einstein doing in the company of such a nefarious individual as Lawrence Kronis?

"Excuse me, miss. The church is closed. You'll have to leave."

A nun in a black habit loomed over her.

"Closed?" Lucy asked, as if trying to understand the meaning of the word. "The church is closed?"

"Yes, the church is closed right now. You'll have to come back after three."

"Closed," Lucy said again. "God has hours?"

The nun stood over Lucy without an expression and simply pointed the way to the door. Lucy got to her feet and looked again at the stern woman. She motioned to the two men sitting in the second pew. "What about them?"

"They are permitted to be here," the nun said, continuing to point the way to the exit.

Lucy made sure to get in the last word. "Well, I hope God is working, even though the church isn't open for business," she said sarcastically before she walked out the front door.

On overcast evenings, the sunset merely darkened the gray sky. There was no spectacle, no applause, just day turning into night. In the matter of one day, Dollar Bill's had gone from a bustling locale of bright activity and celebration to a hollow room of somber worry. The crew was understandably concerned about the health of the boss' son, though nobody said a word.

Bill sat in the corner reading that day's newspaper account of the rocket launch.

"Can I get you something?" asked Molly.

In a world of his own, Bill continued to fix his gaze on the headline: MARINER 10 LAUNCH IS A BLAST.

"Mr. Connor," Molly tried again.

"Huh? Oh hey, Molly. What?" Bill stammered.

"Get I get you anything?"

"Uh, yes, honey, a coffee," he struggled.

"Yes, sir."

Bill pushed his head back into the newspaper. The sedative the doctor had given him to calm his nerves seemed to be working more on his attention. He rubbed the newspaper and noticed how the ink left a black mark on his fingers. "If they could put a rocket in space, why couldn't they get a newspaper's ink to stop rubbing off on your hand?" he wondered out loud.

A shadow fell over the table and made Bill look up. Orel was standing over him. His bright face was a welcome change from the drab hours of seeing his son lying helplessly in a hospital bed with tubes coming out of various parts of his body.

"Have a seat," Bill offered with a lazy smile.

Orel sat across from Bill with a questioning look.

"A coma brought on by hyperinsulinism. Whatever the hell that means," Bill slurred. "Hyper…insulinism. I can't even say it without laughing. Funny word."

Orel smiled kindly.

"Running tests and more tests. Christ, the kid's had more tests today than he's probably had in his whole time in school." Bill's feigned laugh turned into a sob. "They say he's comfortable. How do they know that? They don't know that." His voice was beginning to get loud enough to be heard throughout the bar.

"Here's your coffee, Mr. Connor," interrupted Molly.

"Thanks…thank you, honey. Thank you," Bill said, nodding and touching her hand in appreciation.

As he slowly stirred some powdered cream into the coffee, he looked at Orel. "This life can be a pretty cruel joke sometimes," he said. Then, he pulled his hands close to his face and noticed his pinky ring. "You just can't have it all, can ya? You just can't have it all. I spent my whole life busting my ass to pay the bills. Keep my wife from killing herself every other week. I work my junk business to stay afloat. Take a chance, thanks to your help. Get somewhat successful. My wife starts to feel better… Now my only son is lying in a ffffaa…a hospital bed. It's just no goddamned fair." Bill's eyes filled with tears that worked their way down his cheeks.

"Bill, why don't we get you home so you can rest?" Orel said. "Everything's gonna work out fine. I'll take care of business tonight, buddy."

"I appreciate that, Orel."

Bill struggled to find his feet after a while and slowly made his way to the door. Orel watched his partner walk away. Then he reached in his breast pocket and pulled out a yellowed business envelope with worn edges. "Attn: Lawrence Kronis" was typewritten on the front. He ran a finger over the stamp in the upper right hand corner. The left corner held no return address, but there were marks of having been rubbed for many years.

Of the many effects his father had left him, the envelope was something of a mystery. Orel thought of what his dad had written in his journal. If you've gotten here, you need to finish the job that I started.

He was sure his dad had intended for him to be far out of town by the time this letter was sent, but circumstances had made that not possible. He had gotten himself dug back into the place from which his father had removed him all those years ago, and he had no desire to leave until the mission was complete.

After hearing what his uncle Harry had told him and considering the implications, Orel decided it was time for the addressee to get the letter. He would finish what his dad had never gotten the chance to do, regardless of the consequences.

Chapter 19

His hand rubbed at the smudge where a return address should have been on the envelope. The six-cents stamp was worn well into the paper and held similar dirt marks. The two-cents stamp was bright and clean by comparison. His name, Lawrence Kronis, stared at him in mockery. It wasn't so much the envelope that bothered him, but the message inside.

> *I have hesitated for years to send this to you. If you are reading it, apparently I have gotten up the nerve. You took from me, so I took from you. Your just rewards lie beneath your nose or more specifically your feet. They can be found under the Nearvana stage. Two hands two fingers left off the main spot... two hands two fingers down.*
> *With respect due to someone of your ilk,*
>
> *Jonny*

"Where would you like to go, sir?" the driver asked into the rearview mirror of the black limousine.

Kronis looked up from the envelope and did not immediately respond. His eyes wandered about, looking at nothing in particular, but his mind raced with options.

After a long silence, he finally blurted out two simple words. "Dollar Bill's."

Lucy stared at Rudy's pale face. A flap in a cylinder on a machine next to his bed moved up and down each time he took a breath. She thought of the scariness of the words, *life support*. The fact that an electric plug that made her *Suzy Bake Oven* light bulb hot was now the same thing helping Rudy breathe was too much to comprehend.

This was the third day Rudy was in a coma. He had not moved a muscle since the night of the rocket launch. The doctor had told Lucy that people in comas could actually hear what was going on around them, so she read *Mad Magazine* to Rudy during her visits.

She had found the October edition in his backpack. The cover had a picture of a ship sinking in the background with Alfred E. Newman overboard and his feet dangling above water in an S.S. Poseidon life ring. In many ways, Rudy was Alfred E. Newman. "What, Me Worry?" was a motto that fit both of them perfectly. Even in a coma, Rudy looked as if he did not have a care in the world.

"How long have you been here, honey?" Lillian asked, slowly pushing her slender frame against the heavy hospital room door.

"About an hour, I guess, Mrs. Connor," Lucy replied. "I was just reading Rudy, *The Lighter Side of Sinking Ships.*"

Lillian looked at her motionless son connected to the machines. She did not seem to hear what Lucy said, but nodded politely as if to say, "that's nice." A Bible in her hand and rosary beads around her wrist indicated how she intended to spend the evening with Rudy.

"Okay, Mrs. Connor. I'll leave you two alone now. I need to get some schoolwork done anyway. If the Rude Man wakes up when I'm not here, tell him to get his butt out of bed already," rambled Lucy in her best effort to sound nonchalant.

Lillian smiled kindly but sucked her lips to her teeth to hold back the urge to cry.

On her way out, Lucy bumped into Bill. "Oh, excuse me. I was just...just leaving," she huffed excitedly.

Bill looked down at her and smiled. "We both appreciate the time you spend here with Rudy. It means a lot to us," he said nodding at Lillian for agreement. "He has a good friend in you."

"Thanks, Mr. Connor. I really need to get going."

Bill looked after Lucy leaving. She went through the swinging door, which opened immediately again as Rudy's doctor entered.

With clipboard in hand, he started right in. "Thanks for getting down here on such short notice, Mr. Connor."

"Doctor, you remember my wife, Lillian."

"Yes, Mrs. Connor. Randal McKenzie. Nice to see you again." He hardly broke his stride. "Your son has been doing very well considering the circumstances. We're monitoring his vital statistics, and he seems to be getting stronger every day. It should just be a matter of time until he wakes from this comatose state. As I told your husband, his body was exposed to an alarmingly high rate of insulin, which caused a condition called hyperinsulinism."

Bill shook his head as he listened. Lillian looked at him for comfort. He squeezed her hand to let her know it would all be okay.

The beeping of the machines monitoring Rudy built to a crescendo as Doctor McKenzie gave a thorough review of possible diabetes, dialysis, pancreatic malfunctioning and kidney disease. Bill and Lillian had a difficult time keeping up with all he was telling them.

"So, you're saying he's going to be okay?" Lillian finally asked. Her fingers played rapidly at a rosary bead as she looked at the doctor. "I mean, is he going to live?"

"Well, we won't know his true situation until he emerges from the comatose state," the doctor said gently. "We won't know the proper treatment until he wakes up."

The larger of the two boxes on the dolly presented a struggle for the delivery man to squeeze through the door. When he finally managed to get his load inside and in the back room of the restaurant, he wiped his brow with a handkerchief and looked for the person in charge.

Orel was focused on finishing a complicated doodle. He scrawled lines frantically and glanced occasionally at a magazine on his desk. From time to time, he would turn the paper over and fold it in half. It was not until the delivery man piped up that Orel snapped out of his creative trance.

"One CCTV camera and one Philips video cassette recorder. Making a movie?" asked the deliveryman, placing a packing slip on the desk to be signed.

"Eh? Ha. No, more trying to catch a culprit," Orel said, signing with a flourish. "We've had some suspicious activity in the back area over the past few weeks. Boxes of produce missing. Looks like the lock on the walk-in cooler door was picked, too. I'd like to see if we can't set a trap and catch the bad guy."

The deliveryman nodded.

"The key is going to be hiding it all so that whoever is doing this doesn't know it's there," Orel said. "'Cept yourself, of course. The boss doesn't even know I'm doing this."

"It'll be our little secret, sir. Amazing the technology they've come up with these days, huh? Good luck in your hunt," the deliveryman said as he pushed his dolly out of the restaurant and back to his truck.

A white Fleetwood Cadillac pulled slowly into a parking spot under the Dollar Bill's sign. Kronis stared up at it from the back seat of the vehicle. He paused for a moment, allowing the driver to run around and open the door for him.

"I'll be out in thirty minutes," he mumbled, then made his way toward the front door of the bar.

"Will there only be one today?" asked the cute hostess, ready to help the silver-haired man find a table. Without answering, Kronis continued walking past her.

The place sprawled out before him as he walked closer to the stage. To patrons who looked up from their tables, the man seemed familiar, although they were unsure of where they had seen him before. His eyes squinting in disapproval had them quickly return to their meals as he ambled past.

When he got to the edge of the stage, he tipped his head back to inspect the various lighting configurations on the ceiling. He followed the microphone down to the floor and determined the stage's center. His eyes moved back up to the ceiling and back to the floor again.

"She's a beauty, eh?"

Startled, Kronis turned and saw Orel wiping his hands with a dish towel.

"Had to do a little work on the floorboards, but you kinda expect that sort of thing with a building this old," Orel continued. "Termites and wood rot tend to tear these things up over time."

Not amused by the Canadian's lighthearted conversation, Kronis looked past him toward the bar's office and the empty chair inside. "Where's the boss?" he asked.

"His son has an illness and he's tending to that important matter at the moment."

Kronis pushed past Orel, bumping into his shoulder, and took a seat at the vacant end of the bar. As he unbuttoned his jacket, he searched his pockets for a cigar. He lit the end of the Romeo y Julieta Piramides with a gold-plated lighter. The cigar gave off a heavy white waft. Sucking on the end methodically, Kronis' radiant blue eyes squinted against the irritating burn. He looked up at Orel who was by then leaning an elbow on the bar.

"What can I do for you, sir?" Orel asked, staring back intently.

"Do for me. That's funny."

"Well, you are here either to eat or to have a beer," Orel said with a slight chuckle. "Or is there another motive for your visit?"

"Motive? Interesting choice of words."

Kronis twisted his pinky ring on his finger with his free hand, and spun his chair around to inspect the establishment further.

"Full-time job running one of these joints," he remarked, not engaging Orel for an answer. "Lotta work."

"Yes, sir. Restaurant ownership is a big responsibility," Orel answered, still staring. "Nothing to be entered into lightly."

"Ownership?" said Kronis and guffawed. "Ownership? You're an occupier. You don't own anything. You simply use this place. You're a user. Ownership requires harder work than you could possibly know. You and that junkman are nothing more than maintenance men for the bank. And that bank is me." His face began to redden. "If anybody owns anything, it is I who owns you."

"Ownership is all in who possesses something at the time. And at this point, we possess this place. After all, possession is nine points of the law, sir," Orel said, condescendingly.

Orel's tone stopped Kronis' inspection of the bar. He looked at the ceiling momentarily. Then he dropped his head deliberately until his eyes found Orel's.

"What are your thoughts about the postal service?" Kronis asked as if out of nowhere, two lines of smoke pouring lazily from his nose.

A blank look replaced the little smirk on Orel's face. "Well, I suppose it's a necessary evil," he remarked. "Until something else comes along that can provide correspondence among friends and clients, of course."

Kronis' lip curled as he frowned. "Do you feel the service is timely enough?" he asked blandly. "Say, I sent you a letter. How soon would you expect that letter to be delivered? Two, three, four days tops?"

"I'd say that should be pretty proper service in the States."

Ignoring Orel's take on the United States Postal Service delivery expectations, Kronis plunged his hand into his jacket in search of something else.

"I've found in my business dealings," he started on another tack, "that people possess one of two characteristics when it comes to matters of courage."

Orel remained quiet. The hum of conversation could be heard in the background from the smattering of patrons in the restaurant.

A sheet of white smoke poured out of Kronis' mouth as he continued, "Either they are incredibly *stupid*, or they possess a magnificently large pair...of gonads."

The muscles in Kronis' jaw were beginning to seize and their strands were becoming more defined as they rippled. "Which camp do you feel would best describe your approach, son?" he asked as he dropped the yellowed business envelope onto the bar.

Orel pushed up off his elbow and stood up straight while wrapping the dish towel around one of his hands. He was about to respond when a menu appeared out of nowhere on the bar.

A cheery voice asked, "What will you be drinking today, sir? Our specials include she crab soup and a dozen oysters on the half shell. Can I start you off with an appetizer?"

Kronis' eyes remained locked with Orel's as he politely nodded to the waitress. "Thank you, no, my dear. I am just leaving."

He stood slowly, pushed himself away from the bar and strolled toward the door without further word, paying special attention to the stage on his way. The yellowed envelope remained on the bar.

"Game on," Orel whispered loud enough for the waitress to hear.

"What?" asked the waitress innocently.

He took his eyes off Kronis walking out the door and pointed his head to the television above the bar.

"Game on?" he repeated and deposited the yellowed envelope in the garbage can.

"Sir," the driver greeted his boss, holding the door for him. One last look at the restaurant and the Dollar Bill's sign and Kronis flopped into the back seat of the Cadillac in disgust. Reaching to the floor, he grabbed a briefcase that was pushed up against the back of the front seat.

"Give me a moment," he said to the driver who nodded and remained standing beside the car.

The two clasps made a warm, popping noise as Kronis opened the briefcase positioned on his lap. He picked up the handset of the phone that was mounted to the floor of the case. After seven quick taps on the digital keypad, he stared out the car window in quiet contemplation.

He pulled at the coiled phone cord, waiting for an answer at the other end. After four rings, someone picked up.

"Yeah."

"Enough's enough," Kronis bellowed into the receiver. "The kid's gotta go. We cut off the money supply. We take over Covington's place again. I need to get back in there and take care of some unfinished business. Don't worry how it looks. Just make sure he is hurt enough."

"Yes, sir."

Kronis allowed a long pause to compose his emotions. His breath quickened until he was able to exhale the anger which had been building since his conversation with Orel. "Make sure you…" he started and then stopped.

"Sir?" came the response from the other end.

"He plays, too. I understand he's as good or better'n his old man. Make sure you mangle every one of his fingers."

He threw the phone down into the briefcase.

The setting sun made a silhouette of the car and the driver who stood waiting patiently for his boss to summon him back to work.

Chapter 20

Lucy sat and watched a sparrow leap from bush to bush. There was a large prickly pear cactus in the vicinity, but the bird seemed to know to keep its distance. This was either a lesson learned from experience or one wired into its system by instinct. Occasionally the sparrow would drop down to the pebbles, tilt its head sideways and look in Lucy's direction as if it were seeking her approval to go on.

What is his goal? Why is he here? Why did he come back? These questions, asked of a sparrow, might come with easy answers, but applied to Orel, got a lot more murky replies.

He could have left this place after a few weeks of hanging out to continue what would surely have been a wonderful life. He would meet a beautiful woman, settle down and raise an equally beautiful family. What was his goal in seeing the mission his father laid out through to completion? The risks seemed to outweigh the gain.

Her morning chores of cleaning around the pool deck were already done. This time instead of keeping half-smoked cigarettes for later, Lucy threw them in the garbage. With her smoking partner in the hospital fighting for his life, it seemed like the perfect time to kick the habit.

The verbal dance and towel exchange with Mrs. Hanson, which was becoming an irritating necessity, had transpired just minutes earlier, but Lucy could feel the old lady's eyes burning holes in the back of her head since she sat down at the patio table without finishing her appointed rounds.

It was probably the sparrow which kept her from the next stop, room 17, just over her shoulder. She sat and watched the bird until it suddenly flew past her head in search of better hunting.

A polite nod to Mrs. Hanson and Lucy was on her way to Orel's room. The lock popped with ease and the familiar, soapy scent of cologne pleased her as always.

Lucy uttered the requisite "room service" announcement, more for the sake of nosy Mrs. Hanson than for Orel, since he had been gone since sun up.

Once inside, Lucy put the clean towels on a chair by the door and gathered up the dirty ones that Orel had placed in a neat pile on the floor.

She noticed that the room was more organized than normal. His toiletries were packed neatly in his shave kit and his toothbrush had a travel cap on it. Around the corner, she found his suitcase on the stand for packing next to his bed. A few shirts were folded and sat in a pile next to a stack of nicely pressed slacks. Paired socks of white, tan and black were arranged in a neat circle between the other clothes. Either Orel had just finished laundry or he was thinking about checking out of the motel.

Lucy ducked her head under the bed looking for the gym bag and then scanned around the room. She ran to the foyer, but it was not there either. When she lay on the floor by the bed, she located only the journal. The gym bag with the smiling man spinning a basketball on his finger was nowhere to be found.

Lucy studied the positioning of the journal and the familiar manila envelope by its side. She pulled herself under the bed and assumed the reading position to which she had become accustomed over the months. Drawing her face back slightly, she noticed that there was a piece of notebook paper wedged between two pages of the journal.

Lucy's stomach rumbled as her nerves finally caught up with her. The state of the room, the disappearance of the gym bag and the newly placed notebook paper in the journal all pointed to a change in the status quo. She still had the opportunity to get out from under the bed and go about her business, but something kept her there.

She opened the journal to where the paper had been inserted. As she pulled it out and laid it on top of the journal, she recognized the familiar, beautiful penmanship. Her heart leapt to her mouth when she saw the two words at the top.

Dear Lucy...

The room spun and she was unsure whether to get up and run or to keep reading. Why did Orel write her a letter? And worse. Why did he put it in the journal?

She opted not to run, but started again from the top.

Dear Lucy, I know after all this time, you and I have become quite a fan of reading my father's memoirs.

Lucy's face drained of all its blood and she felt faint. Since she had covered her tracks well enough, it was anyone's guess as to how he knew. Paralyzed by fear and embarrassment, there was no choice but to continue.

I know I have learned a lot about my upbringing, my father's dealings and possible outcomes of becoming intertwined with such nefarious characters as those around these parts. I've been given a tall task by my father to exact revenge on these people for various wrongdoings they have brought upon my family.

The reason for this letter is that in the event that anything were to happen to me, you would be the first to realize it was not an accident. As such, I would hope you would take this journal and the accompanying envelope to the proper authorities. I have followed my father's will and connected the dots of all the bad guys involved. The only thing lacking is a smoking gun. After long, thoughtful contemplation, I've made a decision on how to proceed. At this point there's no turning back. With any luck, my plan goes smoothly and we can go on our merry way.

However, in the possibility I come to harm, I would ask that you stay true to my requests and carry out my wishes. I put this on you only because no one else is as well versed in the history of this matter, and I believe you would see it through to fruition. Assuming you are able to do this anonymously, no harm will come to you in the least. Thank you for being such a good friend over the past months and for allowing me to come into your life.

Love, your buddy, Orel.

Lucy's heart pounded. The thought of anything happening to Orel was too much to stand. Quickly she arranged things the way she found them and scurried out of the room.

The back cage area of Dollar Bill's was a nuisance. Not only did it attract crime, but it was an eyesore as well. Every piece of refuse from the bar and restaurant eventually found its resting spot in this location.

The large, green metal dumpster just outside the cage was usually the center of the mess. Garbage pickups only came by the bar once a week, which meant that things tended to pile up right before trash day and congeal into a black watery pool of noxious odors.

Oftentimes, Bill would assign a member of his crew to make it presentable in case there was a surprise visit from the health inspector. But this time, Orel took it upon himself to tackle the job. A green pickle bucket of chlorine and a common garden hose with a reliable nozzle always proved to be the best weapon against the greasy buildup. Usually, whistling a tune made the time it took to do the mundane chore pass quickly.

This time required something more, however. After considerable hunting among his LPs, Orel pulled out a selection which he thought would do the trick of making a nasty job a little less so. He flipped the power button on the turntable, dropped his choice onto the thin spindle and lowered the needle arm to the third track of the Rolling Stones,' *You Can't Always Get What You Want.*

A dusty, gritty intro of noise peppered the speakers before a beautiful choir sang the first verse.

Orel sang along with the refrain to help things get started. With a slop of soapy bleach and a confident shot of water from the hose, he worked his way around the back area. He had found that the best way to get through a difficult job was to make a game of it. He saw the garbage as the enemy and his to job to banish it from the world.

Lucy wandered toward Dollar Bill's deep in thought over the revelations in Orel's letter. As she got closer, she could make out the slender figure of a man dancing by himself, as if nobody were watching. Orel was lost in the moment. Lucy positioned herself behind the pole of the sign for the best spying position, so she could observe without him noticing.

She suddenly realized she was in a unique situation. He knew she had been sneaking into his room, or so he thought. If she never mentioned the letter he had written, he would never know if she read it or not. If he ever approached her about reading his dad's journal, she could deny the whole thing.

Lucy smiled as she watched Orel. He seemed so innocent and fun-loving while doing such a filthy job. He helped the Stones sing the song while he waded in garbage up to the ankles of his rubber boots.

She quickly left her hiding spot and ran over to Orel. "You get what you need!" Lucy belted.

Startled by the sudden accompaniment, Orel snapped around nervously. When he realized that Lucy was his duet partner, he softened his glare and relaxed his tight lips. "That's right, Lucyball!" he shouted over Mick Jagger's crooning. "Glamorous work, eh?"

"Somebody's gotta do it, right?" she countered.

"How's Rudy?"

"Lazy kid's still sleeping. Just like him to take a nap when there's dirty work to do," she joked. Then, her smile faded and she looked up at Orel. She puffed out her cheeks and let out a long breath.

Orel put down the hose and leaned the mop against the dumpster. He pulled off the heavy rubber gloves and threw them on top of the murky, white mop head. Then he walked to the turntable and lifted the needle so the two could hear each other. With the side of his fist, Orel banged on the wall underneath the record player. It fell open gently, revealing the video cassette recorder hidden behind it.

A single finger pushed a button on the machine, then another button, and an electronic door popped open on top.

Lucy eyed the contraption that had the letters VCR emblazoned on its front. She watched as Orel pulled a black rectangle cassette tape from the door and inserted another in its place. With a gentle push, the door on top of the machine was once again closed.

"About time for a soda, eh?" he offered.

Orel got behind the bar, washed his hands and wiped clean a spot in front of Lucy.

"What'll it be, ma'am?"

"7-Up. With a cherry," she said meekly.

Orel's abilities as a bartender had progressed to the point of easy comfort with the tricks of the trade. He scooped ice into the glass with one smooth swipe and popped the top from the 7-up bottle. Glass in one hand and bottle in the other, he poured in a long arc and stopped just in time before the soda ran over the rim of the glass. A splash of bubbles erupted into the air as he expertly plopped a cherry into the drink. For a final touch, he inserted a bendy paper straw and slid the glass down the bar. It made a half circle to the left, then a half circle to the right and came to a proper stop in front of Lucy. Finishing off his trick, Orel placed a napkin neatly next to the glass with the half full 7-Up bottle on top.

Lucy looked at the drink that appeared in front of her in amazement. "Are you good at everything you do?" she asked inquisitively. "I mean, you make everything look so easy. If I were to do that, there would be ice and glass all over the place."

"All is possible to which we apply our mind," Orel answered with a deep, silky voice and a confident gaze.

An involuntary grin spread over Lucy's sullen face. "It's pretty funny," she started. "I didn't realize how much I hang out with that jerk, Rude, until he decides to sleep the day away."

"Ahhh, a classic case of phantom limb," Orel responded.

"Phantom…limb?"

"Well, yours, of course, is very temporary," Orel started. "There is a condition which people who lose an arm or a leg—amputees—go through. They won't have, say, a leg for years. But one day they feel the need to scratch an itch down the side of the calf on the leg that is no longer there. It becomes sort of a phantom. A ghost. The leg is still there in the mind, despite the fact that it's not there in body. Rudy's not present at the moment for you, but you still have an itch like he's there."

Lucy's eyes widened. "I was never big on ghosts stories," she said, laughing.

Orel gave Lucy a wink and finished cleaning a pile of glasses in the sink. "What are they saying?" he asked, looking up through a steamy haze. "How long's he gonna be in the hospital?"

"I didn't really hear anything. They just said they have to wait until he wakes up," Lucy rambled with a half-bitten straw hanging out of her mouth. She continued to watch as Orel worked his way through the tasks of cleaning up Dollar Bill's. The rest of the crew was not due in for a few more hours. But he was hard at work and probably had been since early in the morning.

"I saw a guy at the hospital who Rudy fishes with," Lucy said, poking at the cherry in her 7-UP. "Leroy…is his name. He said he knew that Rudy was sick for a long time. Said he kept falling down and puking all over. How do you think he kept it from me for so long? I never knew there was anything wrong with him. At least till we went tomato picking. He laughed so hard that blood came out his mouth. He said he had something going on with him. I told him to go to the doctor, but he wouldn't listen." Lucy sat quietly, drawing lines in the condensation on her glass. "Well, he's at the doctor now."

"Leroy couldn't get him to go to the doctor either," Orel said from beneath the counter. "Maybe Rudy just didn't want you to worry about him."

"Yeah. Mr. *What, Me Worry?*"

"What's that, honey?"

"Nothing."

Orel pulled himself from under the counter and pushed a box out of the way so he could move more freely behind the bar. He pulled a ballpoint pen from behind his ear and started to make a list.

"You think he's gonna die?" Lucy asked abruptly.

Nibbling on the pen, Orel stopped what he was doing and leaned forward on the bar in front of Lucy's face. "No," he said firmly.

Lucy stopped playing with the condensation bubbles on the side of her glass and leaned back on her barstool. "What makes you so sure?"

"I get a vibration about it."

"A vibration? What are you talking about?" Lucy asked, shaking her head.

"A sense," Orel explained. "Rudy's a survivor."

Lucy grinned.

"His story is not finished. He is going to do something. What it is, we don't know yet. But his story is not finished," said Orel waving his arms gently in the air. "He's got more pond to ripple yet. Trust me on this one. My vibrations are about ninety-five percent correct."

Seeing Orel's confidence, Lucy sat up straighter in her chair and felt a warm rush of hope surge through her body. It was a feeling she had not had since Rudy became ill.

"Besides, he can't go anywhere till he gets the present I have for him," Orel said, tapping his side.

Lucy pushed herself over the bar to see the outline of a rectangle in Orel's flowery shorts. It looked like some sort of box. She gave a long slow nod and smiled at Orel. Her smile quickly faded when she began to remember the things he had written in the letter. She watched him go about the work of washing glasses that were left over from the night before. Her mind told her to keep her mouth shut, but her heart blurted it out.

"Why are you doing this?" A hot flush spread over her face when she realized she had broken the promise to her herself. "What's in it for you?" she continued.

"This?"

"Yes, this!" she answered incredulously. "You're a very talented person and you are washing dishes and hosing off garbage. What are you doing this for? You could be playing the piano or teaching people how to live. You are wasting your life here. You could be making a lot of money with all the things you are good at."

Lucy sat back realizing she had opened a can of worms and they were wriggling about everywhere. She watched as Orel wrestled with the question he had obviously posed to himself many times.

The silence that hung in the air was broken only by the whine of the hose in the back area.

"Well," he started, careful to measure his words and demeanor. "Talent and ability are just things that are loaned to us. What we do with them is our own business, I suppose."

Lucy was seeing a side of Orel that had not presented itself before. His statements sounded well thought out and well-rehearsed. He seemed to have waited for someone to ask the question, almost at peace with himself.

"Some people know what they are supposed to do in life," he persisted. "I think you are one of those people, Lucy. Your life will unfold in a few short years. It will all make sense about what you're supposed to do with it. Like water rolling downhill in dry dirt, it will find the way to its proper level. Others, like myself, have it thrust upon us and must make a decision on which path to take. We have to figure out the puzzle for ourselves."

His eyes got a faraway look, as if he had already made the decision about which path he had chosen.

"It's sort of like Dorothy in the *Wizard of Oz*," he continued. "She got to the fork in the road where the Scarecrow was hanging. She asked him which way to go. The Scarecrow made a case for either path. But ultimately, it was her choice they ended up following. Those are the decisions we have to live…or die with."

The last three words scared Lucy. She squirmed on the barstool and could not look him in the eye. There was an uneasiness growing between them—he wondering if she had read the letter and she holding back that she had.

"I gotta go now. I need to…. My dad's gonna get upset with me…if I don't," Lucy stammered, pushing the stool away from the bar. "I need to go."

The letter and subsequent conversation were too much for her to handle in one morning. She was feeling the weight of the world on her shoulders and the only person she could discuss it with was standing right in front of her. For some reason, however, she lacked the strength or experience to take the conversation any further.

"Wait. You didn't finish your 7-UP. Here. Put it in a to-go cup."

Orel pulled a wax paper cup from a long stack, spun it in the air, and bounced it off his knee. It landed squarely on the bar. Tilting the cup sideways, he poured the liquid and ice from the glass. He then picked up the bottle of 7-UP and topped off the drink with the remainder. With a Frisbee motion, he topped the cup with a plastic lid and spun the container to Lucy.

Lucy smiled admiringly. "Thanks for the drink and the pep talk," she said.

"All part of the bartenders' code and job description," Orel replied, laughing. "And, Lucyball…"

Lucy stopped and looked at Orel before she got to the door. "Yes?"

"Don't forget to do some pond rippling, darling."

"You can't always get what you want," Lucy answered with a sad smile. The pit of her stomach knotted with tension as she turned and walked out the door.

Lucy was experiencing conflicting moods on her way back to the motel. While Orel's outlook on Rudy's future seemed so bright, his own seemed anything but. *Could it be that anything was possible?*

A slow rumbling noise interrupted her thoughts. In the distance, she could see an old car coming toward her. It was Einstein in his old jalopy.

He pulled the dirty Ford Fairlane close to the curb next to her and called to her, "Little girl, where are you off to this fine afternoon?"

Lucy did not answer immediately, but then stopped and looked in his direction. "Heading back home, if you must know."

"Why don't you like me?" asked Einstein, thrusting out his lower lip to feign a sad face. "I never did anything to you!"

Lucy always had an uneasy feeling around Einstein, but on this occasion it seemed to be worse. She felt violated by his sickening stare. She thought for a moment about possible smart answers, but did not offer a reply. Instead, she turned deliberately away from the car and continued on at a faster pace toward her home.

The old painter watched her for a few steps and stroked his paint-stained mustache. "I never did anything to you," he whispered again. He suppressed the huff of a laugh and pulled the car away from the curb.

When she felt she was far enough away, Lucy looked over her shoulder and saw the eggshell Ford Fairlane drive off toward where she had just been.

After dealing with a pesky phone solicitor for several minutes, Orel went back to the job of cleaning up the greasy mess in the trash area out back. When he opened the door, he noticed the nozzle of the hose whining from the pressure of the water. A trail of greasy, off-white soap made a path down the hill to the dumpster.

Though the mess seemed to be a bigger job than he had anticipated, he walked over to the record player and dropped the needle to let the Rolling Stones accompany him the rest of the way. Underneath the record player he used two fingers to press play and record on the Philips VCR. Carefully, he pushed the false wall back over the machine to conceal its existence.

A grainy melody restarted in the speakers. Orel sang along as he shuffled in the watery muck to retrieve his rubber gloves from on top of the mop.

He slowly pulled the first one up to his wrist. As he reached for the second, he felt a jolt and hot numbness in the back of his head. Another jolt followed. Then a sharp flare in his side.

The record kept spinning and the blows kept coming. Another jolt to his head. A white flash hit his eye. The jolts kept getting hotter. The blows kept getting faster. A sledge hammer bludgeoning one hand. A heel stomping the other.

The greasy trail of water continued to flow down to the dumpster, turning from off-white to pink and then bright red.

The hose whined as the water pressure built. The Stones' song about unfulfilled desire and need trailed off into an instrumental interlude.

There was a movement, she was sure of it. Ever so slight, but it was noticeable. Lillian had been there almost every waking hour, looking for signs of change in Rudy's condition. This is the first time she noticed anything at all. She pulled her face closer and could see an eyelid flutter.

"Bill!" she screamed. "Bill!"

A nurse pushed the door open quickly and Bill followed seconds later.

"He's moving!" Lillian yelled, waving her arms frantically for him to come. "He's waking up!"

Another nurse pushed her way in, followed by a doctor. The first nurse politely pulled Lillian away from the bed, so the doctor could get a better look at what was happening. Lillian found Bill and he wrapped his arms around her.

Rudy's eyelids fluttered some more. Then he pulled his hand to his head to wipe them and was startled by the people looking at him. His eyes darted around the room and his face was full of questions.

"You're at Palms of Pasadena Hospital, son," Doctor McKenzie explained in a calm voice.

Rudy made an effort to speak, but life-giving machinery in his mouth and throat made it impossible.

"You're going to be okay, honey," said Lillian, her voice scratchy and tears running down her cheeks.

Bill's face was a mix of smiles, tears and relief. He bit his lip to hold back the rush of emotion that wanted to come out. Grabbing his son's hand and squeezing it tightly he nodded in reassurance that everything would be okay. His expression spoke the words his mouth could not utter.

A slow whir grew in the distance. A siren. An ambulance pulled up to the Emergency Room entrance downstairs. Bill walked over to the window to see what was happening. A team of nurses and doctors rushed through the door to meet the arrival.

"We have a white male, early twenties," barked a nurse pushing a gurney through the double doors of the Emergency Room. "He's lost a lot of blood. Unconscious for undetermined amount of time! Severe trauma to the head, chest and abdomen. Massive trauma to the extremities, too!" When the nurse got inside, she flipped a box to the admin at the counter. "This, and a wallet is all we found on his person."

The receptionist behind the counter looked at the box the nurse had given her. "Jujyfruits?" she mumbled and then read the note on top.

> *To Rudy,*
> *A little treat for after you wake up. Just remember to save me the black ones.*
> *Love, Orel.*

Chapter 21

A good Florida rainstorm in the winter usually means a cold front is right behind. Although the temperature drops, the sky gets clear and the sun shines.

Lucy sat on the edge of the pool watching the chilly November breeze blow tiny waves across the water. She dangled her toes in the deep end to see how long she could tolerate the numbing cold. She wanted to make her toes feel the same as the rest of her body.

Her best friend was still in the hospital, but he was finally awake. Another friend, to whom she looked up to for guidance, was in the same hospital. The whole thing made no sense.

She repeatedly snapped a tape measure in her hand. Occasionally, she would look at one inch. She had heard her dad say that "Orel was beaten within an inch of his life." *What must it have been like to get hit by a crowbar, a sledge hammer and the tool which twists the nuts off a car tire.* The three weapons of choice seemed so heavy and dirty.

If Molly had gotten there and found him fifteen minutes later, Orel would have been dead. As it was, machines were keeping him alive. She thought about why. She felt ill at the thought that Mr. Kronis had offered to help with running Dollar Bill's since the owners were going through such hard times.

She had probably been the last person to talk to Orel. His last words rang in her head and haunted her. "Don't forget to do some pond rippling, Lucyball." The more she thought it, the more she said it. "Lucyball." The more she said it, the more she wanted to let it all go.

So she said it again. "Lucyball." And again. "Lucyball." One time it was angry. The next time it was sad. With each growing utterance came a new wave of emotion. "Lucyball! Lucyball!" She thought of Rudy. She thought of her mom. She thought of her dad. She thought of Mr. Connor and Mrs. Connor. She thought of those bastards who beat up Orel.

"It's okay, honey," came a warm voice from above her. Gene untangled his daughter from her fetal position under the patio table where she had crawled. His strong, tan arms wrapped around her while his cologne provided comfort, too. "It's okay, sweetie," he said. "We'll make it through this."

Tears welled up between the blue slits of Lucy's eyes. Her mouth was pasty, wet and sad. "I've gotta do what he asked," she mumbled. "I gotta do what he asked me to do."

Gene held his daughter, unsure of what she was rambling on about. Her crying picked up and the only thing she could get out was a barely audible, "I love you, Daddy." She hugged her father tighter than she had ever hugged him before. It seemed they were hugging for more than just Rudy and Orel. They were hugging for the first time in a long time.

Einstein pulled his car slowly into the tavern parking lot. A cloud of dust followed in a slow circle as the car came to a halt in one of the many available spots. A creaking sound accompanied him as he pushed the door open. Paint cans and rollers clattered when he slammed it behind him. His gas stick lay buried under a collection of unfolded drop cloths. He slowly wobbled his way to the outside counter of the tavern and hailed the bartender.

"Wally, start me off with a Cutty and we'll see where the sails take us," he slurred, making it obvious that he had already set sail for some time.

Placing the glass of Scotch in front of him, Wally said, "It seems you've had a few a dese already taday. So you're on a two-drink limit."

Einstein looked at him with a tilted head. One eye stayed closed as his lips turned downward, but he could not muster an appropriate comeback.

Wally stood in front of the painter for another moment, waiting for a wisecrack, then walked away when none came.

"Happy day, ma'am," Einstein yelled across to the bar to Dorothy, inappropriately loud for the mood of the place.

Dorothy looked up briefly and put her head back down, staring at her drink.

"Whas' da matta," Einstein slurred. "Cat gotchure tongue?"

Wally pushed his face in front of him. "She's quite upset," he said. "She's not too happy about the Canadian…being plugged into a wall ta stay alive."

"Ahhh, the Canadian," answered Einstein, perking up to the subject matter. "We shoulda done a better job…ahhh, never mind."

"You better get outta here," Wally said grabbing the glass from him. "I think it'd be best if you go home an' sleep it off. You may say somethin' you end up regrettin'."

Einstein's mouth turned down again. He pursed his lips and pushed himself away from the bar. "Suit'ch your self. Jus' money outta your pocket."

Wally turned his back on Einstein who stumbled back to his car.

"I'm sorry, ma'am. You din't need to listen to him taday," Wally whispered, exhibiting unprecedented compassion.

Dorothy did not answer. She only smiled with puffy eyes and nodded from behind a wall of smoke.

Deep furrows lined her face from lack of sleep, but Lillian still found a way to remain attentive as Dr. McKenzie threw out a barrage of words that went right over her head.

"Rudy's going to require dialysis sessions and several insulin injections on a daily basis. His kidneys are in bad shape and his pancreas is not functioning properly," Doctor McKenzie said. "It's not supplying adequate amounts of insulin needed to sustain sufficient sugar levels in his system."

Bill listened from the window in the same way he would have if the doctor were a mechanic telling him how many things were wrong with his truck. While he trusted the man's opinion, he still felt like he was being sold a bill of goods regarding his son's health.

Dr. McKenzie rifled through the clipboard of charts and notes, as if seeking reassurance among the papers. "It appears that Rudy's kidneys have deteriorated to the point that it would be necessary to place him on a donor's list if a family member did not qualify as a suitable host. As I previously stated, the pancreas is an issue as well and may require replacing. This would force us to look in other directions."

Lillian glanced at Bill who by now was deep in contemplative stare.

"In this scenario, we would look at options for a cadaver donor," The doctor continued.

"Cadaver?" yelled Bill jumping back from the window. "What? A dead person?" He paced anxiously around the room. "A dead person!"

Doctor McKenzie took a moment to allow him to digest the information. It was obvious he had experience with volatile reactions of this kind.

"Yes, Mr. Connor," he answered calmly. "The second option would be more ideal if a double transplant were to be required. Since pancreatic transplants are still in the experimental stage at this point and it requires the entire organ, deceased hosts are the only viable option. Therefore, the cadaver donor would be the source of the kidney donation as well."

"And if we didn't decide to go for a transplant?" Lillian started quietly. "Rudy…What should we expect for Rudy?"

"Dialysis to be certain, ma'am," Doctor McKenzie replied. "A greatly compromised quality of life. A considerable amount of daily pain or discomfort and ultimately, premature mortality. Rudy would not live much past his late twenties, I'm afraid, ma'am."

Lillian gasped as she raised a worn tissue to her mouth and nose.

"The main concern here is the waiting list. Since there are far more people in need of organs than there are donors, there is a considerable line of people on the list ahead of him," the doctor said, looking over a pair of bifocal glasses.

Lillian and Bill looked at each other. The two were stranded alone in their despair. The options were obvious. The solution near impossible.

The sound of a pair of worn-out shoes shuffling into the room was drowned out by the beeps and blips from the life support equipment. A thin-skinned, old hand touched the dark purple, bloodied knuckles. They were the knuckles of someone who put up a good fight. The mangled fingers told another story. A soft creak joined the other noises as Uncle Harry lowered himself into the chair beside the hospital bed.

He sat there silently for a moment looking at Orel's face, which was collapsed inward and not recognizable. Had he not heard the stories and not been told by the nurses that this was the correct room, Harry would not have believed that he was looking at Jonny's boy.

His head shaking from side to side in disbelief accompanied the up and down motion from Parkinson's. Harry's head rotated in a complete circle as he looked at the horrific damage that had been inflicted.

"God help 'em," he whispered. "God help 'em."

He had heard the prognosis several times already, from the doctor in charge to the nurses who changed the dressings. They all said the same thing in different words. Even if by some miracle Orel opened his eyes, the brain trauma would likely cause him to remain a vegetable the rest of his days. Man made electricity was the only thing keeping Orel from dying.

"Ya know what your daddy's favorite song was?" Harry asked the inert shape lying before him. He waited a moment in case Orel figured out the answer, then continued. "He played it with such passion. Barely touched the keys. Tickled them. His eyes always closed when he played it."

Harry closed his own eyes and started to sing softly, *Oh Lord My God, when I in awesome wonder consider all the worlds Thy hands have made…how great thou art…how great thou art…*

A light tap at the door startled him, ending his whispered rendition.

"Pardon me, sir?" said Bill, looking disheveled. "Sorry to bother you, sir, but I wanted to visit for a moment with Orel."

Harry motioned for him to come in. "Of course," he said, struggling to get to his feet.

"No need to stand, sir," Bill said, meeting him in the middle of the room. "Hello."

"Hi ya," said Harry with a hand extended. "I'm Orel's uncle, Harry."

"Uncle?" Bill asked, surprised. "Orel talked about uncles all the time, but he didn't mention a Harry. Are you from Canada? I didn't realize anyone had come into town yet."

"Harry..." he said with his hand still extended. "Harry Covington. Nice to meet you."

"Harry Covington?" Bill asked. "Harry *Covington*? Orel's *uncle*?" He paused awkwardly before he grasped the old man's hand, realizing he was face to face with the legendary owner of the Nearvana who just happened to be Orel's uncle.

The old man pointed to the chair next to Orel's bed. "You mind?"

"No, sure," said Bill.

Harry shuffled back to the chair and eased himself down gently. The same, soft creak whined as Harry got himself comfortable again.

Bill looked at Orel's crushed face and shook his head.

"Good partner?" Harry asked.

"Him? He was..." Bill caught himself. "He is amazing. His zest for life is unbelievable." His voice quivered as he spoke. "I've gone over this in my mind a thousand times and I can't figure it out. He didn't have any enemies. Who would have done this? And nothing from the joint was taken. The register wasn't touched."

Harry's gaze remained fixed on Orel's face as he began, "They're dangerous men. Powerful men. It's much bigger than you would imagine."

His head began to shake in circles again. "I made mistakes. With them. They never considered me all that smart. So I wasn't a threat. Smart scares them."

"Well, shit, they must think I'm a pussy cat," huffed Bill, biting his lip when he realized his profane utterance. "Sorry."

Harry shook his head. "Orel came back," he started.

"Came back? From where?"

"His daddy, Jonny, was in the inner circle with them. He realized things were getting out of hand. Somewhere along the line, his daddy knew this was no place for a child. So he moved Orel up to live with some relatives in Canada."

Bill's mouth opened wider with each new revelation about his battered partner.

"Jonny was hoping to join him, but it didn't pan out," Harry said with a slight cough. "As they say, accidents happen." He pushed his chin down to his chest. "One cliché after another. He spent a few years hopping from family to family."

"So why did Orel come back?"

"Probably the same reason you drive slow past a car accident. You know something really bad has happened, but you wanna see for yourself." Harry wiped his lip with the bottom of his palm.

The beeps from the machines continued. A red dot formed a line, signifying that there was life at the other end. A sucking noise indicated that air was being forced into Orel's lungs.

"But that doesn't answer why..." Bill gestured with a hand in the direction of the bed. "I mean, if these guys did this, why? What's the point?"

Harry laid his chin in his hand. "This looks like an accident," he said reluctantly. "You have anything vested in that joint? If you do, you may be best off to get it out."

"I didn't put up any money if that's what you mean. Orel staked the whole project," Bill explained. "Sweat and goodwill is all I brought to the table. And Kronis is taking care of things right now."

The color drained from Harry's face. "Kronis," he gasped. "You gotta walk away. No…run!"

"What?" Bill shook his head. "What are you talking about? He's the damned landlord. Giving me a hand till I can get through this bumpy period. As soon as my son's better, I'll be back to work."

"No. Listen to me," Harry said, his eyes fixed intently on Bill's face. "Go there. Get whatever means anything to you and walk away. Don't say a word. Just walk away. Go back to whatever it was you did before and don't look back."

He pointed his head at Orel in the bed, as if to drive his point home. "I've just signed some papers. This will be over soon."

Bill stood in the middle of the room. The beeps were loud, sending a message. The words spoke louder.

The sun had nowhere to hide on this evening. Although the view from the hospital window was not as spectacular as from the seawall, it stirred Rudy's heart and comforted him as a reminder of a normal world outside.

"Got any kings?" he asked.

Lucy looked through the pile of cards she was juggling.

"Go fish."

"Got any eights?" she said after a pause.

"Aww, man. Yes." Rudy exhaled. "Got any threes?"

"Go fish," Lucy answered and then looked over the top of her cards at Rudy. "You scared?"

"Picked up a three!" Rudy yelled. "Got any aces?"

"One ace." Lucy slowly handed him the card, but didn't let go, still expecting an answer to her question.

"You think Orel's scared?" Rudy countered.

"I don't think he knows enough to be scared."

"You think he was scared when he got beat up?"

"I don't think he had a chance to be scared."

"Then I'm not scared," Rudy insisted. "Got any sevens?"

"Go fish."

The hospital room door swung open and Rudy's parents arrived full of energy.

"Could we have a moment, Lucy?" Lillian asked. Her face was vibrant and her hair was brushed back neatly. "We've got to talk with you, Rudy." She turned to her son, not waiting for an answer.

Lucy threw her cards into the big pile. "Sure. I'm gonna go down to the snack machine. Anyone want anything?"

"Pop Rocks if they got 'em, Loose," yelled Rudy after her. He looked at his parents, not sure what to expect. "I hope she heard me."

"Sweetie, I hope she didn't, because sugar is not your best friend right now," Lillian said.

"We've got some great news, Sport," Bill started, unable to contain his enthusiasm. "We've got a donor!"

As Lucy walked down the hall, she nodded to each nurse she passed. They all seemed so nice. But the lime green walls gave her a sick feeling. *How odd to have a hospital make you feel ill.* People were gathered at the main desk as she came to an opening in the hall-way. Nurses and secretaries conversed about their personal lives and daily activities at the hospital. Behind the desk on the wall, Lucy noticed a big bulletin board with names. She looked for Rudy's.

"Con…nor," she said under her breath as she worked her way down the board. "Connor, there it is, room 402." Then another name jumped out at her. "Oh, God," she mumbled. "Hughes… room 417." She looked back and forth around the square desk. *He's on this floor. He's right here.* "Oh, God," she mumbled again. For a moment, Lucy stood motionless in the middle of the floor.

"Can I help you, miss?" asked one of the women behind the desk. "Is there something I can do for you?"

Lucy did not answer at first, her mind racing. Then she blurted out, "Candy machine! Which…way's the candy machine?"

The woman pointed toward the end of the adjacent hall. "About three quarters of the way down the corridor."

Lucy nodded in acknowledgement and headed slowly in that direction. Out of curiosity, she looked at the first door in the hallway. "411," she read. Noticing the candy machine four doors away, she put her head down and made a beeline to it.

When she got there, she looked at the choices. Bit O' Honey sounded good, but there was also a Three Musketeers bar. As she reached up to insert a quarter, she saw the backward reflection of the numbers seven one four in the candy machine glass. She stood frozen for a moment and exhaled slowly, then spun deliberately around and mumbled, "417."

Lucy put her hand on the dark green door, her heart pound-ing. She leaned heavily on the door, which resisted her slender body at first. Pushing harder, she entered the room with her eyes to the floor. Her stomach felt as if it had been kicked and turned upside down. When she got all the way in, she worked up the courage and lifted her head.

"Oh, God!" she gasped. "Oh, God!"

She saw the bandages, the blood, the collapsed face. She saw it all. Her eyes darted every which way. She wanted to run, but she could not move. Her breathing was rapid, and it made her dizzy. "Oh, God!" she repeated again.

She forced herself to slow down. She owed this to herself. She owed this to Orel. For a moment, she closed her eyes and regulated her breaths. When she had regained her composure, she raised her eyes and looked at her friend. She had to steady herself again before taking the chair next to Orel's bed. It gave off a light creak when she settled completely into it.

As Lucy's eyes moved up and down Orel's body, a blood blister on his forehead made her wince and her mouth fell open in shock at the sight of his bloodied knuckles. His fingers pointed in all the wrong directions. It was as if each wound told a story. She looked at the disfigured face and thought how beautiful it was only days earlier.

"You..." she started as a single tear trickled down her cheek. "You never got back to me—about who ripples your pond."

The room was deathly quiet when Lucy noticed the mangled left hand stir. She held her breath, unsure whether to call a nurse or wait and see what it was trying to communicate. She opted for the latter when it pointed to a tray next to the bed.

On it was a water glass, a small flashlight and a pen with *Palms of Pasadena Hospital* written on the side. Lucy scooped up all three items to present them to Orel. She held up the water glass to his one open eye. A hand with mangled fingers wrapped in gauze waved it off. The small flashlight got the same response.

Lucy was left standing with the pen in her hand. When she placed it on Orel's stomach, his hand began gyrating again, this time toward a chair in the corner of the room, where a clear plastic bag with his personal effects lay flat against the chair's flowery cushion.

Lucy gathered it up and placed this on his stomach, too. Her heart sank as she shuffled through the contents. A pair of flip flops with dried blood were surely not needed at the moment, and a pack of gum was of no use. The only item left was Orel's billfold. She held it up and the deformed hand seemed pleased.

Holding the wallet open for him to inspect, she rooted among American and Canadian dollars bills, finally landing on a piece of paper wedged between them. Orel's hand motioned for Lucy to remove it. She tweezed the paper out with her newly painted fingernails and unfurled it.

Orel opened his curled hand and allowed Lucy to place the unfolded paper in his palm. She looked at his open blue eye, the white of it blood red, and allowed her hand to stay on his for a moment.

With all the strength he still possessed, Orel clasped the pen and scrawled on the paper. His hand moved fluidly, as if not attached to his otherwise lifeless body. Stopping and starting up again painstakingly, he managed to draw two parallel lines, then drew some more. When the message was done, his hand fell limp and dropped the pen to the floor.

Lucy stood in front of Orel, tears streaming down her face. No sounds came as she mouthed the words, "I love you."

Then she removed the paper from his stiff right hand, stuffed it in her jeans pocket and ran from the room.

Chapter 22

Through the metal Venetian blinds of the large cold room of the Veterans Hospital, the full moon seemed sliced into blue slivers. It was far more austere here than in the cozier surroundings of the Palms of Pasadena Hospital. The smell of moldy walls mixed with alcohol added little to the atmosphere. But the fact that the VA was a better facility to perform a double transplant made it seem more bearable.

Bill had been sitting next to Orel's comatose body for three hours, watching the red line jump and fall. The beeps were exactly one second apart. Every once in awhile, Bill would look at the second hand move on the big ugly clock over the bed to make sure this was the case.

At this point, it seemed like a countdown. The operation was scheduled to be performed in five hours—8 a.m. sharp—which meant there were only about eighteen thousand more beeps till it was over. Math is easy when there is nothing else to do but think.

Bill pushed back the greasy strands of hair, which fell in front of his eyes every time he leaned forward. Occasionally, he looked down at the scribble he made on the mini note pad—*O negative*. It was what the nurse had told him about Orel's blood type. "O negative is the blood type of the universal donor," she had said.

Orel was the universal donor.

"I really 'preciate this, partner," Bill whispered in a shaky rasp. "You've…" He started, then looked over his shoulder to make sure the door was closed. "You've done so much," he started again. "You've done so much for me and my family. But this is big time. And you don't really have much say in the matter. I…uh…wish I had a better chance to thank you." Bill laid his chin in his hand and stared at Orel's crushed face. "I mean, if all he needed was a kidney, I'da been the first one on the table to give it to him." Bill's eyes pooled with tears. "I'm not the most sensitive sonofabitch in the world, but that kid's all I got."

Abruptly the machines beeped faster, startling Bill. He looked at the clock. The pace was now at two beeps a second. He sat up in the chair and looked at the door, wondering if he should get help. He jumped up and paced the room. "I met your uncle. Nice man," he said. "This whole thing was really his idea. Something about 'surrogate decision maker.' Said he can make these decisions for you, since you can't make 'em for yourself." He stopped and looked at Orel. "He told me about your dad. He sounded like a good guy, too. Wonder why you never told me about him."

The beeps returned to normal, and Bill cautiously sat back in the chair to resume his vigil.

Lucy stared at the television as a blond weatherman bubbled over with enthusiasm. "It's going to be a wonderful day in the Bay area today, folks. Highs in the middle eighties with a slight chop along the coastal waters. This is what I like to call JAPDIP—just another perfect day in paradise."

Perfect weather in paradise the day Orel was going to die. It felt strange not having to sneak around number 17 for a change. This sense of freedom was the lone bright spot in the entire drama.

It seemed like a good idea at the time, gathering up Orel's belongings, especially since her father did not think so. But now that she was in the middle of the job, Lucy could think of a thousand other places she'd rather to be.

Before starting the morbid process of packing a person's life into a suitcase, she looked around the room to see how Orel had left it. A single plate and a milk-stained glass on the night stand. She walked out of the bedroom into the living area. The clutter on the coffee table almost had an order to it, with a black comb, nail clippers, a box of tissues and a pack of Wrigley's spearmint gum surrounding an old TV guide lying sideways in the center. Lucy picked up the TV Guide. The pages were worn and dog-eared. It was an issue from March 31, 1973 with Lucille Ball and Desi Arnaz on the cover.

She sat on the sleeper couch and wondered why Orel had an eight-month old TV Guide on his coffee table. She pulled at the cover and the dog-eared page opened to an article about the star of *I Love Lucy* and her son. Her eyes wandered around the pictures for a few moments and then she put it back down on the table.

Over by the hall closet, she could see a jacket hanging on the door handle. A pair of shoes was directly under the jacket. She admired how organized it all looked. Inside the closet, two flannel shirts in plastic, two pairs of pressed and plastic covered corduroy pants and three flowered shirts hung on wire hangers.

Lucy walked into the bedroom. It was unchanged since the last time she had been in it. The bed was neatly made, with the spread making a perfect line under the pillows. She walked to the bureau and ran her fingers over its finely polished top. The first drawer made a dry, scratchy sound when she pulled at it. It was empty. She slid open the second drawer. The only item of clothing in it was the Weenie Bender. Lucy started to smile. *Rudy hated this thing.*

She unzipped the plaid suitcase, sitting on the stand next to the bed as Orel had left it. First she put in the shoes. Then she laid the pants down flat on the bottom, followed by the shirts. *How silly Orel looked wearing flannel and corduroy in Florida. Rudy did well to convince him to change his clothing style.*

Carefully, Lucy picked up the bathing suit and with her arms extended, placed it in the center of the flannel.

Then she took the flowered shirts off the hangers and laid them flat on the bed. She worked out the wrinkles methodically until the fabrics were the same texture as the bedspread. Her eyes moved over them as she was reminded of something Orel had done in each of the colors.

The orange one he wore to Ruskin to pick tomatoes. The green one he had on when he showed her how to play the piano. The blue one he wore for the opening of Dollar Bill's. Lucy bit her lip when she came to the purple shirt. Small flecks of glitter dotted the collar. Glitter from Rudy's costume had gotten on it while Orel held him till the ambulance arrived. The red flowered shirt was not among them. It ended up in the trash receptacle in the emergency room after the paramedics cut it off his bloody body.

Lucy stood over the shirts and admired their beauty. One by one she picked them up, folded them and placed them at each edge in the bottom of the suitcase.

Then she found the grocery bag she had brought with her. She reached inside it and felt around for her blonde-haired Skipper doll. When she pulled it out, she stared at it momentarily, then straightened the lapel of the its black dress and ran her thumb softly across the hair and coordinating black bow.

Pulling Skipper close to her chest, she closed her eyes, and started awkwardly, "God…thank you."

Squeezing the doll tightly, she tried to find the proper words. "Thank you for letting me meet this person. Thank you for letting him help Rudy. Thank you. I owe you a year…no, two," she said with a slight laugh.

A sense of calm grew over her as she nestled Skipper in the fabric bed of flowers and zipped the suitcase shut.

She knelt on the bed and picked up Jonny's Journal, caressing it softly. How much more worn it had become since the time she had first found it. She thumbed the book to the final page to find out the ending.

12-24-72

Been a while since I've seen or heard from you Orie. I'm sorry. If you end up finding this, I obviously have made the right decision. Your life would have been much different if I didn't make you leave. Not in a good way though. After your mother died I lost my rudder. Nobody needs a father without direction. Deep down I knew that all along. Sometimes you're smart…sometimes you're lucky. I guess I was a little of both. Smart's in the blood anyway. I wish I would have known that all along. I did a lot of things in my life that were not so smart. I'd love to be able to sit here and write down everything and tell you exactly what to do but I can't. That's the pain in the ass that this life can be sometimes. The only thing I can tell you is…go out there and change things. Don't be afraid to take those chances in your life. A life full of failure in trying is better than a life full of regret in not. I hope you forgive me.

I love you…Jonny…Dad.

Lucy closed the journal on the final words and rubbed a palm over the cover. Breathing slowly allowed her to keep from crying. After she composed herself, she got up and walked to the living room with the journal by her side.

Peaking out the window, she could see Mrs. Hanson walking around the pool chatting with guests on lounge chairs. Her arms gyrated and her mouth was large as she seemed to be telling each of them how things were supposed to be done at the Gulfside Oasis.

Mrs. Hanson's eccentricities did not bother Lucy as much as usual since she had a lot on her mind. She was looking once again at the confusing ink and pencil picture Orel had given to her in the hospital, a mural of lines, sunshine and faces. It was obvious from the details that he had been doodling it for some time.

While it was a nice keepsake from him, she could not understand its meaning. More puzzling was why he had felt the need to scrawl two parallel lines on the paper, one completely down the middle, and the second to its right, bisecting the distance from first line to the edge of the paper.

And while the drawing was beautiful, it was also disturbing. Orel had never shown any inclination toward violence. Then, *why would there be a drawing of a gun in the middle of all the beauty? And a coiled line issuing from the barrel indicating that it had been fired. Who had fired it? At whom?*

Thinking about it made her head hurt, so Lucy lay down for a moment on the floor. She pulled the *Mad Magazine* from her back pocket in hopes that a little silly reading might make her feel better. She stared at the cover and thought about Rudy. *What, Me Worry?*

Giggling sadly, she thumbed through the magazine. She glanced at Spy vs. Spy, not sure for which one she ever rooted.

Suddenly she jumped up and threw the magazine to the floor in disgust. Two of her favorite people were fighting for their lives in the hospital and she was lying on the floor reading a comic book. She stormed around the room, dumping the suitcase she had just packed on the floor, overturning a chair and the lamp next to the bed and kicking an empty trash can into the wall. Eventually the tears came in an explosion of grief. Her face became puffy and her nose ran uncontrollably. Finally, Lucy sank to her knees, exhausted.

After a while, she got to her feet to pick up the things she had upended and got about the business of normalizing the room. On her way into the living room, she noticed the first victim of her aggression lying face down in the middle of the carpet—the *Mad Magazine*. The fold-in on the back cover was twisted and creased from the many times of trying to make a new picture out of the original one.

Lucy stared at the back page for what seemed like an eternity. She saw how the folds were not symmetrical. There was one down the middle. The second one was to the right of the first fold, bisecting the distance between it and the edge of the page.

Her body tingled with excitement from the epiphany.

She ran back to the dining table and snatched Orel's drawing. Flopping to the floor, she compared the two parallel lines Orel had drawn with the folds on the *Mad Magazine's* back page. They were an exact match.

With extreme care, Lucy folded Orel's drawing in half along the middle line. Then, she creased the right line. As she folded the paper in on itself along the lines, a new drawing appeared.

It was simple in its art and clear in its message. The top image was a dollar bill. The middle image was a box with what appeared to be a cord. Under it were three horizontal letters that spelled VCR. A line from the bottom of the page curved and pointed to the box in the middle.

Lucy started to hyperventilate and took deep breaths to calm herself. Then she opened up the paper again. She looked at the detailed picture with a gun in the middle. Then she creased the paper closed and read the message aloud. "Dollar bill, VCR." She opened the paper again. "Gun," she said awkwardly. "Gun, dollar bill, VCR!"

Lucy ran to Jonny's journal and rifled through the pages until she found the letter which Orel had left for her days earlier and read feverishly, "I have followed my father's will and connected the dots…of all the bad guys involved." Her eyes widened when she came to the last line. "The only thing lacking…is a smoking gun."

She took the journal to the drawing, still locked on the final words. Dropping to her knees, she placed it on the floor next to her and took the folded drawing into her hand. Fixing on the message, she recited once again, "Dollar bill, VCR." And then she opened the folded paper. In the middle of the beautiful doodle was a smoking gun!

The flat line of red transmitted the message. At exactly 7:59 the plug was pulled, but a strong life does not always go quickly or quietly. It took until 8:12 for the machine to finally stop beeping.

Orel was gone.

At 8:13 a surgical team swarmed the room with the precision of a pit crew at a race track. Harry had been permitted to be present when the plug was pulled, but was whisked away as soon as the harvesting of the organs started.

Bill looked at his son's heavy eyelids, which seemed to be the first thing affected by the medication. He just kept watching them blink long and slow.

"Didja thank him, Dad?" Rudy slurred, fighting the fog taking over his own brain. "I never..."

"Rudy, you don't need to talk."

"I nev'...really thank'd 'im. Rail shot. Hugged 'im," Rudy continued, grabbing at something he saw in front of his face. "Think he gotta thank you, outta that?"

Bill looked at Lillian at the other side of the bed. "Don't use your energy to talk, buddy," he said, comforting. "I'll make sure I thank him for ya."

The door flew open and a man in a green outfit emerged. "It's time to get this boy better," he said cheerfully.

Rudy's eyes closed. He tried his best to keep them open, but his cheeks and mouth were the only things that moved.

"You're gonna do great, honey," Lillian said, squeezing his hands folded over his chest.

"You'll be fishing in no time, big man," Bill stated confidently, though his voice trailed off at the end.

The man in the green outfit lifted a metal rail on each side of Rudy's bed and pushed him into the hallway. Bill and Lillian followed until they saw Harry leaning against a wall, staring down at his shoes.

Lillian whispered to Bill, gave him a kiss and ran to catch up with Rudy before they wheeled him into surgery.

Harry looked up from the floor and smiled a sad smile at Bill. "He's gone," he said.

Bill looked at Harry, at a loss for words.

After considerable silence, he said, simply, "I'm sorry."

"Thank you. I appreciate that," Harry said through a handkerchief. "I'm more sorry for you, though. I hadn't seen Orel since he was a youngster. I didn't really get to know him as an adult. Sure, I knew his father, but not him."

Bill nodded and put his hand on Harry's shoulder.

The old man continued, "Today you lost a good friend, Bill. A good person. Heaven's a better place for it, though."

Bill sucked in a breath. "I'd like to really tell you how much my wife and I appreciate you pulling the proper strings on this thing," he said, struggling. "I mean, with the waiting list and the next of kin thing. If it hadn't have been for you...Orel's life...and death would have been a waste."

Harry reached for Bill's hand and shook it firmly. "I gotta go take care of something, my friend. I hope it all goes well," he said with a wink and walked out the door.

Two big lights turned into one as Rudy was wheeled into the operating room. The cold chill of the room woke him enough to make him aware of his surroundings. He could hear voices but could not decipher what they were saying. The smell of chemicals invaded his nostrils as he breathed more rapidly.

"Maaaah," Rudy wailed, but emitted little sound.

In the reflection of an overhead mirror, he could see that he was not the only patient in the room. He turned his head to the other person lying beside him on a similar rolling bed with a sheet covering his head.

"Is that? Is tha' 'im?" Rudy struggled, doing his best to get the attention of the people in the room. When they didn't respond, he looked back into the mirror, then turned again toward the sheeted body.

"Thhhanks," he said. "I nev' sed thhhanks."

A gloved hand gently patted Rudy on the forehead.

"Hello, pal. I'm Mike, your anesthesiologist," said a distant voice.

Rudy offered a lethargic smile. "Danks," he muttered.

The hand remained on his forehead as a plastic breathing mask was placed over his face.

"This won't hurt a bit. Just a little sleepy stuff," the voice said from even farther away. "It will be over before you know it."

Rudy closed his eyes.

"Danks," he said again, and then faded off.

Chapter 23

After the revelation, Lucy could not sleep. Getting involved with Orel's family problems was really none of her business. He was a friend, though. He asked for her to help. She lay there staring at the ceiling in hopes that it would provide an answer. Her eventual decision was not something her dad would support. Sneaking out at this hour was the only option.

A large moon illuminated her bike with the flowery basket in front of the green shed. The early morning, humid air left a little moisture on the bike seat, which she tried to wipe off with the back of her hand. She took one last look at her home and pedaled into the darkness.

As she pulled her bike close to the back cage of Dollar Bill's, a sense of doubt invaded her mind. Several deep breaths and sighs seemed to give comfort to her confused thoughts.

The squeak of the bike kickstand made an ear-shattering shriek against the silence of the night. She closed her eyes and waited a moment to see if anyone had noticed. Surely she was insane for attempting this.

Craning her neck around the side of the building, she could see a blue Thunderbird with a white convertible top parked by the front door. At four a.m., a shut gate and a lock with a key in it made no sense. Who would be up at this hour anyway? Lucy carefully turned the gold key on the Schlage lock and heard it click open. She pocketed the key and pulled the chain-link gate toward her, wincing at the whiny creak it made.

She stopped one more time to reconsider what she was about to do. She could still turn and run away from this whole thing, but an unexpected feeling of determination deep inside her made that option no longer possible.

She tiptoed her way through the mess of garbage in the back of the bar. This was the place where Orel had been beaten. A bleak, bitter feeling knotted her stomach. The dirt and stink of the area were bad enough when standing over it. She could only imagine what it must have been like to be in agony, thrust face down into the vile morass of restaurant waste.

The hallway was dark with a sliver of light at the end. Lucy plunged ahead with unexpected courage. A confidence she never felt before made her moves stealthy and swift. As she got closer to the main bar area, she could hear the voice of a man talking to himself. She knew whose voice it was. The sound of it made her ill, but curiosity kept her intrigued.

Lucy touched the wall as she carefully inched closer to the ice chest behind the bar. The slightest bump would give her away. Her pulse quickened as she carefully peered over the countertop.

In the beam of a single spotlight illuminating the stage, she could make out Kronis' bent over shape. Dust particles danced and defined the edges of the beam of light.

Sucking a slow drag on a soggy cigar, the man was staring at the stage floor as if were a target. "A man is given his time here to do with what he wishes," he mumbled. Then a moan escaped his lips. "The only love I ever knew you stole from me. I asked nothing of you but a song."

Lucy trembled. She was in the belly of the beast. And right now, another beast was in the same room spouting what sounded like the ravings of a madman.

She remembered her mission and told herself not to let fear be a distraction. Slowly she pushed her hand along the wall, feeling around in the darkness until she thought she was in the proper place. She remembered where Orel had turned on the record player and how he had turned off the machine under it the last time they spoke. Biting her upper lip, she closed her eyes. The conversation was vivid in her mind. He had mentioned *solving puzzles.* Lucy had solved the puzzle and the result had gotten her to this exact place and moment in time.

An earsplitting wallop jolted Lucy back to the present. Another bang startled her again. Peering over the bar, she could see Kronis was enraged. He was emitting angry noises, and unleashing his wrath on the stage floor.

Sweat poured from his red face and his hair fell down in front of his eyes as he raised a sledgehammer high above his head. The same hammer which mangled Orel's fingers. He slammed it into the stage. And again. With each blow, another board flew into the air and splintered as it fell to the floor.

Using the noise as her cover, Lucy banged at the wall with the side of her hand. She timed her knocking to coincide with the whacks of the sledgehammer. It was the last bang that did the trick and opened the compartment in the wall. The cover flapped down abruptly and hit Lucy on the shoulder, revealing the hidden VCR.

With one more blow from the sledgehammer, the stage gave way and shattered in front of Kronis. He could see the picture of a green man with his fists ready for a fight staring from the hollow of the hole he'd made. A green man was on the side of a gym bag. Underneath him were printed the words *Fighting Irish*.

A man in a worn pair of flat-soled shoes spilled gasoline from a can in a dark, zigzagging line along the walls of the building. Dark splashes glistened and discolored the paint. The smell was strong and heavy, especially in the area around the dumpster. The man shuffled around the parking lot, spilling more gas.

Then, he struck a single match and dropped it onto the ground. A small blue-orange flame erupted and quickly raced along the zigzagging line. In a matter of seconds, the building was encircled in a ring of fire.

Impatiently, the flames spidered across the wet, glistening walls and climbed up to the awnings. As soon as the wood started to burn, black smoke billowed under the rafters and worked its way into the upper portion of the building. The flames were living, breathing creatures with unquenchable appetites, devouring Dollar Bill's.

Lucy held her breath at the first smell of smoke. She wanted to cough but was afraid she'd get caught by the madman. Frantically, her hands flopped on top of the large VCR machine. Gagging for breath, she felt for buttons. Finally, she managed to push the right one and the machine released a black rectangular object.

She grabbed it and stumbled into the wall. The smoke now hovered above her head. She felt blindly for an opening. Blinking, she saw Kronis hunched by the stage in the single beam of light.

Impervious to the smoke, he reached a long furry arm into the hole of the stage. With a single jerk he pulled out the gym bag with the green man on it and dumped it on the surviving planks. He unzipped the bag slowly and pushed a fat hand inside. Feeling smooth round spheres, he dug through the contents more viciously.

Suddenly, he bellowed at the ceiling like a wounded animal. "Bo-lita balls. Goddamned bolita balls!" he screamed. "He buried god-damned bolita balls!"

Lucy jumped in surprise and tripped over a garbage can. The metal rattling resonated over the billowing smoke and crackling flames. Kronis spun around toward the noise. As he dumped the bag on the floor, bolita ping pong balls bounced everywhere. Wobbling to the bar, he saw a small female figure struggling to get away from the garbage can.

Lucy gasped, realizing he had noticed her. She crawled toward an open doorway as Kronis swung at her and missed. She stumbled over fountain drink canisters and cardboard boxes, but managed to get to her feet. She threw the aluminum cylinders down on the floor behind her as she made her escape. A dim beacon of light over the cage near the back door was the only indication she was heading in the right direction.

"Piss-ant!" Kronis yelled through the smoke and darkness. He regained his feet and dodged a flame which had erupted from the gas line by the stove. His blackened nostrils seethed and he coughed smoke from his lungs.

Lucy's shoulder hit the doorjamb on the way to the cage behind the bar and she tripped, falling into a pile of wet garbage bags. She gagged from the foul smell. Over her shoulder she could see Kronis regaining his feet. He was almost on top of her. With the flames rising behind him, his scowling face took on monstrous proportions.

As Lucy pushed on a slimy bag to get up, she felt a large paw grab her ankle. With her free foot, she kicked out, but the hand only gripped tighter. She kicked again with all her might, and this time her foot landed on Kronis' face. His hand relinquished its grip.

Lucy jumped to her feet, snatched up the black object she had dropped in the garbage pile and raced to the gate. She slung the chain door closed behind her and clamped the lock shut. Kronis lunged and threw his entire weight against the gate. He reached through the gap in the fence for her blouse, but it was just beyond his grasp.

"Open the lock, piss-ant," he commanded. "Open the goddamned gate!"

Lucy's breath quickened and a stream of tears rolled down her cheeks.

"Sweetheart," Kronis tried again, with more honey than vinegar this time. "Please open the gate and everything will be okay."

The black smoke billowed from the back door of Dollar Bill's and the flames rose around his shoulders. Lucy's eyes turned to slivers as she pulled the key from her pocket and showed it to Kronis. She held it there long enough to watch his face melt into momentary despair.

"You'll have to go back to where you came from to get it," she said calmly and threw the key into a sewer drain next to the fence.

Kronis' face reddened and he pushed harder against the chain link, causing it to bow. "Piss-ant," he yelled, twitching and sputtering.

Lucy turned her back on him. She swiped at the kickstand of her bike and hopped on. A small explosion made her jump again.

"Piss-ant!" Kronis continued to yell.

Lucy pedaled her bike as fast as she could until she was a block from Dollar Bill's. Then she stopped, far enough from harm, but still close enough to see. A large explosion thundered in the early morning air, followed by a muffled cry for help.

The flames danced on the wooden roof and shingles until they reached the Dollar Bill's sign. As the plastic melted inward, Bill's face on the sign became grotesquely distorted. The neon lights surrounding it exploded, sending shards of glass into the air. Slowly, the weight of the sign caused it to fall over sideways as Bill's face burned and the dollar signs in his eyes faded to black.

A huge explosion erupted in the dumpster area, followed by a desperate howl and screams. Then silence. Several smaller explosions echoed from inside the bar. For a few moments, the fire seemed content to burn itself out. Then, it reached the gas main and a gigantic fireball blasted through the entire building, sending debris skyward.

A rain of paper bits fell from the sky. At first it was just pieces of menus, napkins and cups. Eventually, it turned to countless charred bits of five-, ten-, and twenty-dollar bills. There were no more pleas for help when the sounds of sirens in the distance invaded the small pops and bangs that erupted into mini explosions at the burn site.

Lucy wiped the tears from her face and reached in her bike basket for the manila envelope. She opened it and slid the black object, a video tape cassette, inside. She closed the gold metal tee on the back and turned the envelope over. The block letters written in black magic marker read: "Attention: Michael Sullivan, St. Petersburg Beach Florida Chief of Police."

Lucy put the manila envelope back in her flowery bike basket. She took one last look at what used to be Dollar Bill's. Her mouth sagged at the thought of how much was lost over the past few days. She pushed off the curb and pedaled away from the flames.

A man wearing a worn pair of flat-soled shoes stepped from behind the tree where he had been hiding and looked after her.

Then, he cast his eyes toward the smouldering remains of the bar. After several moments of reflection, he turned and shuffled off into the distance.

"Mr. Connor, Mrs. Connor," said the exhausted looking doctor in the waiting room of the hospital. "Things went brilliantly. Your son is recovering fine. We will just have to monitor him for several days to insure that there is no rejection of the organs. I feel, based on your son's physical condition, the outlook is very positive for a complete recovery."

Bill turned to Lillian, who started laughing through her tears. She was laughing at Bill because he started crying through his laughter. Somewhere they met in the middle and hugged in celebration of their son's recovery. The all-night wait was over.

Behind them, on the black-and-white television mounted on the wall, a newscaster announced, "A popular real estate mogul dies in a tragic local landmark fire! This and all your local news, weather and sports on First Break This Morning."

Chapter 24

"Yassir. Thank you very much, sir. This is something he would have wanted. Thank you… You, too." Dorothy hung up the phone and started back to her seat at the bar.

"Hey, Dot. You in da pool?" barked Wally from behind the bar.

"Sure, hon. Put me down for two boxes and I'll take the over," she answered. "Won't be able to watch all of the Super Bowl today though, dahlin'."

"What, you gotta date or something?"

"Yes, Wall. Yes, I do."

She took a sip of her Dewar's and nodded politely with a confident smile to a new face at the bar.

Wally walked away shaking his head.

With a second gulp, the Dewar's was gone. "Cash me out, Wall. I need to get going. I'll talk to you later," Dorothy said.

She pushed her stool away from the bar, put down a five-dollar bill and walked out of the Sunset Tavern.

"Goddamned women," Wally said, looking at the other customer at the bar for a show of support. "Back in my day, when Joe D. and I were in the service together, women knew their place."

The man nodded politely and gently tapped at his drink, asking for another.

January 13th seemed the right day for taking down the Christmas decorations. The fifty degree temperature was brisk, but the sun warmed things up nicely. Lillian finished with the last strand of lights around the awnings, but there was one more decoration that needed to come down.

She grinned as she looked at the happy Santa by the front door. She remembered how Orel had set him upright months earlier. A memory of his introduction. The Santa had not moved from that spot in five years, but somewhere deep in her heart, Lillian realized now was the time for him to go.

"Well, big guy, I'll have to show you to the attic till next year," she said as she started to pluck him from the gravel flower bed. She pulled hard, but the Santa did not give way immediately. Lillian, realizing it required more force, gave one strong tug, and Santa finally gave up the ground. Lillian fell back with the decoration on her lap.

"Wow! You were really in there," she said to the bearded man who smiled back at her, seemingly unfazed.

Bill was putting the finishing touches on the freshly washed red pickup truck, paying special attention to waxing the logo on the door. The fire at the restaurant had put him back once again in the junk business, so he wanted to be make sure his truck stayed in good shape.

"Bill!" he heard Lillian yell from across the yard. "You gotta see this!"

"Oh, Christ!" he yelled back, afraid that Lillian was hurt.

"Bill!" she continued to shout.

"What?" he answered, running as fast as he could to her. "What?"

When he finally got to her, he found Lillian sitting by the sidewalk, leaning over a gym bag. On it was a smiling man in a green hat who was spinning a basketball on one finger. A gym bag full of green rectangles. More than he had ever seen in one place. Too many to count. The impish, green man on the faded white leather pouch just stared back at him and continued to smile.

Lillian looked at Bill in disbelief.

"There's a note," she said with a puzzled face and handed a piece of paper to him.

Bill unfolded the letter and read the familiar handwriting.

> *Hey Boss, I came across this during the clean-out of Nearvana. I figured Mr. Claus could keep an eye on it till you thought it would come in handy. If anyone can keep a secret, he sure can. Use it in good health. Remember to "ripple the pond."*
>
> *Orel*

Bill sat down next to his wife and they both ran their fingers over the money. After some whispers, Lillian pulled the handles of the gym bag together and closed the zipper. She dusted off her hands, fixed her hair and carefully carried the bag inside the duplex.

Bill stayed behind, filled in the hole and put Santa back in the spot where he had been standing on his head for years.

Lucy hardly paid attention to the new visitor as she entered the office. "Hi, sweetie," greeted her father. This is Mr. Wolfinger. He's going to be staying with us for the next few weeks."

Lucy nodded politely, yet indifferently at a thin man with pale skin and a dim sense of fashion. "Gonna go down to the tavern and do some fishing and crabbing, I think," she said to Gene.

"Okay. Don't stay out too late."

"I'm…" she started. "I'm probably just gonna catch up with Rudy," she said and gave her dad a sad smile.

"You got some mail today," Gene said, handing her an envelope with no return address. "Who's it from?"

Lucy scanned the handwritten envelope. It was sloppy and hurried. She rubbed her thumb where the return address should have been.

"Not sure. Started a pen pal thing a while back. Probably something from that," she said nonchalantly, her mind racing with possibilities. She bit her lip and gave a slight nod to the new guest. "Gotta get going, Dad."

Lucy kissed Gene on the cheek, grabbed the envelope, and dashed out the door.

Wandering through the courtyard, she encountered a familiar guest. "Morning, Mrs. Hanson," she greeted.

"Young lady," the old woman acknowledged snidely. "Off to mutilate some more crustaceans?"

Acquiescence seemed the best response, and Lucy continued on her way without a word. When she was far enough out of sight from the office and Mrs. Hanson, she leaned against a beat-up Coke machine to take another look at the envelope. For some reason, she felt in no hurry to open it. Not that she knew its contents. If anything, she was afraid of them.

When she slid her thumb along the sealed fold, the sharp edge of the paper gave her a cut. She jumped slightly and sucked the injured thumb. The paper inside was thin and flimsy. A simple trifold document she had seen before, full of words she did not really understand. She did see the name Orel Benjamin Hughes next to "power of attorney" and another signature below it, Harold Samuel Covington. Beside the ownership column was the name Lucille Rae Lewis. At the top of the document were the simple words "Parcel 57."

A police car with a flashing light zipped past, breaking Lucy's concentration. The beach was not known for crime or dramatics, so when she heard the siren chirping a couple of times, she ran after it.

By the time Lucy caught up to police car, it had stopped behind an old vehicle on the other side of the street. The officer was approaching the driver's side door with care.

"License and registration," he said deliberately.

"Good morning, officer. Was I speeding?" came from the man inside.

"License and registration," the police officer flatly requested again.

A paint-speckled hand reached out the window with the proper documents.

The officer looked them over with satisfaction, and said, "Please step out of the vehicle, Mr. Rose."

Einstein took a long time to get his lanky body out of the vehicle and looked at the officer with a pair of questioning eyes.

"Is there something...?" he started.

"You have the right to remain silent," the policeman interrupted. "Anything you say can be used against you in a court of law."

"On what charge?" Einstein asked.

A second police car pulled up behind the first. When the officer finished reading the old painter his Miranda rights, he stared straight at the man and said, "First degree murder. Please turn and face the vehicle."

Lucy edged closer as handcuffs were snapped on the bony wrists of the painter and he was pushed into the back seat of the second police car. Her eyes locked on his. With his three-day-old beard and baggy eyes, he looked more sinister than before he was under arrest.

Einstein stared back at her. "I never did nuthin' to you," he mouthed.

Lucy looked away briefly, then locked eyes with the painter again. So many things she could say. Instead, she turned and walked away, stuffing the flimsy piece of paper in her back pocket.

The bright, rainbow-colored cloth rolled on the beach as the men did their best to fight the wind. The cool, gentle breeze blew through Dorothy's thin hair as she kept her chin strong, determined not to make this a sad occasion.

"This isn't the first time I've done this," Dorothy bragged to the muscular man who was checking the information on her form. "I did it a few months back with a friend of mine. We figured we'd do it again," she said holding up an urn with her bony fingers.

"Well, ma'am, you do realize that the Beach Patrol frowns on that type of thing," the man said.

"Yes, I know. I'll make sure I'm downwind," she answered sarcastically.

"Yes, ma'am." Here are your goggles. And if you'd like to let me strap you in, we'll be ready to go."

Dorothy put the urn down on the sand momentarily while she pulled the goggles over her thin hair. With a long step, she got one leg into the harness, and then the other. The man politely picked up the urn and handed it back to her.

"You are set for take off, ma'am," he said, flashing her a brilliant, white smile.

"Let's do it!" Dorothy yelled over the wind and the revving of the motor.

As the boat pulled into the Gulf waters, Dorothy felt a strong tug forward. She bounded twice off the sand before becoming airborne.

"Here we go!" she yelled excitedly.

The boat got smaller and the January breeze got cooler as she ascended into the air. By the time she almost reached the full extent of the rope, the waves were mere white puffs below.

When the rope was completely taut, it was time.

"Well, kiddo," Dorothy started. "You made quite an impact on the people you met here. That's not an easy thing to accomplish. I know. I've been trying to do it for sixty something years now. You pulled it off in a matter of months."

Dorothy looked around at the beautiful view. As the boat started making a turn, she noticed Sunset Island approaching over her left shoulder. She could see the mouth of the intercoastal waterway that led to Sunset Tavern. This was the perfect spot to open the urn.

Remembering the wind from the last time, she stuck her forefinger in her mouth and wet it. In a deliberate motion she felt carefully for the right direction. This time the wind was blowing straight toward her, so she decided to empty the urn between her legs. Slowly she opened the lid and watched it drop into the water. With two hands around the urn, she raised it toward the sky.

"Every time I look at this water, I'll think of you, Orel," Dorothy said. Then she brought the urn down and emptied its contents over the Gulf. The ashes floated in the air as it plunged below.

A single tear rolled down her face as her old cheeks formed into a wrinkly smile.

It was only eight weeks since the surgery, but Rudy was already doing his best to get back to fishing. He sat in a special chair

Bill had found on his route, which gave excellent support to his back and stomach.

"So, I gotta tell ya, I was pretty scared," Lucy said, looking at him slumped in the chair. "I mean, you can't find a good fishing buddy right down the street, ya know. It takes time and patience. You need to learn each other's moves."

Rudy looked at Lucy with a pained smile and pointed toward the horizon. "You ever think you'd like to try that?" he asked.

"What, parasail? Nah, looks scary," she answered.

"I'd like to try."

Lucy smiled at Rudy as she cast her line into the water.

"So, whatta you think the Fins chances are today?" Rudy asked, not sure if Lucy was still into sports or not.

"I think Shoes'll get 'em a win," she answered. "By about three or four touchdowns, I bet."

Rudy tossed one Jujyfruit after another into his mouth.

"You miss him?" he asked suddenly.

"Who, Shula, what?" Lucy said, confused.

"No, Orel! You miss him?"

"Sure, don't you? I mean, I've got a pretty good case of phantom limb going on right now."

"Phantom what?" he asked.

"Nothing. I'll explain it someday."

Rudy's eyes winced in momentary pain.

"I feel like he's all around me," he said. "Of course, part of him is in me. But it's different."

Lucy gave Rudy a questioning look as he shoveled more Jujyfruits into his mouth. Red ones and green ones by the handful, but it was the black ones that held her attention. One by one he piled them up on his knee as he talked to her.

"I can't really put my finger on it," he continued, holding the yellow candy box to his eye to see if there were any left. When it was obvious the supply was depleted, he reached for a black one from the collection on his leg. "I really can't put my finger on it," he repeated as he tossed the black candy into his mouth, savoring the taste.

Lucy smiled sadly as she finished removing the claw from a crab she had caught. She pulled her arm back as far as she could and heaved it back into the bay.

Rudy looked at the crab he had in his hand, about to do the same to its claw. He stared it in the eyes for a moment and then gently dropped it back into the water.

A loud, beeping sound came across the Sunset Tavern parking lot. Through a whirl of sand, Lucy and Rudy could see Bill's red truck making its way toward them. Several more beeps followed until it pulled to a quick stop next to them.

"Who wants to go to Three Swings?" yelled Bill from the driver's side.

Gene was next to him in the cab, and Lillian sat in the back with a big smile.

Lucy and Rudy looked at each other. "We do!" they chimed in unison.

"We have to get rid of the crabs first," Lucy said and flung three of them into the water at once. Then they gathered their fishing gear. Lillian gave Rudy a hand and pulled him slowly into the back of the truck. Lucy hopped in effortlessly. Her dad smiled warmly at her in the side mirror. Bill gave thumbs up, which looked eerily like the Dollar Bill's sign.

Lucy glanced over at Rudy, who had found the comfort of his mother's arms and loving touch.

As the truck chugged away from the seawall, Lucy stared back at the bay. The splashes from the crabs had left circles where they hit the water. As the circles grew and intersected one another, each changed.

Some were big and some were small. Some were round and some were not.

It was their differences that made them the same.

Acknowledgments

Since this was my first effort at writing a narrative of this length and breadth, I had no idea what the experience would be like. I can only compare it to running the marathon, which I was able to check off my bucket list a few years back. There were times when quitting seemed the best option. There were also times when the finish line seemed nowhere in sight. Fortunately, these are normal emotions encountered in any worthwhile process. Fighting through the walls of self doubt and frustration come with the territory.

Once I felt the story was complete, I realized I lacked an apparatus to take my manuscript to the next level. Writing, it turned out, seemed to be the easy part. Editing and publishing require an entirely different approach. Thankfully, through happenstance and good luck, my sister Dianne was smart enough to hook me up with my book doctor, final editor and layout designer, Chris Angermann. Without his help, I am sure my story would still be languishing with many holes in the plot and rambling with characters who needed more development. His commitment to seeing this project to completion is unmatched. I owe him an enormous debt of gratitude for "shepherding" this story to the printed page.

Chris also introduced me to my editor, Susan Hicks, who was the first writing professional to look at *Another Man's Treasure* with a critical eye regarding its prose. Her calm reassurance that my story was on the right track and her continual confidence kept me focused in the final months of the editing process. She worked diligently at "polishing" my sentences and paragraphs despite going through a tough time in her life personally. I believe I have found a lifelong friend in Susan and look forward to working with her on future projects.

And last, yet foremost, I want to thank my family. It is not easy being around a creative person in general. Being around someone who is writing his first novel is another matter altogether. My parents, Mary and Charlie, provided encouragement along with plenty of material for stories through the years. My two sons, CJ and Nick, grew from children to adults as they cheered me on along the way. My wife, Lisa, deserves the biggest thank you, since she has had to hear me dream aloud for thirteen years about this project. In all my creative endeavors throughout our marriage, she has been by my side giving me inspiration, motivation and countless smiles. Thank you, Sweetie. I love you more than anything in this world.

And as always, a big thank you goes to the Good Lord, who kept me in good health, mind and spirit throughout this journey.

www.ingramcontent.com/pod-product-compliance
Lightning Source LLC
Chambersburg PA
CBHW030931260626

47169CB00002B/435